S.J. MARTIN

Ravensworth

Rebellion. Revenge. Romance

Contents

Prologue

I n 1071, England was once again a country under occupation by a foreign invader. The Normans defeated the Saxon King Harold's forces at Hastings in 1066 and, Harold was slain. Duke William of Normandy was now King and, he began a campaign of suppression and control.

Five years on, the people of England are still living with rebellion, warfare, and slaughter. They are subject to Norman domination, their lives changing with new laws, a different language, and a new culture imposed upon them.

King William and his half-brother Odo have spent the last few years ruthlessly suppressing rebellions against his rule in several parts of the country. Northern England is undergoing harsh punishment after the revolt of the Northern Earls in 1069-70. The people are suffering from what is known as the 'Harrying of the North'. This included the almost wilful razing of villages to the ground, from the River Humber to the River Tyne. Along with the destruction of crops and slaughter of livestock that blighted the inhabitants' lives for generations to come, tens of thousands died from famine during these years.

There are winners and losers during this time. The Saxon Thegns, who fought against the King at Hastings, lost their lands, livelihood, and for some, their lives. The Norman and

Breton Lords who fought with the King have been rewarded with land taken from the Saxons.

One of those Breton Lords was Alain Rufus, the King's nephew, who saved William's life at Hastings. The land awarded to him is a huge area, vast swathes of North Yorkshire, known as the 'Honour of Richmond'. This is still a troubled area, with much resentment against the Norman overlords, so Alain has sent his Breton Horse Warriors north to kill and capture the escaping rebels under the command of Luc De Malvais.

Alain is building defensive castles across the north on William's orders. He has established himself at Richmond on the River Swale, where he is constructing a large castle. Several others are planned in strategic positions across his lands to control the errant population. One of these is about to be built in the village of Ravensworth...

Chapter One

June 1071 - Ravensworth Village in the North of England

Merewyn Eymer lay on her back in a hollow amongst the high meadow's grass and clover. It was a perfectly still English summer's day with barely a cloud in the sky. This peaceful, pastoral scene around her was in complete contrast to the raging turmoil she felt inside her. She could scarcely contain it.

She squeezed her eyes tight shut, gritted her teeth, and clenched her fists in rage. She wanted to scream, but that would give her position away to those just below her in the village. She felt consumed by waves of anger and pure frustration at the situation. Worse still was the mounting hollow feeling of fear, making her stomach clench; fear of losing everything she loved in her way of life, fear of change, and fear for her village and its people. She put her head down and drummed her heels on the ground, hard enough to hurt. Then, giving a deep sigh, she turned over and, flooded with a feeling of utter despair, she gazed down through the long grass at her home in the clearing just below the village of

Ravensworth.

She had chosen this hollow spot in the meadow on a slight slope; it was very close to the village but hidden from below. It afforded views looking west and south over the Holme Valley, assuring her a clear sight of anyone approaching without fear of being seen. Her large green eyes darkened with rage as she thought about the troop of armed men who would gallop into her village shortly, the Norman soldiers. These men were the hated enemy; it seemed like every week that the Saxon Thegns received alarming news that the Normans were burning Saxon villages. They were killing people, farm animals and even burning crops in the fields all over the North of England.

The Normans had invaded England and defeated the Saxon King, Harold Godwinson, nearly five years ago at Senlac Hill, near Hastings. William of Normandy was subsequently crowned on Christmas Day 1066 as the new King of England. Everything she knew and heard about them told her these Normans were a warlike and ruthless race. They had set out to systematically destroy and subjugate the people of England and, in particular, to punish the people of the north for daring to rise against them after the most recent rebellion of the Earls in Northumberland. The new King seemed determined to wipe out most of the population north of the Humber.

Her father repeatedly asked why the invaders did not yet touch Richmond, Ravensworth, and the surrounding villages? Today they would find out why or was it their turn to have their village razed to the ground and their animals put to the sword so that the people would starve this winter. The fear for the last few days had been palpable amongst the villagers, although her father had done his best to alleviate

4

their concerns. She swept back her long, unruly silver-blonde plait, which seemed to come unbound continually, and gazed critically down onto her home and surroundings.

It was a large village, mainly a collection of a few dozen thatched houses and huts, some very large, like her father's Hall, some small dwellings for the cottars, who worked on her father's land. Standing in the centre was a substantial new Hearth Hall, just completed last year by their Thegn, Thorfinn Le Gunn. On its own was the church, with its wooden shingle roof, standing out as the only stone building. A sturdy high wattle fence surrounded the whole village to discourage the wild boar and the wolves who might venture from the nearby ancient forests.

She kept her head down and watched a few women moving nervously around the village, carrying out their daily tasks. Most of the menfolk would usually be in the fields, tending their strips and the crops. However, today, a troubled and apprehensive group of them gathered in front of the Hearth Hall, most of the women clustered anxiously around the doorways of their houses, with their children close. They were hoping for reassurance from their Thegn, Thorfinn. Reassurance that Merewyn knew Thorfinn could not give them. Her heart went out to him; he was a brave warrior and a just and fair Thegn. However, according to her father, Thorfinn was to lose all of his lands and manors to a Norman Lord. She knew that his authority would be taken away, replaced by the hated Norman rule and law, along with their Norman customs and language; this had happened elsewhere in England, the travelling pedlars brought such tales of horror and destruction.

Merewyn narrowed her eyes as she gazed down. She could

clearly see Thorfinn, a massive bear of a man with a mane of reddish-gold hair, now tinged with grey, his Huscarls placed defensively behind him, standing at the top of the steps, leading into the Hearth Hall. She could make out the figure of her father, just as impressive, standing a step below him, always ready to support his friend and fellow warrior of old. She knew her father would be angry and dismayed that she was not safe behind barred doors at home, but she could not stay cooped up, and she wanted to watch what would happen when they arrived.

Her heart bled for Thorfinn and his family; they would be dispossessed of everything they owned by the Normans. Where would they go? Would they go back to Denmark? She would miss Thorfinn's daughter, Ardith, her dearest friend and confidant. Thorfinn had been there her whole life, her father's friend; he welcomed Merewyn into his Hall like another daughter following her mother's death. She received instruction and learning from the priest alongside his daughter, and she always sat in the Hall at the top table with the family. Her father, a Thegn in his own right, had stayed in Yorkshire, becoming indispensable as Thorfinn's Steward, managing his dozens of scattered manors and lands.

Thorfinn had fought alongside her father at the battle of Hasting for King Harold Godwinson against the Normans. They had been defending their country and King. However, they were defeated by the Normans, and Thorfinn and her father had been amongst the Lords and Thegns who had eventually surrendered to William of Normandy at Berkhamstead in October 1066. Since then, they had been living on borrowed time; the recent rebellions across the country bringing everything to a head, as William and his men brutally suppressed them.

As she gazed down at the village, she could see the tension in her father's posture as he talked, in an animated way, to Thorfinn and to the assembled village men, who stood in a large group around the hall doors. They all kept glancing apprehensively down the road towards Richmond. Lord Alain Rufus's messenger in Richmond had arrived several days ago announcing the imminent arrival today of a new Norman overlord and his entourage, and they were not sure what to expect or what would happen.

Suddenly, in the distance, she heard hunting horns blown, the crowd below her stilled, all looking anxiously towards the road from the south.

They were here.

She hunched further down in the long grass; her eyes fixed on the road south where it entered the forest. Soon she could hear and almost feel the thud of horses' hooves galloping relentlessly towards her village and family.

She found her hands tightly gripping the turf as they burst from the forest galloping down Kirby Hill into the full sunshine, dozens and dozens of mounted riders clad in chain mail, conical metal helmets, and wielding swords and long pear-shaped shields. She could see a small group of Norman lords or knights at the front, their mail covered by expensive cloth tunics emblazoned with their colours and designs, and their bright pennants and standards flying in the wind beside them, held by retainers and squires. These Lords rode horses that were impressive heavy beasts, huge war destriers built to carry men into battle, nothing like the small, sturdy ponies in the villages. It was striking and overwhelming to see but, at the same time, terrifying.

Merewyn covered her ears to cut out the harsh sounds of the blaring horns and the thunderous thud of the hooves, and still, they streamed out of the forest. The large contingent did not slow as it approached the village, and she could see the village men cowering back towards the Hearth Hall, the women pulling their children indoors. She held her breath; would they now massacre everyone in the village as they had done elsewhere in the north before burning the buildings and killing the animals? Had she done the wrong thing coming up here and leaving her small brother in the house with Helga, their servant?

She watched, transfixed, as suddenly, the Knight in the lead flung his arm to the left, and the force split into two groups. Half of them galloping across the long meadow grass and round the wattle fence to encircle the village, no doubt she thought, to prevent any terrified villagers escaping from the northern gate. The rest of the group galloped into the village, raising a huge dust cloud in the summer heat and scattering the people; the second group of riders galloped up through the northern gate scattering dogs and chickens in their wake. Merewyn took her hands from her ears and waited for the screaming to begin; she heard harsh laughter and shouts from the Norman knights as swords drawn; they surrounded the men on the green, pushing them into a tight group. The dust cloud began to settle, and she could now make out the shapes of people in front of the Hall. She felt proud that Thorfinn and her father, two huge Saxon warriors, had not moved a muscle; they stood their ground as the mounted Norman Lords looked down at them.

Merewyn felt faint. There was a ringing in her ears and a pain across her chest. She was gritting her teeth, and she realised she was still holding her breath. She let it go and gulped in mouthfuls of air, making her head swim; she needed to calm herself. She knew that Thorfinn and her father would not be intimidated. Her gaze swept the village, concerned to see what was happening. She watched the Norman Lord gesticulating and could see the ring of horses tighten round the Saxon men, several of whom were now brandishing weapons. She watched as Thorfinn and her father tried to calm their people. A dozen of the soldiers now dismounted, and swords drawn, they advanced on the steps of the Hearth Hall. She saw her father raise his hands in a peaceful gesture as they bundled him down the steps to join the encircled group on the green.

Their leader shouted orders; she could not make out his features clearly, but he seemed surprisingly young, mounted on a large grey warhorse, his auburn hair shining in the morning sun. Following his orders, a group of Norman soldiers systematically searched the village houses for any more menfolk. The young boys and even the elderly thatcher Eadric, crippled with age, were dragged out from their homes and pushed towards the green. The old man fell heavily after only a few steps and his granddaughter Emera tried to stop them, running out and pulling on the soldier's arm until the man turned and brutally hit her down to the ground. She lay dazed, the deep bleeding marks from his mailed fist evident on her face as he stood over her.

Merewyn could almost feel the hostility coming from the twenty or so gathered Saxon men on the green as they watched on, fists clenched and raised in anger. Without warning, Emera's young husband ducked under the belly of the nearest horse, avoiding the slashing sword of its rider, and raced across the green towards his house. He drew a large dagger from his belt as he ran at the two soldiers in the doorway, standing over his wife. Merewyn cried with alarm as she saw the fully armed men step forward to meet him, and within seconds, one had thrust his sword through the throat of the young Saxon before calmly putting a foot on the chest of the fallen man to pull it out. Emera screamed with horror as she looked down at her husband's body while the blood pooled around his head and shoulders. With clawed hands, she grabbed the dagger on the ground and threw herself at the soldier, who stood calmly wiping the blood from his sword on the young man's tunic. The man sidestepped quickly, laughing as he reached out, grabbing her by her long blonde hair. He brutally twisted the dagger from her hand and dragged her screaming into the hut, followed by the grinning second soldier.

A stunned silence hung on the village green as her screams gradually died and turned into cries and moans. The corralled Saxon men averted their eyes from the scene behind them. The elderly thatcher, still on the ground where he had fallen, had now pulled himself over to cradle the bloodied head of his granddaughter's young husband; while the two soldiers were still loudly taking their pleasure with the young Saxon's wife. The Norman Leader, undaunted, stood up in his stirrups and loudly ordered the Saxon men to disarm or their wives and daughters would suffer the same fate. Merewyn watched as the village men reluctantly dropped their weapons, which the Norman soldiers collected as she heard the Normans telling the men to sit on the ground.

At this point, the Norman Lord dismounted and, with two of his knights, went up the steps to the Hearth Hall, spoke fleetingly to an angry Thorfinn, and gestured for him to come inside, allowing him to bring his Huscarls with him. Meanwhile, several soldiers searched the men on the green to check there were no further hidden weapons. Merewyn prayed that none of the men would fight back, and she could see her father counselling the men to obey. As she watched, the village men were counted into groups of five. Their hands bound, they were tied together and marched out of the village, forced to sit in groups on the open ground well beyond the village fence to the southwest. Merewyn's heart was pounding as she wondered what they would do to them. Would they be taken away or killed? She asked in a rising panic how she would keep the Normans out of her home with her father gone.

She went cold at the thought of what she had just witnessed with Emera, and as she shuddered, the two Norman soldiers came out of the hut laughing, with one still fastening his braies, before he pulled down his chain mail hauberk. She put her hands to her cheeks in horror and was not surprised to find them wet with tears of shock and anger.

All of the Normans had dismounted; there was a sudden hive of activity as a large group began to make camp outside the fence, to the village's southeast. Several huge wagons, drawn by oxen, now emerged from the forest and rumbled along the road towards the green, piled high with goods and barrels of wine and beer; it certainly now looked as if they were here to stay and occupy, rather than destroy the village. As she watched, some of the men started collecting wood from the forest floor for fires, and several tents were being unpacked, rolled out and erected, including what looked like a vast, colourful pavilion, which lay on the grass.

There must be well over sixty of them, thought Merewyn, far outnumbering the men of the village since the recent battles and rebellions had claimed so many lives, young and old. She watched the squires and grooms unsaddle the horses, including the enormous destriers, a group of men started leading the horses along the track north out of the village and towards her. At first, she panicked and looked around her for an escape route, but then she realised that they must be heading down to the river, the Holme Beck below, to water and rub down the animals. She stayed still warily watching them just below her.

She had never seen a Norman before but, of course, had heard much about these ruthless and warlike men. However, watching this group of young men splashing with the horses in the beck, shouting, laughing, and joking, they seemed like young men anywhere. It was difficult to believe that these same men could slaughter villagers and their animals, or they could casually rape a young woman and kill her husband without a second thought. She knew, however, that this was the reality of war; she was not naïve, and her people were the defeated race, while these Normans were the conquerors, and they could do as they pleased. Merewyn sighed, but it turned into a half sob; she knew their life would never be the same again.

Suddenly, one individual caught her eye; he was standing on the bridge, directing the young men in the river. He was tall, blond, and muscular with his hair slightly longer than his compatriots, who favoured the short Norman style. With a sharp intake of breath, she realised he looked just like Braxton, Thorfinn's arrogant, handsome son, who was missing since the rebellions. A frisson of fear and apprehension coursed through her body.

Braxton Le Gunn, the name reverberated through her...

She shook her head to clear the memories of him, but to no avail, his face and hard cruel eyes rose unbidden. Merewyn had put all thoughts of him out of her mind over the last six months. For several years, he had pursued her relentlessly, determined that she should be his wife when he returned from the rebellions in Northumberland.

However, Braxton was an arrogant and cruel bully who enjoyed tormenting the young village youths and animals alike; he was his father's heir. He made sure everyone treated him accordingly. There was no doubt that he was a striking figure; with his father's colossal warrior build and long plaited blond hair and beard, he looked every inch a Thegns son. However, there the resemblance to his handsome father ended, for Braxton had his mother's narrow ice-cold eyes along with her cruelty and sly cunning character. He was a boor, and he wanted Merewyn, mainly because she despised him; she had kept him at bay with the backing of her influential father for several years.

Her father, Arlo, was in a difficult position; this was his friend's eldest son, who would inherit all of the manors and estates, which Arlo managed. Fortunately, Thorfinn Le Gunn recognised the flaws in his son's character, and he watched his son's attempt to woo Merewyn with interest, laughing at his repeated attempts to win her over. This had infuriated Braxton even more until he became obsessed with possessing her and even more determined to have her.

Arlo, however, knew things would come to a head. Since their mother died in childbirth, he had used the excuse that he needed Merewyn to stay at home to manage the household and raise his youngest son Durkin, who was now five. However, pressure had come recently from the priest; Father Giffard could see all the advantages of the match for Merewyn, who was now twenty and needed to be wed. The priest liked Merewyn, despite her occasional wild and wayward lapses; he was hoping that she might be suitable for Braxton, that she would curb his cruel excesses and sweeten his temper.

Arlo was aware of the priest's thoughts, and after lengthy discussions with Thorfinn, he had finally given in. Therefore, there had been a hand-fasting ceremony, which took place in the Hearth Hall before Braxton left for the north to support the Earl's rebellion. Merewyn went cold as she thought of it. She knew that she had to follow her father's wishes, but she could clearly remember how Braxton's lust-filled eyes had raked her body, as he gripped both of her wrists tightly enough to bruise them, and he promised her a wedding night to remember when he returned. Merewyn shuddered; she was not naive about bedsport but the thought of her body being at his mercy every night filled her with dread.

As the unpleasant thoughts of Braxton lingered, her thoughts turned to Garrett, her elder brother, causing her brow to furrow. Garrett was, unfortunately, in sway to the bold brashness of Braxton. Along with three other young men from the village, he joined Braxton to fight in the rebellions in Northumbria. Now they were both missing, presumed dead, along with several other young men from the villages around.

Alain Rufus and his Norman forces had harshly crushed the rebellion of Earl Edwin and Earl Morcar nearly nine months ago. Hundreds of rebels had been imprisoned, executed, or sold as slaves, but not a word had filtered back about the boys' fate from their villages. King William had rewarded Alain Rufus for the swift suppression of the revolt in Northumberland with the extensive 'Honour of Richmond', including hundreds of manors and all of Thegn Thorfinn Le Gunn's lands.

Conflicting emotions tore her. She would certainly not miss Braxton, and part of her hoped he had fallen in battle, but Merewyn's eyes filled with angry tears as she thought of her handsome lost brother. She brushed them away with her grass-stained hands and turned a glare of hatred onto the Normans below who had invaded her home, killed or imprisoned her older brother, and who had now taken her father as well.

The young Normans had now taken the horses back up the road, through the village to the camp, and the bridge below was clear, so it was time to make her way down the slope and try to get back home unseen through a village full of Norman soldiers. She knelt upright and then gazed down with dismay at her grass-stained linen over-tunic. Her long, silver-blonde hair had come loose from its plait again and hung in her face; the hair was so fine it rarely stayed in place unless bound with a kerchief or band.

She stood and tried to shake and brush as much vegetation off her clothes and hair as possible, then slowly she turned, ready to descend the hill down to the bridge. Suddenly, she heard a sound behind her, and she looked up, thinking it was one of the grazing sheep. Instead, she froze as she saw a tall, imposing Norman soldier in chain mail directly behind her. He was quietly walking through the long meadow grass, leading a huge dark dappled horse, which is why she had not

15

heard him arrive, and now, his eyes narrowed as he spotted her, he turned, and he was coming straight towards her.

Chapter Two

Luc de Malvais was tired, a bone-deep tiredness, following months of brutal fighting, tracking down rebels, and sleeping rough night after night, often in the open with his men. He had led his Breton Horse Warriors from Durham up to the border with Scotland and back, crisscrossing Northumberland. The last group of rebels they captured had looked just as weary of it all as they were, as he had escorted them to captivity in the Norman stronghold of Durham.

A messenger had found him there, and the missive had ordered him to proceed south with haste, to join up with other Norman Lords at Ravensworth, north-west of Richmond. The message explained that Luc was to oversee the building of several necessary new fortifications in the area. Now, he was looking forward to a few months of more peaceful work, establishing Norman rule in the north for his 'Patron', Count Alan Rufus. Luc was also tired of war; these Saxons should know when they are defeated, not still rebelling after five years, they should know when to give up and go back to their farms. There had been enough deaths, he thought as he made his way south, riding towards Richmond.

Luc thought of the mammoth task ahead of winning these

people over. King Williams 'Harrying of the North' following the rebellions had not helped. While he understood his King's anger and the wish to punish the northern Lords by depriving them of further men and supplies, he could not understand the continuing wilful destruction of the villages, the burning of standing crops in the fields, and the slaughter of good farm animals. When it came to winter, many of the surviving people would starve. It would leave a legacy of famine for several years to come as well, with no seed gathered for planting in the spring and no way of replacing their stock.

He sat up in the saddle, stretched his back and dropped the reins to let his horse crop some grass. He held that thought for a few seconds. Would he give up so quickly in their position? Alternatively, on the other hand, would he fight until his last breath to defend his land? He laughed aloud. He probably would fight; in fact, he definitely would! He did have some empathy for them, but it was now part of his job to bring peace to these troubled lands, to make this land productive and profitable again for the King.

Luc rolled his broad, muscular shoulders to try to loosen some of the tension and tiredness; he had been riding at a steady pace for many hours, since just after daybreak. His warhorse, Espirit Noir, was feeling the strain as well after the last few months of relentless riding. Usually, Espirit continued unflaggingly, but it was hot, and now even this horse's proud head was swinging low. Luc picked up the reins again and continued travelling south-west. Perceiving a low hill ahead, he decided to dismount and lead Espirit for a while; they must be getting close to their destination, and it would do him good to stretch his long legs and give his horse a breather.

He reached the top of the hill and gazed down at the scene

below. It was a peaceful and prosperous-looking valley, the large village surrounded by dozens of cleared cultivated fields divided into the usual strips. There seemed to be an orchard of sorts, and a church stood slightly apart, enclosed by a low, drystone wall. The village was on a slight slope, which ran down to a small river with a stone packhorse bridge spanning it at its narrowest point. However, he could not see many villagers, and no men were working the fields, which was odd, then he spotted the activity south of the village, close to the edge of the forest; dozens of Norman soldiers were setting up camp. He was relieved, and he leaned against Espirit's powerful neck and patted it gently. 'Not long now, boy, to a good rub down and a bag full of sweet oats and hay,' he murmured.

He began to descend the hill slowly when his eye caught a sudden movement over to his right; someone was there, only yards away.

With warrior reactions, his hand automatically came up to grasp the hilt of one of the swords strapped across his back, but then he saw it was a Saxon peasant girl; she was kneeling up brushing grass from her clothes, it was clear she was neglecting her duties at this time of day. He started towards her, and Espirit snorted, shaking his head and rattling his bridal.

The girl turned to face him, and her body went rigid, her face registering total shock and then fear at seeing him there. He moved closer, only feet away, but she stood like a statue, then she dropped her head, staring at the ground, her hands clasped tightly in front of her.

'You girl, what village is this?' he demanded.

She showed no sign of having heard a word he said, and

then he realised he had spoken in French. He switched to English, which he thought a hard guttural language compared to his own, but he knew it was vital to talk and communicate with the English Saxons he was to rule.

'What is the name of this village?' he said

He spoke slowly so that she would understand him, and he reached out a hand grasping her chin to raise her head, but she suddenly jerked her head away and stepped back, glaring up at him. Luc was taken aback.

It was a grubby face, but beneath the tears and grass stains, he discerned an exceptional ethereal beauty. She had the largest green eyes he had ever seen, an unusual combination with her fine silver-blonde hair. She was older than he had initially thought, quite tall with a pleasing figure and his eyes paused on her heaving, well-rounded breasts. His gaze returned to her face, and he was astounded by the look of pure venom and hatred she gave him; this was way beyond the sullen glares and anger he had come to expect from the peasants or captured rebels he had thus far encountered.

'Ravensworth!' She spat the word out at him like a hissing cat and then picking up her skirts; she turned and ran, fleet as a hare, down through the meadow.

His eyes followed her willowy shape and her long bare legs as she raced over the bridge and into the narrow streets of the village, where he then lost sight of her. He watched her go, both astonished and bemused at her reaction. Then uttering a bark of laughter, he turned to Espirit and said, 'Well, that may be one local that we don't win over no matter how comely she is.'

He started back down the slope towards the village, thinking about a pair of deep green eyes. How long had it been since he had lain with a beautiful woman, he mused that maybe he would just go and find this rebellious Saxon girl and teach her a lesson in manners. He smiled, thinking of how he might enjoy doing that, with those bare white legs wrapped around him. Then he paused. Was he ready to be entangled with any woman after the pain he had gone through with the death of his beautiful wife, Heloise? As he descended the hill and reached the bridge, his thoughts refocussed on finding a hot meal and a roof over his head for a change; he had done enough sleeping rough this year.

* * *

Merewyn ran as if the devil was on her heels, and in a way, it felt as if he was. She had been caught unaware and unprepared by an enemy Norman soldier. She raced down the narrow ginnels behind the village houses and towards her father's Hall, continually looking back over her shoulder, her skirts still bunched above her knees, impervious to the shocked glances of the village womenfolk she passed. She was aware that she already had a reputation for being a bold and wayward girl; no doubt, they would now be nodding their heads and muttering that she was over-indulged by her father and should be married by now to a husband who would tame her. She smiled wryly at the thought.

She crept along the side of her father's Hall and then made a dash along the front; she pushed open the large, heavy oak door of her home and shut it firmly behind her, levering the hefty wooden bar firmly down into place. She leaned her head back against the solid security of the substantial rough timbered door, her palms flat against the wood, her brow

21

beaded with sweat, while she tried to catch her breath in the cool, dark interior of the Hall. Her eyes suddenly widened; would he come looking for her because of her disrespectful attitude? Then she realised he did not know who she was or where she lived, and she breathed again.

She could hear voices; it was her little brother, Durkin, with Helga, their servant, out in the vegetable patch feeding the chickens. Everything sounded and seemed almost normal, but it was not and never would be after what she had seen today, and her eyes filled, yet again, with angry tears.

Unwillingly, she replayed the scene in the meadow and the man who had accosted her. Surprisingly, the horse's image came first; it was the most stunning animal she had ever seen, a huge, dappled steel-grey stallion, almost black in places. He had a proud and noble head, quite different from the horses she had ever encountered before, topped by a long black mane and huge limpid and intelligent eyes.

This man was not just a Norman soldier; no ordinary man could afford a horse like that. The trappings, too, she had seen in that first glance, were of the finest woven decorated leather. Although muddied and well ridden, the long saddlecloth was blue and silver; these must be his colours. This man was a knight of substance. Why had he not arrived with the main contingent, who had galloped into the village an hour ago? Who was he?

At first, she was puzzled; because this man did not look like a Norman. He was very tall, with broad shoulders arrayed in chain mail, covered by a sleeveless worn, stained leather doublet. His double swords and scabbards were crossed and strapped across his back. Just like the foreign mercenaries her father and Thorfinn had fought against at Hastings. Is this what he was? A paid mercenary, a killer, who did the work of the Normans, no questions asked.

At first, his dark, almost saturnine unshaved features seemed harsh as he had narrowed his steel-blue eyes at her and snapped out the questions. She knew exactly what he had asked her the first time, her education from Father Giffard had included French and Latin, and she could read and write well in both. She did not answer him at first because she was still in shock at finding him so close to her, without warning. Then when he gave a harsh laugh and repeated the question slowly in English, her fear dissipated, and her anger flared at the contempt and arrogance of this man.

This Knight was the epitome of everything she hated about the Normans. When he dared to reach out to touch her face, she gave him the attitude and response he deserved and fled, but not before she had seen the shock register on his face. She had to admit it was an attractive face. He had dark winged brows, a shock of even darker hair, which fell across his forehead, a full and sensual mouth, and a firm jaw and chin, which along with his demeanour suggested a strong character, a knight who was used to getting his own way. It was evident that he had thought her just a peasant girl, and as her eyes dropped to gaze ruefully at her hands and clothes, she could understand why.

She shook her head to clear herself of such fanciful thoughts and snorted in disdain. He was the enemy, probably responsible for her older brother Garrett's death; she was a Thegns daughter who would have a Saxon husband found for her, now that Braxton was dead. She pushed herself away from the door, headed through to the back of the house to wash and change. She decided to send their servant boy Bjorn to find

23

out what had happened to her father and if or when he would be released. She also wanted to know the fate of Thorfinn and what lay ahead for them all in this new Norman-dominated world.

Chapter Three

Merewyn stood in the cool of the small bedroom she sometimes shared with their servant Helga. She was rebraiding her long fine hair, which was often difficult to hold in place, and she knew she had several neglected tasks to do and oversee in the house today. Her mind kept returning unbidden to the events in the meadow and the tall, dark, Norman mercenary when she was brought out of her reverie by the sound of frantic pounding on the front door. Her first reaction was to panic. Had he found out where she lived, had he come to punish her for her disrespect?

She clung to the sturdy wooden doorpost of her room, afraid to answer the repeated hammering. Then, she heard her father's angry voice, 'Merewyn, where are you? Unbar this door!' He shouted.

She flew across the expansive Hall to the door, lifting the heavy bar with some difficulty, the angry frustration in her father's voice spurring her on.

Usually, Arlo was a genial man, firm but fair, respected by the villagers and his friends alike for his sage counsel and patience when dealing with cases at the Moot Courts. What's more, he was a Thegn in his own right and had been a fearless warrior, fighting at Thorfinn's side at Hastings. His missing son, Garrett, had inherited his tall build and his good looks but had to gain the experience and wisdom of his father.

Arlo pushed the door open quite violently, and Merewyn jumped back out of the way as it clattered, with a bang, against the plastered timber wall. Merewyn was surprised. She had not seen him this angry since her mother's death when he drank for days at a time, and he had blamed everything and everyone for the premature death of the woman he loved. It had not helped that he was away with Thorfinn taking part in the surrender of the Saxon Thegns to the Normans at Berkamstead when she had died in childbirth, so he blamed himself as well for her death. He stomped into the room, frustration evident on his face but defeat and exasperation even more apparent in his demeanour and his slumped shoulders.

'I am so pleased you are safe. I am sorry I did not answer sooner, father, but I was afraid, and I wanted to keep the house secure with so many Norman soldiers wandering around the village, I saw what happened to Emera.' She said. He raised his eyebrows in concern as he looked at her but then grunted in acceptance and threw himself down on the wooden settle with weary resignation,

'Bring me some ale, girl! I need to think. Make it mead; I need something stronger!'

Merewyn returned with a leather tankard full of mead. Her father was sitting, leaning forward with his head in his hands. Now she was frightened. She had never seen him like this; he was usually so brave and fearless, always in control in any situation.

'What is it, father? What has happened?' she asked.

It took a few minutes to respond as he took a long draught

from the tankard and wiped his mouth. 'Thorfinn explained to this new Lord exactly who I was, my position in the villages, so he sent his men to find, release me and bring me to the Hearth Hall as well to listen to his orders and plans. The rest of the village men and boys are still out there, hands bound in the sweltering heat of the southern meadow with no water.'

Merewyn felt dismayed but relieved that her father was here and unharmed; she sat beside him and took his arm, laying her head on his shoulder.

'Our lives will be changing, Merewyn. Thorfinn and his family will leave Ravensworth tomorrow. As we thought, he has lost nearly all of his land and manors'.

'But where will they go, father?' She said as she sat down on the wooden settle facing him, immediately concerned for her friend Ardith.

'Lord Bodin has graciously allowed Thorfinn to keep one small manor at Melsonby, but, of course, Thorfinn will be paying tithes and will give fealty to his Norman Overlord.'

'Who is this Lord Bodin father? I thought all of the Honour of Richmond had been given to Alain Le Roux or Rufus as they call him?'

'It was, but Lord Bodin is one of Alain Le Roux's younger half-brothers, a soldier, but also more of a courtier. He tells me he wants peace for this area; how Thorfinn and I stayed quiet at that point, I do not know. Do they think they will get peace by killing young Saxon men and raping their wives?'

Merewyn nodded. 'But what of us, father? Will we lose everything, our house, our lands and livestock as well? Will we go to Melsonby? Will there be room there for all of us?'

Arlo sighed and stretched his long legs in front of him, ignoring her spate of questions at first. Merewyn thought her father looked exhausted, not surprisingly, since he had been at Thorfinn's side since dawn, supporting his friend and trying to calm the village men.

'Thorfinn, I am sure, would be happy for us to go with them, but I would be no more than a retainer on such a small Manor. I will think on this, Merewyn and we will discuss it later.' Privately, Merewyn thought her father would never be 'just a retainer', but they would undoubtedly be considerably more impoverished than they were at present. With little or no land in England, would they go to their lands in Denmark, she wondered. Arlo had closed his eyes, and Merewyn left him to rest. She had just reached the door when he spoke:

'There is to be a welcoming banquet tonight in the Hearth Hall; tell Helga and young Bjorn to take several of our pigs over for slaughter, the Huscarls will see to the mead and ale, and the Normans have brought many butts and skins of their red wine with them'.

Merewyn headed out to find their young servant Bjorn, who had managed to stay hidden during the search, to arrange the animals for the feast. It was a generous gesture from her father for his friend, particularly if they were about to lose everything. She saw that the Normans were already setting up huge roasting pits outside on the village green, and she knew that Thorfinn would be setting a larger one up in the centre of the Hearth Hall as well, for a whole ox, as they usually did on feast days.

Her thoughts raced ahead; they may have to leave their home tomorrow! She could hardly imagine not being here in Ravensworth. She had been born here, as had her brothers. Arlo Eymer was a wealthy man, owning dozens of hides of land here and even more back in the family lands in Denmark.

This wealth was reflected by his position in the community, by their large house, plastered in white inside and decorated with tapestries embroidered by her mother. Their clothes and household linen were of a more refined quality; they even had decorated glassware to drink out of at the table. Were they to lose all of this? What could they take with them? What would happen to their servants? Could they take them or, would the Normans claim them?

However, on reflection, Merewyn knew that these material and practical losses were nothing compared to Garrett's loss. What had happened to him? Was he a slave or prisoner in Norman hands, or was he dead? The not knowing was the hardest thing to bear, and she cursed Braxton Le Gunn for taking her brother away to the doomed rebellion. Her mind in turmoil, Merewyn felt her anger building inside her again against the Norman invaders who now occupied her village.

Her tasks completed, she called Durkin in for his meal; he was only five years old and would not be at tonight's feast. She, however, would have to be there. How would she cope? To have to sit, eat, and drink with these cruel and arrogant Normans after what she had witnessed today! However, she would do her best to support her father, Thorfinn and her friend Ardith, who would also be devastated at being forced from her home here in Ravensworth.

Suddenly, a thought flashed through her mind. Would he be there, the dark Norman knight with the crossed swords? In her mind's eye, she could see those steel-blue eyes looking at her in amazement and annoyance as she turned and raced off down the hill. Her cheeks burned with embarrassment at how she had reacted. Her father must not know about that; her conduct would mortify him. This Norman Knight thought she was a peasant girl, and she had undoubtedly looked and acted like one, but tonight she would be dressed as befitted her station as a Thegns daughter; if he was there, indeed there was no way he would recognise her.

* * *

Luc walked into the centre of the bustling village leading Espirit. He saw they were setting up large spits over fire pits, and servants carried a wide range of furniture and foodstuffs into the large Hall. Luc stood watching the hive of activity around him and scanned the large village green. He was pleased to note that men at arms were stationed at strategic points around the village. The men on the northern gate had been Bretons like himself, part of the large contingent belonging to his Patron Alain Rufus, so he had stopped to chat with the officer he recognised and catch up on recent news. He was aware that one of Alain's knights was here, and he wondered who it would be, they were a small but loyal group that surrounded Alain, and as one of the chosen few, he knew and liked them all.

As he stood on the village green, he assessed his surroundings. It was a large and prosperous-looking village, well kept, the thatched rooves of the houses in good repair and the fences sound and secure. The Hearth Hall was impressive; it was a substantial new building, which dominated the village's eastern side. Recently built, it had a unique design with large, wide side doors on both sides instead of at each end, letting the light in and the airflow through. Wide wooden steps led up to the entrances suggesting that the floor inside had been raised and planked. It was plastered with white lime and thickly thatched. The Thegn who held these lands was obviously very wealthy; the land seemed well managed and productive, and there was even a squat stone church over near the edge of the forest.

He set off towards the southern gate, suddenly conscious of the angry glances of the Saxon womenfolk; he would have stopped to challenge them, but he needed to take his tired horse out to the camp for a well-earned rub down and rest. Just then, two people appeared in the wide doorway of the Hearth Hall. One was a priest with a robe and shaved tonsure that was protesting and gesticulating, but the other man gave a loud shout of welcome and recognition.

'I would recognise that horse anywhere! Malvais! At long last!'

He ran lightly down the steps to greet Luc, engulfing him in a bear hug and clapping him on the back. He then held Luc at arm's length to look at him.

'We thought we had lost you in the wilds of the north; we have heard so little from you in the last months.' He said.

Luc laughed, 'I am not that easy to kill off Bodin. It is good to see you, my friend. I had not realised they had brought someone of your importance here to oversee this area.'

Luc had not seen Bodin for nearly nine months. Bodin had stayed in the south with King William's court while Alain Rufus had come north with his mainly Breton army to crush the King's northern rebellion. Bodin was one of Alain's two half-brothers, the quieter of the two, a diplomat and a committed Christian, as well as a formidable and loyal knight. Luc thought that Bodin was looking well; the good living in court had paid off. He was well fed and the picture of military elegance. Luc, looking down at his own tired clothes and tarnished mail sighed, he felt like a ragamuffin mercenary standing alongside the polished Bodin.

'So, is there any chance of a bed, or will I have to bivouac in the woods again tonight, my friend?' he asked.

Bodin laughed, 'You do look as if you could do with a good meal and a bath Malvais, and you are very welcome to share my pavilion. My servant, Francois, is in residence, and he will be delighted to see you despite your blood-spattered doublet and unshaven visage. Tomorrow, we will be moving into the Hall; the resident Thegn, Thorfinn Le Gunn, will be leaving, and you will have a large bed in there.'

Luc smiled, 'Many thanks, but first I have to get Espirit rubbed down and fed.' Bodin stood back and looked at Espirit with open admiration.

'So be it, your noble and famous horse looks in far better condition than you do,' he laughed. 'I have unfinished business with Father Giffard here who seems to think that we shouldn't kill Saxon men who attack us with daggers, but I will join you shortly for a cup of wine and hear your news from the north.' He said, turning back to the Hall and the hand wringing priest.

However, it was to be several hours before Bodin reappeared. This gave Luc the time he needed to see to both his horse and himself. Francois had come up trumps with some hot water, a tub and lye soap to remove the layers of ingrained dirt, blood and sweat from his aching body. He felt transformed once he had shaved, changed into a loose clean tunic and settled into a camp chair with a cup of wine. He was busily tearing chunks from a large, roast fowl when Bodin came to join him.

'Sorry for the delay Malvais. It took longer to sort out the details and agreement for the move tomorrow. Father Giffard is now helping to facilitate this; his French is excellent which is useful.' He flung himself into a chair and helped himself to wine.

It was a large pavilion divided into several rooms as befitted a Norman Lord, but inside, it was a military and male environment. Folding camp furniture and sturdy trestle beds were in evidence rubbing shoulders with stands for weapons and chain mail. Various documents and a map lay on a larger table, and colourful Normandy and Breton pennants hung from poles in the corners.

Luc smiled as he looked around. It felt like home and reminded him of when they had been on a campaign together in France. Then he became serious, 'So where exactly is this Saxon Thegn, Thorfinn Le Gunn, going tomorrow?' He asked with a raised eyebrow.

'Alain has been generous to the defeated Thegns. He now owns these Manors and lands, but he needs them to stay prosperous to produce an income to build several fortifications. Therefore, he aims to establish a relationship with the leading Saxon families to avoid further rebellions. Thorfinn and his family will move to a smaller manor at Melsonby, but he will pay tithes and fealty to Alain,' answered Bodin.

Luc raised his eyebrows, 'And this wealthy Thegn, he has agreed to this, without a fight or demands for reparation?'

Bodin smiled. 'Thorfinn is a wise old warrior, and he knows when it is pointless to keep fighting. His wife is dead, his son is missing or killed in the 'Northern Rebellions', and his daughter, Huscarls and servants, will go with him to Melsonby. However, it is not too far, and he will, no doubt, prove to be very useful to us in helping to understand the customs and geography of the area.'

Luc frowned. 'It all sounds somewhat suspicious to me and somewhat naive to think we can trust them. We know that hundreds of the rebels came from this area; many like Thorfinn fought at Hastings and even more recently in the rebellions in Northumberland, that we have spent almost a year putting down.'

Bodin sighed. 'I understand your view, Luc, especially as you have been on the front line in this, but the people here are tired of war, and William's policy of destroying and burning has had an effect; they don't want that to happen here. Yes, we had an unfortunate incident here today, and a young Saxon died, but we had to be firm and show them the consequences if they openly resist and attack us.'

Luc twirled the wine in his cup and gazed into the deep red liquid. He was not convinced; he knew there was still several pockets of rebel Saxons, some of which they had relentlessly pursued, but they had fled east to the coast, and he had lost their trail. What's more, he had travelled back and forth across the north for months; there was still smouldering anger and resentment out there, ready to flare up at any time.

He had seen that just today in the reaction of a local peasant girl. Suddenly, her face came back to him, huge green eyes opened in shock at first but then narrowed in hatred. She had been magnificent, especially when she was angry and spitting words out at him. He imagined holding that face in his hands and kissing away the anger. He smiled but then suddenly remembered other eyes, deep dark blue ones, those of the woman he had loved and lost, and a wave of sadness came over him again. Bodin watched the emotions chasing across his friend's face, 'You don't look convinced, Luc, and you are now miles away,' he commented.

Luc smiled ruefully, 'I am sorry, Bodin, I just remembered an encounter with a beautiful Saxon girl outside the village this morning, and she obviously hated us. Nothing for you to be concerned with, but I do not think winning them around will be easy. However, you know my loyalty is to my Patron, and I will do everything in my power to support his plans.'

Bodin smiled; he was not worried, as he knew that Luc was not only his friend but also one of Alain's most trusted knights, his unbeaten champion and the Leader of the Breton Horse Warriors. Privately, he thought it would do Luc good to get involved with any girl; he had grieved for the death of his wife, Heloise, for several years, far too many.

'Where is Alain? I had not heard from him for over a month until yesterday. Has he gone to re-join William?' asked Luc.

'No, not at all,' said Bodin. 'William wants to ensure that the North is secure and stable, so Alain is at Richmond. He is building a large castle, and quite a community is growing up around it. I am leaving in two days to join him back there, then, next week; I will travel as his emissary to William. Therefore, for me, it is back to the intrigues of the King's court and his delightful half-brother Odo. I hope to return to Richmond in early autumn.'

Luc's grey eyes narrowed, and he looked puzzled. 'You are leaving? So who is in charge of all of Thorfinn's Manors and land? I presumed Alain sent me here to help them?'

Bodin laughed. 'Why, you, of course Malvais. You are to be Alain's Marechal of not only this village but at least a dozen other Manors in the area until my brother Bardolf arrives in a year or so. Alain depends on you to crush any further rebellious tendencies, to show them how Norman culture and customs can enrich and improve their lives. You are to build a fortification here at Ravensworth, a castle for future defence. Win over the Thegns and their Huscarls for us Luc, I expect you to turn this into a peaceful, prosperous area.' Luc smiled in a resigned way; privately, he thought it could take a generation or two.

'You can start immediately,' said Bodin. 'Tonight, there is to be a feast in the Hearth Hall for the village to say farewell to Thorfinn and to welcome their new Norman overlords.' Luc rolled his eyes in mock horror, 'so that will be a festive feast then!' Both men laughed.

'Now I must go and arrange the release of the village men and boys. I think I have subdued and punished them for long enough,' said Bodin.

'Release? Where are they imprisoned?' asked a surprised Luc.

'Not imprisoned as such but held and bound in small groups, they have sat in the sun for several hours, things became quite heated for a while when we first arrived, emotions were running high so I had to take more heavy-handed action than I would have liked' he explained.

Luc raised an eyebrow and was about to enquire further when Bodin's servant, Francois, returned. He was a soldier and a Steward; he had been with Bodin since he was a boy and believed that all knights should dress to reflect their station in life. He bowed and spoke to Luc, 'My Lord, I took the liberty of having one of your chests brought with us so that you will have suitable attire for this evening and your standards are in the Hall.' Luc smiled ruefully, knowing the state of the rumpled and stained clothes in his saddlebags, so in reality, his sojourn at Ravensworth had been carefully planned by

Bodin and was well known to many others, except him! This was so typical of Alain Rufus; they were all pawns in his hands to be moved around the board as he willed.

'Sir Gerard and your men from Richmond are travelling with the baggage trains and supplies and will be here in a day or so,' added Francois as he left.

'Ah, the noble Gerard,' laughed Bodin. 'He is still by your side then?'

'Of course,' said Luc. 'I did try to send him back to Brittany last year, but he sulked for days.'

Sir Gerard was Luc's Vavasseur, his right-hand man and his second in command of over a hundred Horse Warriors. He was a battle-scarred warrior in his forties who had served as a young man with Luc's father; he had been at his side since Luc was only ten years old. He was his tutor, his sword master, and his friend all rolled into one. Luc smiled as he went to get ready for the feast, especially at the thought of Sir Gerard escorting baggage and slow ox-drawn carts. He would be like a surly bear when he arrived.

Chapter Four

The Hearth Hall was packed to capacity, extra benches were brought, but there were still men standing and talking in the far aisles behind the solid wooden Y shaped uprights that held up the impressive roof. As Merewyn entered with her father, the same familiar smells assailed her. The sharp tang of fresh rushes on the floor bruised by many feet, interspersed with the whiffs of wood smoke from the fires under the large spit in the centre of the Hall where an ox was roasting. This was being turned continuously by two red-faced village boys. The smell of the roasting beef was enticing, with several expectant faces turned towards it. The rays of the setting sun slanted down from the many high window slots in the walls, the motes of dust dancing in the beams of soft light that sliced across the Hall.

Although it was a summer evening, the large doors were open on either side to allow a flow of air, and the torches were being lit in the sconces around the walls. For Merewyn, there were the same poignant memories of many happy nights spent here over the winter and spring with her family and friends listening to stories and songs from the travelling skalds.

However, now it was different. The tension was tangible in the Hall, and she knew that it would never be the same again. She noticed that the Norman soldiers had taken up all of the benches and tables down the eastern side of the Hall. Without their stark helmets and chain mail, she had to admit they looked like any other group of young men, except that most of them wore their hair cut very short and were auburn-haired, or very dark like the knight she had met in the meadow. She quickly scanned that section of the Hall to see if he was here, but it was not easy when the Hall was so full of people, with at least a dozen serving men and women moving around the tables with pitchers of ale or wineskins. However, she was sure that he would stand out, she could not see him, and she breathed a sigh of relief. Maybe he was exactly what he had looked like, a mercenary passing through on his way to Richmond.

A few of the released village men and Thorfinn's warriors had taken the benches on the western side of the Hall. The difference was stark; the Saxons, with their long blond hair and beards, an occasional redhead amongst them, were subdued. She was aware of the glowering surly looks passing back and forth between the two sides of the Hall. She had been pleased to note the pile of weapons in the porch when they came in, the men being asked to disarm on entry under the watchful eye of several burly armed Norman soldiers. Merewyn's father stopped and surveyed the scene through narrowed eyes; she could see him mentally checking that everything was in place for Thorfinn's last night of hospitality in Ravensworth. Arlo pulled a serving-man over to one side and gave him several further instructions.

Merewyn had dressed with great care for this feast. She had a tall willowy figure, which was shown off to perfection by an embroidered powder blue over-tunic. Her long silver-blonde hair was unbound, as befitted an unmarried maiden, covered by a gossamer-thin delicate white veil held back from her face by a silver clasp. She was aware that heads had turned on both sides of the Hall to look at her as she stood beside her father. She also heard the lip-smacking and disrespectful bawdy comments in French from the Eastern side of the Hall, just the behaviour she expected from Normans, as she cast them a haughty, dismissive glance. The looks and stares from the Saxon benches were admiring but respectful, with nods and smiles; they knew her position in the village. She was one of their own, their local beauty, and many scowls were directed at the Norman men who dared to disrespect her.

The top table on the dais was empty at present, and as they threaded their way towards it, Merewyn eyed the large new Norman carved wooden chairs placed behind the table; she realised that she would not be sitting up there with Thorfinn and her father. Instead, Arlo led her to one of the adjacent tables close to the long top table. Father Giffard and two of the senior Huscarls were already seated; they greeted her father and Merewyn warmly. Merewyn slipped gracefully onto the bench where her father indicated, with her back to the aisle, so she had a good view of the Hall and the comings and goings.

There was a subdued atmosphere for so many men, with only low conversation rumbling in the background. None of the usual shouted banter, the guffaws and raucous laughter of a feast night; instead, there was uncertainty and apprehension, nervous, angry glances darted at the line of armed Norman Knights in position behind the top table. Two of the Knights held long coloured pennants or gonfalon, one of them a flaming red and gold and the other a bright blue and silver.

She eyed this mail-clad honour guard with disgust. There were no young boys or squires there; instead, she could see that all of the men chosen were seasoned warriors, with faces of stone; two of them were young knights sporting their newly acquired colours. There was no doubt that this was an army of occupation and this honour guard was for protection in case things became heated again, this time in the Hall.

A scurry of activity at the southern end of the Hall turned heads in anticipation, but it proved to be her friend, Ardith, who was descending the steps from the solar with her servant. As they wended their way down the Hall, Ardith stopped to talk to Arlo, who was still standing beside them. 'They are coming down presently, and my father wants you beside him on the top table tonight, as usual, Arlo Eymer.' Arlo nodded in response but looked uncharacteristically grim.

She then turned, and, smiling; she slipped in beside Merewyn, who was surprised that Ardith would be sitting at this table with her and not with her father on the top table. However, at that moment, Thorfinn's entry caused a stir, two of his tall blond Saxon Huscarls were flanking him, and a group of Normans accompanied him.

The group of Normans were tense as they entered the packed Hearth Hall, a situation not helped when a giant Saxon warrior stood up from his bench and punched his fist in the air, shouting,

'Thorfinn... Thorfinn!'

Within minutes, the whole of the Hall's Saxon side were on their feet, shouting their Thegns name in unison and banging on the tables. Merewyn glanced at her father, his face creased with anxiety, and at Ardith, who now had a hand over her mouth and tears in her eyes as she watched her father stride sternly but proudly down the Hall. The Norman contingent watched in subdued but concerned silence, although Merewyn could see awe and respect on some of their faces for this impressive and renowned Saxon warrior. Reaching the top table, he raised his tankard and shouted for silence. He then saluted his people. He thanked them for their service and loyalty but told them they must now look to the future and a peaceful England, that there had been too much war for too long. He then sat while the Norman Lords settled on his right and Arlo on his left, although one chair at the top table remained empty next to Lord Bodin.

Merewyn realised that she also had silent tears running down her face; she had looked up to this wise warrior for the whole of her life, and here he was doing the only thing he could, advocating peace to protect his people. The message was that they were to put war and conflict behind them and work with their new Norman overlords to bring peace back to the region. Thorfinn now banged on the table and introduced Lord Bodin to the assembled Hall. Merewyn brushed away her tears to examine the Norman who now stood on Thorfinn's right hand. This, then, was the man who would rule Ravensworth and its surrounding manors and, more importantly, order their lives now and in the future.

Bodin Le Ver was of medium height with dark curly auburn hair cut in the short, almost brutal, Norman style. Still, he had attractive features and dressed in expensive garments - a red silk tunic with gold banding. Bodin spoke in fluent English, which surprised her. He thanked Thorfinn for his speech and the welcome; under what were difficult circumstances, a low growl of anger rippled through the Hall as the events of that morning were fresh in the Saxons' minds.

'The man is obviously a diplomat', whispered Merewyn cynically to Ardith, who smiled and nodded her head in agreement.

He finished by saying that they would all be prepared to work together for a prosperous peace and that their Patron, Count Alain Rufus, would ensure their safety and wellbeing as long as they abided by and followed Norman law.

Merewyn could not imagine he thought it would be that easy, especially after the killing of young Sweyn that morning, and she turned to look at Ardith in disbelief. By doing so, she missed the arrival of the tall, dark figure that mounted the dais and took his place in the empty chair besides Bodin. She turned back to hear his last words,

'And so I introduce Lord Luc De Malvais who will be the Marechal of this area and therefore your overlord for Count Alain'. Bodin swept a hand towards Luc and smiled down at him.

Luc did not speak but nodded in acknowledgement of Bodin's words, gazing enigmatically but with an assessing eye out over the crowd. She turned to see the new arrival, and there was the dark Norman knight she had encountered in the meadow. She gave such a gasp that Ardith and Father Giffard looked round at her in surprise.

'What is it, Merewyn?' Said Ardith as she followed Merewyn's shocked gaze to the top table, 'Do you know him?' she asked in amazement.

Merewyn could only shake her head; she could not speak; she was in shock. He was not just a lowly Norman Knight and retainer. She recalled that she had even thought at one point that he might be just a mercenary, considering the state he arrived in, but no, he was a Norman Lord in his own right.

Also, he was the new Norman Marechal, the Overlord of this whole area, he would make decisions about their lives and future, and she had treated him with disdain and contempt.

She looked up and found a disturbingly familiar pair of steel-blue eyes staring down at her as she realised that her gasp, and the concern that followed it, had drawn the attention of some of the top table.

There was a smattering of applause from his Norman followers as Bodin sat down, and the men on both sides applied themselves to their drink and the enormous trenchers of roast meats and fresh bread that was carried to the tables. On daring to raise her eyes, Merewyn realised that Luc De Malvais was staring at her with unfeigned interest, a small smile on his lips that now reflected in his eyes. He had recognised her, she was sure of it, and she was determined not to look at him again.

Merewyn sat like a statue; it took her several moments to realise that Father Giffard offered her and Ardith the choicest morsels from a selection of roast pork and fowl. She weakly shook her head; she could not possibly eat a thing. Her stomach was in knots. However, she took a large gulp from her cup instead. She was surprised to find a rich, warm, full-bodied, intense red wine and not the watered ale or mead she was expecting. She felt the heat of it spread through her body, and she finished the cup to have it filled immediately by the smiling serving boy behind. A second cup took the edge off her anxiety, and she felt emboldened enough to risk another glance up at Luc De Malvais through her partly lowered lids.

He was dark and handsome with a longer hairstyle than his compatriots, one that reached his tunic's collar and fell forward over his brow. He had shaved and dressed in a blue and silver tunic held by an unusual, sizeable Celtic-style silver clasp on one of his broad shoulders. He was now deep in animated conversation with Thorfinn and Bodin. She watched, mesmerised, as he used his long, strong hands to describe what he meant. She was close enough to catch snatches of the conversation as he made sweeping gestures to the roof, and she realised he was admiring the design of the new Hearth Hall.

'He is handsome, isn't he,' said a smiling Ardith.

Merewyn jumped as she realised that Ardith had been watching her. 'I suppose so. I have encountered him before, in the meadow this morning. But he is a Norman and arrogant,' she sneered.

'A Norman who is now our new Overlord, that is not going to change; we need to accept it and move forward. Also, men are men the world over, Merewyn, no matter their origins, and women will always be in thrall to them,' said Ardith. Merewyn knew Ardith was only a year older than she was, but her friend seemed so calm and mature, while Merewyn knew that she could still act like a hoyden at times. She gave an exasperated sigh, 'He is still the enemy, and no-one will force me to be pleasant to them while they have occupied our lands and slaughtered our menfolk.'

Ardith smiled. 'Bodin is very courtly, a true knight who engaged me in conversation while we were waiting for my father in the solar.' Merewyn felt her anger rise and gazed at Ardith in amazement. 'Ardith, you liked him! How could you when they are Normans? They are throwing you out of your home tomorrow and stealing your villages, land and animals. These Normans have only a veneer of civilisation; they are warlike ruthless savages who murder our men, and today they raped one of our women!' she emphatically cried at her.

She almost forgot where she was; she was so astonished and frustrated with her friend, who could seem so quick to brush aside the wrongs done to them. Father Giffard leaned over, grasped her wrist and told her harshly to be quiet, and Merewyn realised that she had raised her voice when there was a lull in the conversation. At the top table, they had heard what she said; she narrowed her eyes in dislike as she turned in scorn to glare at the top table, but her father's stern stare in her direction and his tight lips said it all. Thorfinn was gazing into the distance, down the Hall away from her. Lord Bodin commented loudly in French to Luc that he was surprised that such licence was allowed to a young unmarried girl to be so outspoken. De Malvais contemplated her in cold hard stony silence; his eyes narrowed in what was anger, and his lip curled in distaste. She felt the hot colour flood up into her face, and she dropped her eyes. She heard her father stand and apologise to the table for his daughter's lack of courtesy, assuring them it would not happen again.

It was just too much for Merewyn; the tension, fear and anxiety of the long day had taken its toll, combined with this public chastisement from her father. She knew that she had to get out of there. She sat for a further five minutes; head bowed, as conversation resumed, and then she drained another full goblet of wine. However, her mind made up; she spoke to the priest. 'I do not feel well, Father Giffard. Please tell my father I have gone out for some air.' The priest nodded as Merewyn squeezed slowly out of the bench, gave a swift bow to the top table and backed into the aisle, forcing herself to walk slowly, albeit slightly unsteadily, as she was unused to such strong red wine. Inside, she felt the panic building and the shame, she felt like running.

* * *

Luc had approached the Hall with very mixed feelings that evening; he was apprehensive about a large Hearth Hall full of angry Huscarls and Saxon villagers, so he had purposefully attached a dagger to his belt beneath his tunic. However, having met Thorfinn and his family, his fears had been somewhat allayed; Bodin was right; this was a wise old Thegn who wanted to work with them to protect his people and maintain the peace. As he entered the Hall behind Bodin, this did not prevent him scanning the crowd like a warrior, assessing every escape route and taking time to reposition some of the Norman guards until he finally followed the others and headed to the top table.

Once the feast was underway, he relaxed slightly and found the food and wine to be excellent. Thorfinn introduced him to Arlo Eymer, his friend and Steward, a wealthy Thegn in his own right. Luc thought this Thegn would prove to be very useful to him over the coming year; he must arrange for him to stay at Ravensworth and work with him, rather than leaving with Thorfinn to go to Melsonby. He then had time to sit and assess his surroundings and the display of apparent wealth. The Hearth Hall was very impressive, with substantial oak pillars holding up the roof's cross beams. It was plastered white inside, making it far lighter than other halls he had seen; the walls covered in places with large colourful tapestries and banners. His eyes finally roamed over the occupants of the Hall; he immediately spotted and assessed the large warrior Huscarls on one adjacent table, huge Saxon men wearing many torcs as badges of battles fought. The garrulous priest sat beside them, and then he saw her.

He blinked and stared at the girl who was sitting on the front bench beside Thorfinn's daughter. Could it be her, the beautiful but wilful peasant girl from the meadow? It must be. No one else had that unusual fine silver-blonde hair. He watched her as she was deep in conversation with Ardith. He thought she must be a maidservant, although she was in similar fine clothes to her mistress. She looked up at him at that point, and he found himself staring down at her, aware that she now recognised him as well. She had a special kind of beauty that he found captivating; her deep green eyes were now wide with trepidation, and he watched her biting her lower lip in apprehension. He enjoyed watching that for a few seconds, recognising the effect he was having upon her. He decided to visit Thorfinn at Melsonby in future to see more of this maidservant.

His attention was suddenly brought back by Bodin asking his opinion. Bodin complimented Thorfinn on his Hall's design while describing the cathedral's new vaulted roof in Bayeux in Normandy. As he listened and agreed with Bodin, his eyes wandered back to her. He found himself drawn again to look at her; she seemed to be deep in animated conversation with her mistress. At that moment, there was a lull in the discussion at the top table, and everyone could hear what the girl was shouting so emphatically... 'they are warlike and ruthless savages who murder our men and today, they raped one of our women!' Her condemnation of them resonated around the Hall.

He was taken aback; he could not believe that this Saxon girl had the temerity to insult both Bodin and himself in that way, no matter how beautiful she looked when passionate and angry. He sat in seething silence as Bodin made some comment to him on her behaviour and her father apologised for her, but, as he glared down at her, his anger simmering, she suddenly got to her feet, bowed and left. His eyes followed her as she slipped down the far aisle towards the doors.

Arlo on Thorfinn's left was, again, on his feet, 'You must forgive my daughter, my Lords. Her mother died five years ago, her brother is missing or dead in the rebellion, and she is now finding this situation very difficult, especially after today's events. Bodin nodded curtly and thanked Arlo for the apology.

Luc barely registered at first what Arlo said; his anger was too hot. This was the second time this girl had shown disrespect to him and, now, to Lord Bodin and the two young Norman knights sitting on Luc's right. She needed to pay for her insolence; on impulse, he stood, made his excuse briefly and set off after her, moving swiftly down the darker pillared aisles towards the large side doors.

* * *

Merewyn slipped through the gap in the Hall door and stood on the large porch gulping in large mouthfuls of night air and wafting her veil to try to cool her crimson cheeks. She breathed a sigh of relief, but then, suddenly, she heard the noise of the door pushed violently open further behind her and even before she felt the firm hands on her shoulders, she knew it would be him.

Standing very close behind her, he towered over her as she glanced back and upwards; the light from the large summer moon highlighted his stern, unforgiving face. He spoke, and she could hear the anger resonating through the barely controlled words.

'So, not just a shirking peasant girl in a meadow! Instead, you are the daughter of a Saxon Thegn, but with the manners and behaviour of a low serving wench'.

His hands on her shoulders firmly pulled her back towards him as he was speaking, and he slid his hands down her body, gripping both of her upper arms, holding her in place against him. Merewyn now felt very afraid. She turned her head slightly and apprehensively looked up at him, his mouth was a thin, grim line, and she could see from his flashing eyes just how angry he was. She could also feel his hard-muscled body through his tunic as he held her firmly in place against him, his solid muscled thighs pressed through her dress against her lower back and legs. The silence hung for a few seconds, and she could hear and feel his harsh breath on her neck.

'So maybe it would be better if I decided to beat you and treat you like a serving wench. After all, that is what you deserve after the disrespect you showed to me, Lord Bodin and his knights while embarrassing your father at the same time.' He said in an icy tone.

Merewyn stood there partly ashamed but frozen with trepidation and fear; no one had ever spoken to her like this. She found that his proximity was having an unexpected and startling effect on her. Her spine tingled from top to bottom from the charged contact of his body pressed hard against hers. She summoned up every ounce of courage and looked up over her shoulder directly into that severe and unyielding face.

'I was only telling the truth. I am not sorry about that; you must know that here in the villages we hate the Normans, you have stolen our land, slaughtered our menfolk, and today your men murdered a young Saxon and raped his wife.' Her voice faltered on the last words as his eyes darkened even further with anger.

'What did you say!' he demanded.

Suddenly, he spun her round to face him, still tightly holding her arms. As she looked up into those hard, steel-blue eyes, she felt her stomach tighten and flip in apprehension; she had gone too far again. Therefore, she said nothing. This was no village boy that she could easily manipulate and push away, this was the new Overlord of Ravensworth, and he could do with her and her family what he wished. She suddenly felt very powerless and apprehensive, new emotions for her, and it showed in her face and wide eyes as she gazed up at him.

He saw it as well, and he suddenly pulled her to him and held her body close in a vice-like grip; she could feel every part of his hard-muscled frame pressed against hers, a wave of heat flooded through her. Holding her with one hand firmly on her lower back, he leaned her slightly backwards; his hand pulled her veil off and gripped her hair tightly at the base of her skull, holding her head in place. Then his lips descended harshly onto hers.

Village boys at the solstice feasts had kissed her before, so she was no novice, but she had never experienced anything like this. He possessed her mouth as his hands began travelling over her body and up through her hair; feelings she had never imagined coursed through her body. His tongue explored every part of her mouth, and, suddenly, he was kissing her throat and moving down over her collarbone, his fingers loosening her tunic and bodice. She clung to him and could feel the heat from his exploring hands, caressing her pale, chaste skin as they moved lower, gently cupping and squeezing her breasts.

She let out a low moan. She could not have stopped him if she had tried, and she was not sure she wanted to; she was bewildered and overwhelmed by the emotions flowing through her body. If he had let her go at that point, she would have fallen, as she had no control over her limbs, which seemed to be shaking. She inhaled the pure masculine smell of him. He groaned, and his hands dropped to clench her buttocks and pull her firmly against his hard manhood. He lifted his head and gazed down into her face. She found herself panting slightly as she stared up into his intense gaze with expectation. She could both see and feel the hunger and need in him. He wanted her, and her body had reached such a fever pitch that she thought at that moment, he could have carried her unprotestingly to the nearest barn. How could this be? He was a Norman; at that moment, a picture flashed into her mind of Emera dragged by her hair into the hut. A wave of cold anger went through her. 'Are you just going to take me as well? Isn't that what Normans usually do,' she gasped.

Immediately he froze; he took a deep breath and straightened up, but he still held her firmly to him, and she felt him lift a handful of her long silken hair and bring it to his face, inhaling the smell and scent of her. Then he took a step back from her, and she realised that his breathing was ragged as well; he looked at her in a puzzled way, a gamut of emotions seeming to race across his tanned, handsome face.

She watched him frown, and to Merewyn, it seemed that he wanted her, but she could see he despised her or himself for that desire at the same time. This reflected her uneasy feelings, she recognised that something about him attracted her despite what he was and what he had done, but it was inconceivable. She watched, apprehensive as he took a deep breath and without another word, he released her, gently pushing her away and turning on his heel; he went swiftly back into the Hall.

Merewyn, now freed, staggered back slightly and stood still, breathing quickly. She could feel her heart hammering as she tried to work out what had just happened. I hate him, she thought. She felt shocked at what he had done, but she knew that more shocking was the fact that she could still feel the excitement he had ignited in her. She brought her hand up to touch her bruised lips. Her cheeks flamed as she remembered how her body had responded to him; she felt ashamed and angry with herself and then furious with him. How dare he put his hands on her, a Thegns daughter? He did not have the right, even if he was their Norman Lord, and they were now his vassals!

This enemy had killed her brother and stolen their land. Thorfinn and her father would hear of this. He would regret ever touching her. She clenched her fists and let the anger flow through her, and, then wrapping her arms tightly around the oak doorpost, she gazed out at her village. The dying embers of the fire pit glowing in the dark, the thatched rooves bathed in strong moonlight but with black hidden shadows between the buildings, the dark, bloodstained mark clearly still to be seen on the dirt ground outside of Sweyn's home where his body had lain.

Seeing this, she sobered and came to her senses; in reality, she knew that what had just happened between her and Luc De Malvais must also stay in the shadows; she could tell no one, or she would put their lives in danger if they decided to defend her honour. Now, she knew that De Malvais was a powerful, wealthy Norman Lord in his own right, a professional knight and a hardened warrior. Still, neither her older father nor Thorfinn, who were both experienced fighters, would be a match for him. It must remain a secret; he would surely keep it a secret. Then she froze. Would he come back for her again?

She released her grip on the post and made her way quickly across the village green, back to her home, her body still ravaged by the physical sensations of the encounter. She repeatedly glanced over her shoulder in trepidation that the Norman might follow her. As she reached the safety of her door and closed it behind her, she thankfully realised that at least they would be leaving Ravensworth tomorrow to accompany Thorfinn and Ardith to live at Melsonby. It would be challenging, but there was some comfort in that move, for at least it meant that she would see very little of Luc de Malvais; she would leave his immediate sphere of influence.

Chapter Five

L uc returned to the Hall with mixed emotions. He shook his head and ran his hands through his hair as he headed back to the top table; he felt perplexed. What had just happened out there, he asked himself? He had gone out intending to threaten and frighten her into submission, to punish her for her insolence and disrespect. He followed her out and opened the door, but the sight of her standing with the moonlight reflecting off that beautiful, long, silver-blonde hair was too much for him. It was madness, and before he realised what he was doing, his righteous anger forgotten, he pulled her into his arms and was kissing her hungrily. At one point, he admitted to himself, he had thought of picking her up and taking her to the nearest bed or mound of straw; then he remembered who she was, a rebel Saxon girl. More importantly, he remembered who he was, the appointed Marechal of Alain Rufus. How could he swive the daughter of one of the Saxon Thegns that he intended to win over? He smiled ruefully at the thought, then her words on the porch came back to him; that was the second time she had implied rape; he determined to ask Bodin what had happened when the men arrived in the village.

The feast was still in full swing as he slipped back into the chair beside his friend Bodin. He emptied his goblet of wine in one go and refilled it. Bodin, noticing his heightened colour and frown, watched him with raised eyebrows and a knowing smile. 'Certainly beautiful, isn't she, our rebellious Saxon?' he said.

Luc scowled at his friend and emptied another goblet of wine, 'I have no idea what you mean, Bodin.'

'Really, so what are these?' said Bodin, as he leaned over and released several long silver blonde hairs from Luc's large Celtic tunic clasp and held them up.

'She is a pretty rebel who needs punishing and teaching a lesson,' said Luc with a sheepish smile. Bodin had eyes like a hawk; he was a consummate court politician and missed very little.

'And are you going to punish her, teach her that lesson, or have you just done so?' asked Bodin, with a smile.

Luc laughed aloud. 'No, I just gave her a very pleasant warning about her behaviour, but, as you are well aware, Bodin, I have no time for a troublesome woman in my life, and she would certainly be trouble. I have work to do here for Alain.'

'Then you should make time, Malvais. How long has it been now since the death of Heloise? Is it six, seven years? Too long for a man to be celibate or on his own, and you should be producing heirs to help you rule all of that land in Brittany.'

'I assure you, Bodin, I have not been celibate. As you know, many women have wanted and enjoyed my company and my bed. Uncomplicated women who needed no attachment or ties. I have time enough to find another wife when I have finished here, when I return home to Brittany, I am sure my mother will have several lined up.'

'That could be several years, Luc. Count Alain has plans for you and this area, and, on that note, I have just arranged with Thorfinn that the Thegn Arlo Eymer will stay here as your Steward for the next year at least. Arlo has status and knowledge of the people and land in this area, and he will prove very useful to you. We will, in return, allow him to stay in his own house in the village and keep his land, paying us the regular tithes and giving us fealty of course,' added Bodin.

Luc tried to look grateful at this news, but he ran his hand over his face and sighed, for he knew that if Arlo Eymer were staying, then so would his family. He would see his beautiful, wilful daughter every day. There was no doubt that she was bewitching, but Luc thought she could also cause trouble in the village with her barely hidden hatred of everything Norman; he could not imagine her wanting to give fealty. Although the way her body had reacted to him, the way she had accepted his passionate kiss did not suggest, she hated him too much. He leaned back in his chair, becoming thoughtful, as the conversations continued around him. He allowed himself a few moments to revisit the feel of her body against his, then he shook his head and drained his wine, determined to forget what had just happened until her words in the porch resonated again.

'Exactly what happened here this morning, Bodin? I have heard mention of a woman who was attacked.' Bodin did not answer for a few moments staring ahead out into the Hall in preoccupation until he turned and regarded Luc solemnly.

'Do you remember our early years together as Mercenaries fighting against the Lombard and Saracens in Sicily?' he asked. Luc nodded and then gazed down at the swirling wine in his cup. He thought he knew what Bodin was about to say.

'There was a Saracen town we laid siege to for several months. They refused to surrender, but still, they sallied out in raiding parties at night, and they captured one of our patrols. They flayed the men alive in front of us on the top of the town walls, where we could all see them; I can still hear their screams when I think of it. We called one of our finest archers to put them out of their misery. The next day you could feel the anger amongst our troops, and we finally smashed through the barbican and entered the town. Our orders were to give no quarter, so we killed every man in it and raped every woman and girl,' he said.

Luc looked up and met Bodin's eyes. 'They were dark years after the death of Heloise and my son; I was young, angry against the world and lost in my own misery. I am not proud of what we did for revenge in the heat of battle, but I like to think that we are different people now,' he said.

'I know. Neither am I, Luc, but in many ways, we are still at war here. Today a young armed Saxon warrior raced across the green to kill two of my men. He died. His woman then went to attack the same men with his dagger, so they dragged her inside and swived her; it was nothing. We have to show them who is in control here, Luc or they will rebel and kill us at the first opportunity.'

Luc looked pensive. 'I will keep your show of force, Bodin, but I will not be using your methods; l will use the Norman law and justice that William is so keen for us to embed,' he said, draining his cup.

* * *

Merewyn woke early; she was always an early riser, especially in summer, when she did not want to miss any of the long summer days. There was much to do today, with the packing up of the house and arranging which animals to take with them; some would have to be left behind. She dressed quickly into practical clothes and braided her hair tightly, pinning it up out of the way. She could hear Helga rattling around in the scullery, readying the pots for the large pan of pottage that always bubbled in the hearth.

She walked through to the front of the house to open the shutters in the Hall. To her surprise, she found her father already there at the table, having a breakfast of bread, cheese and mulled ale. He glanced up at her without a word and returned to his food; she realised he was still angry and ashamed of her behaviour last night.

Merewyn sighed, 'I am sorry, father, and I should not have said what I did, at least not loudly.' He raised an eyebrow and returned to his food. Merewyn persevered,

'I was just angry and not thinking. I didn't expect them to hear me.' She added.

Her father stood up and gave her a tight smile. 'Didn't you?' he asked.

He pushed back his chair and started for the door, and then he stopped and turning he faced her. 'Merewyn, do you not think we are all angry, but what can we do? Should we take up arms again to be maimed or killed and watch our families taken into slavery or serfdom? These men out there, these Normans who have defeated us, they have the power to do that.' He said in an exasperated voice. Merewyn hung her head, he was right, and her actions were putting her family at risk.

'This is my fault in some ways; I have been far too lax with your upbringing, allowed you far too much freedom. I have been too wrapped up in grief and anger for the loss of your mother and then in the affairs and estates of Thorfinn. Now I have to deal with these damned thieving arrogant Normans. Once we have settled Thorfinn and his family into Melsonby today, I promise to look for a Saxon husband for you. I have left it far too long. I wish you had married Braxton before he went to do battle, but, of course, he did not return, and neither did my son.'

Arlo stopped and closed his eyes, overcome with sadness and grief for a moment at the thought of his handsome and impulsive eldest son, Garrett.

Merewyn knew that both Braxton and Thorfinn had pressurised her father for an immediate marriage. Instead, her father had delayed and listened to her wishes. He understood her dislike and misgivings about Braxton. Yet it was a good match, especially as all of their lands would come together. However, now he was gone, killed in the rebellion. She cast her mind quickly around the men on the local manors to try to think of any one of suitable rank but unbidden; her thoughts returned to a pair of steel-blue eyes and the all-consuming feelings of the night before. Again, she felt a rush of heat as she remembered the easy and masterful way he had held her in his grasp and undone her clothes with one hand. She had done nothing to stop him. In fact, for the first five minutes, she had not uttered a sound of protest against this Norman. What did that make her? She was brought back with a start as her father unbarred the door.

'Should I bring all of the chests through for packing, father?' she asked.

Arlo gave an exasperated snort, 'No! We will not be leaving.

If you had not rushed away last night, you would have heard that Lord Bodin has seen fit to leave us here on our land. On condition that I work with the new Marechal to help him administer the manors as I did for Thorfinn.'

Merewyn was taken aback. 'We are not going with Thorfinn and Ardith?' she asked in shocked surprise.

'No, we are staying in our own home and in a far better situation than I had thought possible. I may still despise these Normans, but they are dealing with some of us fairly, given the circumstances,' said Arlo.

He opened the door and stopped on the threshold, looking back at her pale face. 'Now, I must ensure that everything is in place for Thorfinn's departure this morning while you can reflect on your behaviour last night and occupy yourself with tasks today, as befits a dutiful and respectful daughter.' His face softened slightly. 'I am not asking you to fawn over these Normans like Father Giffard seems to be doing, but I am expecting you to say very little unless asked, and I expect you to be respectful and polite when in their company, no matter how much we despise them. Do you understand?'

'Yes, father,' murmured a suspiciously meek and contrite Merewyn. He smiled as he went out. He was not taken in. He knew how headstrong and outspoken his daughter was, just like her beautiful, Irish mother had been. The door closed with a thump behind him, and Merewyn was left standing alone in the middle of the room. She wrapped her arms around herself as if to give herself security, her mind in turmoil.

'Not leaving,' she repeated to herself. 'Not leaving Ravensworth', she whispered. Although she was pleased, they were not leaving their home, and they were allowed to keep their lands; she wondered what would happen when she saw De Malvais again. How could she even look at him and meet his eyes, knowing what had happened between them? What would she say to him? Would he even mention it? She doubted he would, as he thought her beneath him. A thought suddenly struck her. Was he married? Indeed, he must be and have children back in Normandy. The thought slightly unsettled her, and she realised that she did not like the idea of a beautiful, dark, Norman wife waiting for him for some reason. She stood there, bewildered about the reaction she had to this Norman.

What had happened between them was probably nothing to a man like him. She was aware that he was physically aroused last night; she was not naive, and she had acutely felt the hardness of his manhood pressing against her stomach. She had thought at one point that he was not going to stop and, if she was honest with herself, she shamefully admitted to herself that she was not sure she wanted him to either.

She knew that this was no romantic dalliance on his part. She was aware of his position as Marechal; he was now the overlord of dozens of manors and responsible for hundreds of people. If he wanted her, he could take her at any time, and who would stop him? As a young girl, she had overheard the stories from the women of the village; she remembered listening, enthralled, to their shocked voices as they told tales of rape and pillage by the Normans. She had learned from their stories that the French Lords often practised 'Droit De Seignior': the right of any lord to take any maiden or woman in his domain, even on her wedding night. She was sure that was precisely how De Malvais thought of her as an available Saxon girl for his amusement. Well, with her, he would find he was thoroughly mistaken; she would treat him with all the disdain and contempt he deserved.

A cry and smash from the scullery brought her out of her reverie as she realised Durkin was up and causing problems for Helga. He was a delightful child, but already, at five years, he was pushing the boundaries and showing the same wilful streak that both she and her brother, Garret, had inherited. When she entered the small room at the back of the house, she found Helga surrounded by pots and leather buckets sweeping up a broken crock from the floor. Durkin was sitting on a small stool swinging his legs, eating a large chunk of bread and dripping. Merewyn frowned at him and shook her head, 'As soon as you have finished that Durkin, you can come with me to the orchard; you can help me collect the honey.'

Looking after the beehives was a task Merewyn had inherited from her mother, and she had taken it on most willingly; the hives were under the trees in the orchard. In the springtime, the honey was sweet from the apple and pear blossoms and in the late summer, the bees roamed the moors above the village, collecting nectar from the flowering heather. This gave the local honey mead its unique flavour.

Merewyn set out through the quiet village carrying a sizeable wide crock and a sturdy bag with a wooden spatula. Durkin trotted at her heels, carrying a wrap of very fine woven linen cloth. Merewyn knew the bees would be sleepy at this time of the morning. The dew was still on the grass and, if it had not been for the intrusive, leering Norman guards on the gate smacking their lips at her, it would have been like any other summer morning in Ravensworth. On reaching the orchard, Merewyn quickly set to work removing the woven wicker covers off the chosen hives and gently lifting the full honeycombs into the crock, shaking off the sleepy bees. She had covered her head with the gauze-like linen and wore a pair of her father's old leather gauntlets to prevent being stung. They moved systematically across the front row of hives, Durkin giggling and laughing at the honey running down his fingers as he helped Merewyn place them in the crock. She laughed too, enjoying this moment with her young brother, utterly unaware that a tall, dark-clad figure on horseback, invisible in the shadows of the orchard, was watching their every move.

Chapter Six

Luc very rarely had any trouble sleeping, but his experience with Merewyn and the talk with Bodin followed by far too much red wine had left him with a dry mouth and an aching head as he tossed and turned on his truckle bed. He watched the sunrise hit the side of the pavilion and decided to get up and ride out into the countryside around.

He dressed quickly and walked through the early morning ground mist to the horse lines; the soft light was just beginning to filter through the trees. He felt he needed a good gallop to clear his head, and he knew his horse would enjoy it. He was welcomed with a whicker from Espirit; Luc rubbed his nose and fed him a small apple. A sleepy young groom arrived to help, but Luc waved him away and, using just a bridle, he vaulted onto the horse's back and set off out of the village to explore some of the areas he was to oversee.

He rode south at first, over the tops of several small hills, which gave him a vantage point to survey the local area's topography. He could see the village nestled on the Holme River's southern bank, and he could make out the road that led east up the hill on the north side to Melsonby, the village that Thorfinn and his family were moving to today. He rode for several miles in that direction to get the feel of the terrain; then he realised he was beginning to feel hungry, so he cut back through the ancient forest. This route brought him to the edges of the orchard, east of the village. It was wattle-fenced to keep the wild boar and deer out, but Espirit hopped over that with ease.

Luc relaxed his shoulders and arms. He felt better for his hour in the fresh air, and he let the reins go long to give his horse its head to stretch out and nibble at a few flavoursome plants and grasses as they threaded their way through the mature apple and pear fruit trees. Then he heard laughter; it sounded like the village children. He saw a slight clearing ahead and pulled Espirit up under the shade of a large pear tree. He could see what appeared to be a mother and young child and realised they were collecting honey as the woman was veiled and gloved, and he could see the dozen or so wicker hives under the trees. He sat quietly for a while and watched, unable to tear his gaze away as she deftly extracted the honey. Suddenly, he realised it was Merewyn, her tall figure, the graceful way she moved giving her away; she had such a natural elegance.

He took the opportunity to sit and watch her unseen. He was somewhat confused, as he did not think that she had a child or was married. She had dressed demurely at the feast, but with her long hair loose and unbound, as a maiden would, was she a widow with a child, he wondered. Would that explain the hatred and bitterness towards him and all Normans, had her husband died in battle? He then remembered something that Arlo had said when he apologised for his daughter's behaviour; her mother had died in childbirth a few years ago. Was this small child her younger brother?

He watched as she replaced each of the wicker domes on the hives, and then she threw the linen back from her face and sat on the grass with the boy. He heard them laugh as they dipped their fingers in the honey and licked them. Luc sat there mesmerised, entranced by her. She seemed so young and innocent in this setting. Framed by the rising morning sun behind them, she bore no resemblance to the angry, rebellious young woman from the day before.

As he watched them, a dark, hollow feeling rose in his chest. This peaceful scene was probably being re-enacted all over England, across Normandy and in Brittany's home province. It was very different from the brutal reality of the warfare he had seen and experienced for the last twelve years. However, it also resurrected painful memories; it was six years since he had lost both his wife, Heloise and his newborn son in childbirth. He had locked that memory away after raging in anger against fate. Now, he rarely let it out, but watching Merewyn with her young brother brought the memory flooding back. His son would have been a similar age to this child. He let out a harsh shuddering breath for what he had lost that summer.

Espirit, seeming to recognise his master's tense body and distress, snorted and stamped his foot. Luc quickly pulled himself together, gathered his reins and frowning; he rode out into the clearing as it became apparent they had both seen and heard him. The laughter had indeed stopped, and Merewyn had swept her brother safely into her arms. She looked apprehensive and frightened but just as beautiful, while the small, dark, tightly held boy gazed at him and the horse with fearless, frank interest and fascination.

* * *

Merewyn had been enjoying the time with Durkin. He was a delightfully mischievous child, so quick, and he looked enchanting with honey on his nose and eyebrows. They had both been laughing together when the stamping horse startled her.

As the horse and rider emerged from the shadows, she realised at once whom it was. She saw he was riding without a saddle, and his long powerful legs gripped the horse's side, directing him with the lightest touch. However, his stern expression worried her as his horse came on towards them. He did not look pleased to see her there, and he gave an almost cynical sneer as he looked down on them.

Merewyn decided to follow her father's instructions. 'Good day to you, my lord,' she said in a cold, impersonal voice, bowing her head with respect.

Durkin, however, had no such reluctance, 'That is the biggest horse I have ever seen,' he said as he wriggled out of Merewyn's arms and ran forward.

The child darted straight under his horse to Luc's amazement and rested his head on the enormous muscled chest. Equally astonishing was the fact that Espirit, a war-trained Destrier, moved not a muscle. Trained to strike out with those deadly hooves and kill an enemy, he saw the small child as no threat. Instead, he lowered his head and snorted warm air onto the boy's face. Luc, taken aback by the situation, lost any cutting remark he was about to make to Merewyn.

'What a fearless little boy,' he said, and he could not help adding, 'you can tell he is your brother.' He found himself smiling at the thought as he leaned forward. Merewyn's feelings turned to amazement from apprehension as Luc's face lit up with that smile. She could see that it reached those arresting eyes as he leaned over to look down at Durkin, and she could hear the sincerity of his words. This brought about a spate of confusing thoughts; where was the angry dominant overlord of the previous night? This was a side of him; she did not know. A side that made him seem more human as Luc De Malvais the man, rather than an authoritarian Norman overlord. For a few minutes, she watched him, almost mesmerised by him as he interacted with the boy and the horse. He was wearing a loose-lined tunic, open at the top showing his tanned, muscled neck and offering a glimpse of his powerful chest.

'He has no fear of any animals,' said Merewyn. Then she could not stop herself adding a sting in the tail, 'he is too young yet to know and understand the fear of men and what they are capable of.'

She regretted the comment as soon as she made it, watching his smiling face close down into a frown again and, with his mouth grim, he glared down at her. However, Durkin now emerged from under the horse and reached up to stroke its velvet nose.

'What is his name?' he asked Luc. Merewyn held her breath, concerned for her brother with this stern, angry Norman, but Luc just glanced away from her and answered him. 'He is called Espirit Noir, and he is over seventeen hands high,' he said, leaning over to look down at Durkin, 'Which is French for 'Black Spirit' because at times he has a very nasty temper, especially in battle when he is almost impossible to stop,' he said in a stern voice. Durkin only laughed aloud and stood up on tiptoe to stroke the powerful withers of the enormous animal, bringing the smile fleetingly back to Luc's face.

Watching him, Merewyn, to her surprise, found herself almost unwillingly smiling along with him. He glanced at her again; they stared at each other for several moments in an awkward, uncertain way that made her breath catch in her throat. Then, she pulled herself together. 'Come, Durkin, we must get back; there are many tasks to do for father to assist Thegn Thorfinn today.'

She gathered her belongings, gave Luc a bow of her head and set off through the orchard, pulling the reluctant and protesting Durkin with her by the hand. As she went, she felt bemused by the encounter; waves of conflicting emotions washed over her. She hated the Normans and everything they stood for, but this man attracted her like no other she had ever met. It was unforgivable! He was a Norman! She felt the anger against them building again as she thought of her missing brother, Garrett. What was wrong with her?

Luc watched them go, reflecting, with interest, on her pleasant greeting and the sudden smile he had received when talking to her brother. He imagined her father's hand in this; there was no doubt that her father had counselled her to compromise. She must have hated that, as she so clearly despised them. Her father had overindulged her since her mother's death; indeed, she should have been married by now. Why wasn't she? She was undoubtedly outspoken, and there was no doubt she needed a husband's firm hand to show her the error of her ways. He mused for a while on that smile she had given him. He thought about how he would bring her to heel and how much he might enjoy doing that. Then, he laughed as he realised that, beyond the shadow of a doubt, she was entirely capable of making any man's life hell.

Aside from that, she was a Saxon rebel, her father a Thegn who had fought against them; her brother was a rebel that he or and his Breton Horse Warriors had opposed in Northumberland. A young man, whom he had most likely either killed, or imprisoned in the raids. She was best left to some ardent Saxon to control. However, with that thought, he suddenly found that he did not like the idea of her with another man even though she was not, and could never be, for him. There was no denying that she was eerily beautiful, but she was unattainable. As a Breton Lord in King William's forces, he knew that he could never countenance any relationship with her. He needed to put her out of his mind and concentrate on the immense tasks before winning over this domain's people. He found himself feeling somewhat irritated by the encounter, but he was not sure why. He decided he needed food, and he turned Espirit for home.

Arriving back at the pavilion, Luc gave Espirit a rub down and handed him over to the groom to turn out. Going inside the spacious tent, he found Bodin deep in discussion with Arlo Eymer.

'You were up and out early, Malvais, something keeping you awake?' said Bodin with a grin. Luc just smiled, he knew exactly what his friend was alluding to, and he was pleased that it seemed to go over the head of Arlo.

'Thorfinn will be packed and ready to go by mid-afternoon, and Arlo is available to give you a tour of the village and the surrounding demesne lands after that.' Bodin added. Luc nodded, expressed his pleasure that the Steward was now staying in the village and, having agreed to meet Arlo at his house later in the day, sent him on his way. Bodin looked thoughtful, 'He will prove to be very useful, Luc, keep him on side and find out where the real problems lie in this area.' Luc nodded in agreement.

'However, Bodin, it will, of course, be more difficult if you expect me to take my pleasure with his daughter when and where I will,' said Luc shaking his head ruefully.

Bodin laughed, 'We'll win his support first; he might even give her to you. I have seen many times in the past how you can charm the common folk and have them eating out of your hand.'

Luc frowned, 'Yes, but that was on my land in Brittany and on yours in Normandy, not deep in conquered enemy territory where the people hate and resent us. I think it will take much longer than you think, Bodin. These Saxons are very independent and proud. And Arlo is a Thegn, a lesser knight as such, but still a Thegn.'

Bodin laughed, 'Win them over, Luc, just win them over and build the castle that Alain wants.'

Luc washed and dressed with care to see Thorfinn leaving Ravensworth. Gone was the loose tunic. In its place was his full military garb, as befitted the Marechal of Alain Rufus, a shining chainmail hauberk over a soft leather tunic. He went fully armed, his signature crossed swords on his back. He did not expect trouble after Thorfinn's speech; nonetheless, he had doubled the guard for Bodin, as he knew emotions might be running high today. As they approached the Hearth Hall, he could see a half dozen heavily laden carts, over twenty horses and a large crowd of villagers who had gathered. As they pushed their way through to the ground in front of the steps, he could hear the rumblings of discontent from the villagers, and he could see the sullen glances directed at Bodin and himself, so he stayed at a slight distance where he could scan the crowd.

However, Bodin had never lacked confidence, he was a diplomat, and he walked straight up to Thorfinn and grasped his arm and hand in a gesture of farewell and conciliation. Thorfinn enveloped Bodin in a bear hug and slapped him on the back. Luc could see that both sides were surprised by this gesture, and it seemed to relieve the tension somewhat. Thorfinn then descended the steps with his impressive huge muscular Huscarls following to mount their horses. Luc looked at the horses with interest; he had seen the breed before in the Netherlands, stocky striking dun and skewbald larger ponies from the fjords of Scandinavia. Although moderate in size, only fourteen hands or less, they were good draught horses, but swift, with incredible strength and high resilience levels. More recently in Northumberland, he had watched a group of rebel Saxons escape towards the north-east coast on such stocky animals.

He stood slightly apart and found himself involuntarily scanning the crowds for Merewyn, and he soon found her; she was saying her farewells to Ardith, Thorfinn's daughter. Both of them were in tears as Ardith climbed onto the front cart. Thorfinn then raised his arm in salute, and stern-faced, he led his party out of the village, shouts of farewell going up from the assembled crowd as the cavalcade headed down and out of the north gate.

Luc scanned the crowd for any sign of trouble as they began to disperse. He suddenly caught a glance of pure vitriol directed at them from a slightly older scar-faced man who, looking tense, had one hand inside his oversized tunic where Luc caught a glint of metal.

Luc turned away as if he had not seen him, but in reality,

he began to move beyond the crowd towards the steps while reaching up for one of his swords at the same time. In an instant, the man had broken and pushed through the crowd. A short war axe was now in his hand, and he was moving towards Bodin, who had turned his back and was mounting the steps towards the Hearth Hall entrance. Luc was still a few feet away as the man raised the axe towards the unaware Bodin's head. Luc sprang across the short distance, sword drawn; he had no choice but to bring the blade slashing down on the Saxon's wrist. With that devastating blow, the axe attack lost force and momentum. With the man's hand still clutching the handle, the weapon struck the chain mail on Bodin's shoulder hard and clattered onto the steps. There were cries from the crowd as the man screamed and dropped to his knees. The pumping blood from his wrist staining the earth in front of the steps as most of the villagers drew back in alarm.

Bodin spun round, his hand automatically drawing his sword as he dropped into a warriors crouch. He gave a breath of relief as he saw Luc and the blood-soaked scene in front of him. He straightened, and, walking forward, he kicked the offending axe and appendage down on to the earth.

'It seems that yet again, Malvais, I owe you my life,' he said in a light tone. However, Luc could see the apprehension and tension in his friend's face; the attack had been too close for comfort. He waved over two of the soldiers then spoke loudly enough for the shocked crowd to hear.

'Take that man to our physician. That wound will need cauterising immediately and then keep him under guard until we can take him to Richmond. Count Alain will deal harshly with any rebel who attacks a Norman.' He nodded to a very pale Arlo who had put a tight leather strip around the groaning man's elbow and wrapped the bleeding wound in a cloth.

Arlo helped the man to his feet to follow the soldiers. As he did so, the wounded man immediately glared up at Bodin, and Luc could see that the hatred had not diminished in the slightest. He shook his head and then noticed Merewyn staring at them. Her eyes raked over the group of Normans on the steps. She stood slightly apart, her fists clenched, tears unashamedly coursing down her cheeks. Then she turned on her heel, and her maidservant took her arm and led her back towards the house.

* * *

Later that day, Luc felt his mood lighten as he settled into the upper floor bedroom of the Hearth Hall; it opened into another room that could be useful as a solar and business room. Although he was still sharing it with Bodin for another night or two, this would be his home for some considerable time. Thorfinn was a wealthy Thegn and had spared no expense with carved decorated wooden beams and wide shuttered windows, which would have a thin horn covering in winter to let in the light but keep the weather out.

His faithful retainer and friend, Sir Gerard, had arrived with the rest of his belongings. Luc was pleased to see him and smiled as he watched Gerard bring in the chests, grumbling all the while about the heathen Saxons and the slowest of bullock carts over rutted roads…

'How are the men?' Luc enquired, trying to halt this diatribe of complaint.

'Getting fat and lazy after a week of doing nothing,' said

Gerard.

Luc had brought a contingent of thirty Breton horse war-riors with him to the north of England, but, while he travelled south, he had left them to enjoy the delights of Durham's growing city for a week, after several hard months together in the wilds of Northumberland.

'They needed the rest Gerard, as did their mounts. It has been a hard six months pursuing the rebels over the wild terrain of the borderlands, and we never caught the large group that escaped to the coast, despite several sightings of them.' said Luc. Gerard reluctantly nodded his agreement.

'There will be plenty of patrols here and rebels to hunt down to keep them occupied.' Luc added.

Luc stood at the window and looked down on the scene below; the women were already about their daily tasks, but a few men still stood in small groups, directing sullen glances at the Norman guards. Luc knew he needed everyday life here to be back on a regular footing, with the men back in the fields as soon as possible or engaged in 'labour work' on the projects he had in mind, the building of the castle being a priority.

He spotted an enormous, impressive shaggy dyer hound running beside a small boy and realised it was Merewyn's young brother Durkin, who seemed to have the enormous hunting dog to a word of command. This immediately raised thoughts of Merewyn and brought the night outside the Hearth Hall unwillingly to mind. The feel of her body pressed to his rose unbidden, the scent and texture of the long silver hair against his lips. He enjoyed those recollections for a few minutes, and then he pulled himself together. He had to push these thoughts away. She was forbidden territory, as far as he was concerned. On a practical note, he had to visit Arlo to get things moving in the village. He would see Merewyn almost every day, and he needed to handle that in his position as a Marechal, not as a man who had enjoyed a brief few moments of pleasure with a local beauty.

* * *

Merewyn was in the back of the house helping Helga to churn butter. It was a backbreaking task, but it allowed her to vent her anger at the bloodshed on the green and at seeing Ardith forced out of her home and village. Her head told her that Melsonby was only five miles away, but her heart ached for the loss of her only friend and confidant. She wiped her hands and poured her father some ale. Going into the hall, she found him sitting on the settle, looking as dismal as she felt. She knew he was angry and frustrated, as he had snapped at Durkin to take the hound outside for a run. She put the ale down and put her arms around his broad shoulders, kissing his cheek, which brought a smile back to his face. Just then, a loud knock sounded at the door.

'Let him in, Merewyn,' said Arlo in a resigned tone. He had not shared with his daughter that Malvais was coming here to speak with him; it was pointless fanning the flames of fire further; he had seen her anger earlier this afternoon, and he understood it; he felt the same. Merewyn looked at her father in alarm and then opened the heavy wooden door.

Luc stood on the threshold, his large frame almost filling the doorway. Still, in full military garb, he looked all Norman and nothing like the man from last night or in the orchard this morning. She stood frozen on the spot, clutching the door, blinking at him, this Norman Lord who was terrifying with a sword in his hand and now here in her home. She also felt herself go hot at the thought of what he had done to her last night and the colour swept up into her face. She saw a brief smile play on his lips, seeing her obvious discomfort. He seemed to know what she was thinking, and time seemed frozen for several minutes as they stared at each other. Then he spoke. His Saxon English was excellent…

'I give you a good day, Mistress Eymer. I have come to speak to your father. May I come in?'

'Bring our guest in, Merewyn,' shouted her father impatiently across the hall. This brought her to her senses; the laws of hospitality were sacrosanct in Saxon homes, no matter who the visitor might be. She dropped her eyes and stepped back, opening the door wide and indicating to him with her hand that he should enter.

Luc stepped over the threshold and was immediately surprised at the size of the hall he was in; this was a sizeable substantial building with a high vaulted roof and whitewashed walls, hung with colourful, expensive tapestries. There was a balcony or gallery at the far end above several doors, and smoked hams hung from the roof above them. He gazed around, taking in all of the signs of wealth and position and then he took a seat on one of the wooden settles, as indicated by the Saxon Thegn, already seated, and commented,

'This is an imposing home Arlo Eymer,' commented Luc.

Arlo grunted, 'Yes, this was the original village Hearth Hall, but it was replaced by the much larger one seven years ago when Thorfinn moved from Austwicke to make Ravensworth his permanent home, and of course, we came with him.' At that moment, he spotted his daughter, still seemingly rooted to the spot inside the door.

'Merewyn, bring refreshments for our guest,' he barked at her.

Merewyn moved through to the scullery area to fetch the ale, some freshly baked bread and cheese. Her mind was in a whirl. She had never really expected to see him here inside her house. It made the situation in Ravensworth so real. In her heart, she had hoped that they would leave the village and go with Thorfinn, but now they were here to stay, which meant dealing with these murdering Normans daily. On top of that, she found the masculine presence of this man disturbing.

When he entered a room, Malvais dominated it with his impressive frame, but it was more than that, the way he held himself, his long powerful legs, his head held high He was a born leader, and this emanated from him. She could just imagine him riding into battle at the head of his men. She was also very much aware that this tall, chainmail clad Norman, with his dark, good looks and his piercing intelligent steel blue eyes, had touched her in some way that no other man ever had. Her stomach knotted every time she looked at him, and she did not dare to meet his eyes again, but at the same time, she hated everything he was and everything he stood for. She returned with the refreshments, her stomach churning, just in time to hear her father say,

'There are things you need to know Malvais before we begin. I fought with Thorfinn against you at Hastings and would do so again if I had to.' Merewyn held her breath, frightened for her father after what she had seen this morning and now knowing what this man was capable of, but at the same time proud of Arlo's brave warrior spirit.

'I am aware of that,' said Luc. 'However, that was in the

past, over five years ago and, although in some ways those memories are fresh, as one warrior to another, we will work to ensure it does not happen again if possible. I am sure we can respect one another and the roles we played in the armies of our kings, but, as Thorfinn said, now we need to look to the future. I am aware that the last few days' events have not helped, but we cannot allow attacks on our men and especially not on Lord Bodin. You do know he is the brother of Alain Rufus,' asked Luc in exasperation.

Arlo took a deep breath; emotions in the village are running high Malvais, especially after what happened to young Sweyn and his family.'

'The young man who killed yesterday?' he asked.

Arlo inclined his head, 'that was his father who attacked Lord Bodin this morning.'

Luc closed his eyes for a second and let out a breath of chagrin, understanding now the extreme hatred in the man's eyes. 'I know Arlo Eymer, but we must put it behind us.

Arlo nodded and sighed, 'There is more, Malvais. My boy, Garret, left with Thorfinn's son, Braxton, and several men from this and the surrounding villages to fight in the risings of the Earls in the north.'

Luc nodded, and his face became more serious, 'Bodin made me aware of that as well and I am sure you are conscious that Count Alain and I came here to put down that Saxon rebellion. We also lost many men, some of them very close friends. However, I appreciate the difficulties you and your people have, coming to terms with that, as my men stationed here may well have fought against, killed or captured men from these villages.'

Both men heard the sharp intake of breath behind them and

turned to find Merewyn stood pale and wide-eyed. 'So you may have killed or captured my brother Garret?' she said in a breathless whisper.

Arlo immediately jumped in to interrupt her before she could yet again disrespect their guest. 'This is warfare, Merewyn. Your brother and the men who went with him knew the risks they took when they left the villages, against the advice of Thorfinn and me. They were too much in thrall to Braxton's persuasive rhetoric! Why are you still here, girl? Put down the refreshments. Go about your tasks. Malvais and I have much to discuss.' He snapped. Merewyn placed the tray on the table with an audible clatter, turned on her heel and fled. Luc, grim-faced, watched her go.

Arlo shook his head, 'Wounds are not only on the surface, Malvais; many families here have lost loved ones. The worst part of it is not knowing if they are alive or dead. My son was a reckless, headstrong boy, easily led by Braxton, and I hope he died quickly and with honour.'

Luc looked thoughtful, 'I will try to ascertain for you if he was captured or not. There may still be the possibility of a ransom for the son of a Thegn if he has not already been sold into slavery in Normandy.'

Arlo quickly looked up, hope written on his face for the first time. 'We would be grateful for your assistance Malvais,' he said.

The men spent the next hour discussing the two projects Luc had in mind for the village. Arlo was reluctantly impressed with Luc's idea to build a dam and millpond further up the valley. This would mean a millrace could be constructed with a mill further down the river, giving the villagers the ability to grind their corn. However, Luc explained that the priority was the building of the castle. The fortification was a motte and bailey design initially built out of wood on a raised-earth mound. Luc told Arlo that he would need several 'labour days' from the village's men but that, to mitigate this, he would also use his men and any captives on the project. Arlo nodded in agreement; he knew that this was inevitable. The Normans would do everything they could to consolidate their position in the North, and he knew that many new fortifications, such as this one, would be built to help them do so.

Luc then took his leave, thanking him for his hospitality. As he stood up, he glanced towards the doors at the end of the hall, hoping for a sight of Merewyn. 'Please thank your daughter for the refreshments for me as well. Arlo, being no fool, caught that glance with surprise and annoyance.

'It will take a lot of time, Malvais, for some people to forgive and forget the last few years. That's if they ever do,' he said abruptly.

Luc nodded, recognising, again, the hostility that was inevitably still there. He turned on his heel and left.

Arlo sat back down on the settle and took a long draught of his ale. He tried to view it objectively: Malvais owned considerable lands in Brittany; he seemed a straight-speaking young man, and Arlo indeed recognised a formidable warrior when he saw one. However, he dismissed the idea. The whole situation would be impossible. He was a Norman; Merewyn hated Malvais and what he stood for with all of her being, and he knew that he could never countenance any liaison for his daughter with a Norman. It would be unthinkable; she needed to marry into solid Saxon stock. He smiled as he realised that he, himself, had not done that. Instead, ignoring the advice of his parents, he had run away with the wild, beautiful, redheaded daughter of an Irish Lord. Now, all three of his children had inherited her unpredictable temperament.

However, and more importantly, Arlo knew that he had to work with Malvais to preserve the villagers' life and welfare in these unsettled times; as today's events had shown, things were still volatile. As for Merewyn, she had always been headstrong and, at times, a wilful girl. Any man would have his hands full there. He allowed himself a smile at the thought. He needed to find her a husband and, soon. Someone strong enough to handle her, to take her away from Ravensworth and away from these Normans in England. He gave a satisfied sigh; he would talk to Thorfinn tomorrow and put out a few feelers.

Merewyn stood outside in the afternoon sunshine gazing over the kitchen garden and the dark-forested hills that swept up and over the ridge that towered behind the village. She was physically attracted to this man in a way she could not begin to explain, and now she knew that he or his men could have killed her beloved brother, which made her angrier with herself for finding him attractive at all.

Chapter Seven

L uc spent several days in Arlo's company, although he avoided going into his house again. He had received the message loud and clear from Merewyn and Arlo that the villagers were still unforgiving when it came to Normans; the resentment ran deep and would do so for many years. There was no doubt, Merewyn was out of bounds; he resolved to put her out of his mind, although, when he glimpsed her from a distance around the village, he found his eyes following her graceful figure.

The time with Arlo proved to be invaluable. He learnt which of the village Freemen were trustworthy, which of the villeins were hard-working, which were feckless and which of the families it was wise to win over with favours. He needed to build bridges for the future, which meant he needed to know which young men needed a firmer hand to bring them into line. He treated them all fairly, and this began to get him a small amount of respect. He was also aware that he received the odd nod and grudging grunt of approval from the Saxon Thegn himself. Luc was pleased with this because, although he knew that he would have to deliver punishment at times, he planned to win the people around by showing them how they could work together for the good of the village and surrounding manors.

The building of the fortification was a bone of contention; there was no hiding the fact that this was part of a Norman plan to keep tighter control across the north, and Luc could feel the tension and reluctance from the village. Surprisingly, Arlo, for his part, was interested in the Norman process of surveying and pegging out the site for the Motte and Bailey castle to the south of the village and work began almost immediately.

Early on the first morning, Arlo arrived with a group of village men and boys, but both he and the villagers were astonished to see Luc, with his shirt stripped off, helping his men start digging the large ditch that would encircle the castle. Although it was a problematic Breton dialect, Arlo could hear the banter that De Malvais had with his Horse Warriors and the Norman soldiers left behind by Bodin. He could see the respect they had for him. The village men brought for labour work were also somewhat mollified to see their new overlord with a spade in his hand and were slightly less resentful of being taken away from their fields. Others made their feelings known from the outset, a few of them refusing point-blank to leave their strips of land for the Norman invaders. Luc immediately gave the order to have them brought to the castle site, where he had them hogtied and left on the ground for a day in the sun to persuade them to see the error of their ways. Labour or boon days were necessary, and they were the Manor Lord's right, who could demand them at any time.

One of them, Wiyot, became a particular problem. He complained loudly and longly, a known village troublemaker, doing the minimum possible labour until things came to a head. In his late thirties, Wiyot was a large burly man, renowned for his laziness but quick and witty with his mouth. He was using a large hammer to pound the posts into the ground to form the Inner Bailey's palisade fence that would encircle the Donjon of the castle, but he had only completed three during the entire morning. While haphazardly completing his work, Wiyot kept up a stream of abuse at two of the Norman foot soldiers working beside him, attaching the rails for the palings; they stood waiting because of the man's slow work rate. After an abusive rant in Saxon at the two men, which cast aspersions on both their mothers and fathers, the ordinarily calm Norman Serjeant, who had picked up a smattering of the language, walked towards Wiyot who was leaning on the huge hammer and delivered a stunning blow to his jaw. The curmudgeonly Saxon fell to the ground and opened his eyes to see the Serjeant hefting the large hammer to bring it down on to his head. Wiyot yelled loudly and tried to scrabble back along the ground away from the enraged soldier.

Merewyn had just brought her father some bread and cheese for the mid-day break, and they both turned to watch as the loud altercation broke out. She gasped in horror as the Serjeant lifted the hammer above his head; in an instant, Luc, watching in concern, sprinted across the grass, shouting in French for the Serjeant to stop. Reaching the man just in time, Luc pulled the descending hammer from his hands and threw it on the ground. He then turned and berated both groups.

'Hasn't there been enough death in our lives this year? If there is any punishment to be given, then I will be the one dispensing it!' he yelled, as he ordered the shaken Wiyot to be taken away and imprisoned for a few days. Gerard, alerted by the shouts, arrived at Luc's side shaking his head at what he had heard. He took the young Serjeant firmly by the arm and pulled him to one side, hauling him over the coals for losing his temper. Sir Gerard was both highly respected and feared by the men; he was a fearless and ruthless warrior and a hard taskmaster. The Serjeant knew that there would be at least a week of harsh duties or punishments for his actions, and he shamefacedly hung his head under the tirade that fell upon him.

Merewyn and her father had watched all of this with interest and, as they walked back to sit under a nearby tree, Arlo found himself saying, 'I think we have been fortunate to have an overlord such as Malvais. I believe him to be that rare thing, a fair and just man.'

Merewyn did not reply. She thought about what she had just seen, the speed and purpose with which Malvais had raced across to intervene, disarming the Serjeant in seconds. For the first time, she began to consider his words about putting the war and rebellions behind them. They would never forget or forgive, but she knew they had to think about the children, like her brother Durkin, who would grow up in a different world under Norman rule. Did she want his life to be full of rebellion and war as well?

It was backbreaking work on a hot summer's day, but they made good progress with so many men, and Luc called for a break in the mid-afternoon, leaving them all to rest in the shade for a while. He decided to take a walk up to the Holme valley's top to inspect the dam and millpond's proposed site. He had carried out a similar scheme on his lands in Brittany, and there was no reason why it would not work here; the slopes and hills made it ideal. It was peaceful in the top meadow and, at the lower end of the valley where the deep fast running streams merged; there was a natural, slightly deeper ox-bow pond under a high raised bank with reed beds and dark green watercress along one side, an ideal place for fish and eels. The water looked cool and inviting after the hot labour with his men on the castle site, so Luc decided to immerse himself; he needed to remove the sweat and soil from the day's work. He carefully removed his clothes, laying them on the high riverbank, and then strode into the slightly deeper water, revelling in fully submerging his body and head in the cool of the river to remove the soil and dust from his hair.

* * *

Merewyn had returned home from the castle site and had set out with Helga to collect some of the wild blackberries and bilberries that grew in profusion at this time of the year in the scrub areas on the edge of the forest. Durkin occasionally helped pick the fruit, and now his face and hands were stained with juice. Merewyn laughed, 'take him back, Helga and clean him up. I will go and check the eel traps while we are up here'. Their young manservant Bjorn regularly set the long narrow wicker basket traps, pinning them along the riverbank's deeper edges and pools amongst the reeds. If they were lucky, several small eels would go into a delicious stew, or even a small trout, or two.

She emerged from the forest fringes, strolling with her basket down through the scrub gorse bushes and across the flower-filled meadow to the riverbank. The traps were in the usual place. She rolled up her sleeves, laid down on the edge of the bank in a space between the thick gorse bushes, and hung over the edge, gently pulling the wound willow string of the trap towards her. She lifted it carefully onto the bank, draining it of water but keeping all of its precious contents encased. She had just raised the second one onto the bank when she heard the splashing. She presumed it was Durkin, who had probably followed her, disobeying Helga yet again, so she stood up, the traps on the grass at her feet, and looked down the river, ready to scold him for yet more disobedience.

The words died on her lips as she saw that barely thirty feet away, in the deeper water under the edge of the high riverbank, was Luc de Malvais. He had been swimming and was standing, hip-deep in the river. As she watched, he emerged from the water completely naked and stood in the shallows, feet planted firmly apart. She watched as he shook the drops from his body and then ran his hands back through his dark hair to take it away from his face. He closed his eyes, stretched his torso and turned towards her, facing the west to get the warm rays of the late afternoon sun on his body.

Merewyn realised she was holding her breath, but she hardly dared to breathe. She had glimpsed many naked men before in her life, it was inevitable living in a village, but Luc de Malvais was one of the most beautiful men she had ever seen. She stood, transfixed by what she saw in front of her. His broad, powerful shoulders tapered down his ribbed muscled torso to slim hips. His long legs planted firmly on the riverbed had large, firmly muscled thighs and calves from a lifetime spent on horseback. There was no softness to be seen. He was all rock-hard slabs of muscle and sharp planes.

She could feel something that could have been described as desire sweep through her for this man, and an unusually warm sensation began to build as she looked at him.

His eyes were still closed, so; she stared uninterrupted in rapt admiration at his naked body. Her mouth slightly open, she moistened her lips with her tongue as she noticed the water glistening on his muscled thighs and his imposing manhood. Then, slowly moving her gaze up over that broad, powerful chest and corded neck, she realised that he had opened his eyes and was staring intensely back at her.

There was no sudden modesty from him as his manhood began to respond to her gaze, no rush to cover himself; he stood there, proudly, in all his naked glory, still with his feet firmly planted in the river, his powerful arms by his side. She was spellbound. She could not move as she gazed into those stunning but severe blue eyes. She watched as his mouth curved into a slow lazy smile of amusement, and his eyes became dark and intense with desire.

'Do you like what you see?' he asked in an amused voice that was also warm with intent.

Merewyn felt the colour flood to her cheeks as she realised that he had caught her staring unashamedly at his naked body for some time, but somehow, she could not seem to drag her eyes away from his magnificent physique and his intense gaze. She finally lowered her eyes as she realised that he had now become significantly aroused by her watching him, and then she heard the splash as he turned and began to stride, with clear resolve on his face, through the shallows towards her.

Knowing everything would be lost if he came any closer to her, she turned and fled, leaving her basket and the fish on the grass behind her. As she ran, she could hear his laughter echoing down the valley. Her anger flared as she realised he had seen how she desired him, but still, she hated him, oh how she hated him for doing this to her! How could he have this effect on her? How could she have stood there so wanton gazing at his naked body for so long? Her cheeks flushed with heat and colour as she wondered how long he had watched her face as she stared in fascination and awe at his magnificent body. She was horrified that he had caught her in such a situation. How could she ever meet or look at him again without thinking about what was under that tunic of chain mail? She squealed in frustration as she ran down the hill that, yet again, he had wrong-footed her.

Luc watched her go and then lay back on the riverbank in the sun to let his body dry before he dressed. He smiled as he remembered the open admiration on her face, the apparent desire there as well as she bit her bottom lip; maybe he could win her round after all. She was innocent and naive but fiery and ripe for the taking as well; his manhood remained hard and pulsing as he thought about how he would teach her a lesson, but Luc also found he also wanted to teach her to enjoy real lovemaking and pleasure. He smiled to himself. He was a soldier; it would be easy to wage a campaign that would sweep her off her feet and make her come into his arms willingly. The reality, however, intruded on his pleasant thoughts, and he had to ask himself, to what end, though?

Could he justify to himself seducing the daughter of a Saxon Thegn for his pleasure? Bodin would say yes... to the victors – the spoils of war. He could not offer her marriage; his mother in Brittany expected more, and she was already lining up prospective candidates, some with a large dowry and land adjoining his own. Would his family ever accept a semi-heathen Saxon wife, no matter how beautiful or wealthy her father was? Luc sighed, pulled on his clothes and headed back to the village, picking up a discarded basket of berries and two fish traps as he went. On reaching the village green, Luc handed the items to Arlo, who was emerging from his front door.

'Merewyn left these on the river bank,' he said. Arlo, noticing his wet hair, raised an eyebrow, nodded and went back into the house. He found Merewyn in the back with Helga preparing some of the blackberries. He handed her the traps and basket. 'You seem to have added another admirer Merewyn,' he said and frowned at her. 'Was it not enough to have all the young men for miles around at your feet?' Merewyn gave her father a look of pure outrage,

'He's a Norman!' she spat back at him.

'He is, but he is also a man, Merewyn, first and foremost. He is a real man, much more so than many of these young men that claim to love you; a grown man that appreciates a beautiful girl, despite your shameful behaviour.' Merewyn and Helga looked at Arlo, astonished as he gave a bark of laughter, then stood hands on hips regarding the two women.

'However, you are right. Malvais is a Norman and entirely unsuitable; I am going to Melsonby this afternoon to help Thorfinn and his retainers settle in; he also has guests arriving from Denmark today. He and I will be discussing a suitable contender we have found for your marriage, which will take place as soon as possible – possibly within the next month!' he announced. 'I may bring the young man back with me tonight for the feast if I find him suitable.' He turned and went back about his business, leaving them open-mouthed, and Merewyn disconcerted, wondering who this 'suitable suitor' was, she had heard not a word about these guests.

Chapter Eight

Luc had returned to the Hearth Hall to bring Bodin up to speed on how the castle's plans were progressing. This was to be Bodin's last night in Ravensworth before returning to his brother Alain Rufus, in Richmond for a few days and then on to William's Court in London. Bodin was delighted that he had found some musicians to play for them that evening; they were on their way from Durham to Richmond to play for Alain and his knights. Luc smiled; Bodin always had the knack of finding things in the middle of nowhere, from a chicken when they were starving to a stolen cart full of wineskins or a strolling lute player.

'On a serious note, Bodin, I need a favour from you while you are in Richmond. I want you to find out if Garrett Eymer and Braxton Le Gunn are amongst the captives brought down from Durham to be sold or executed. Their fathers wish to ransom them if possible.'

Bodin frowned, 'You want me to do that; you honestly want to bring a couple of young rebel vipers back into your nest here in Ravensworth, Luc?'

Luc nodded, 'I am sure their fathers will pledge surety for their conduct Bodin and Alain will welcome the silver.'

Bodin smiled, 'So is this because you are building bridges

with the main Saxon families as Alain requested, or could it have anything to do with the father of a certain green-eyed maiden?' Luc laughed ruefully, 'maybe a bit of both,' he admitted.

'Well then, I am surprised you want to bring Thorfinn's son back here,' said Bodin. 'Father Giffard told me the girl was hand-fasted to this young rebel, Braxton Le Gunn before he left. There was no marriage ceremony as such, but as with these things, a promise or commitment is given by both sides.'

This was unwelcome news to Luc and made him frown, as he had thought the girl was free of all ties. However, really, what did it matter? It was highly likely that this Braxton was dead; it had been over nine months since the rebellion, and nothing had been seen or heard of them. Bodin watched the play of emotions on Luc's face.

The problem with Luc, he thought to himself, was that he was an honourable man with a conscience. In an exasperated tone, he said, 'Look, either just drag the girl into your bed, swive her and get her out of your system, or get her father to marry her off quickly to someone in another village far away. Alternatively, I can take her to Richmond. As you know, several of mine or Alain's knights would have her off the horse before we reached the stable.' He laughed at Luc's furious expression.

Then Bodin became serious, 'there are too many other things here to concern us, we must finish the building of the castle as soon as possible, Luc, and she is a distraction.' Luc nodded in agreement, but Bodin noticed he remained thoughtful.

* * *

Merewyn had thrown herself into the household tasks with abandon to try to erase the disquieting image of a naked Malvais standing in the river. Still, the scene kept returning as she played over in her mind what she should have done and said, admonishing herself for how she dealt with it. She was delighted, therefore, when Ardith arrived unexpectedly to stay the night. Ardith explained that several Saxon families had been invited for the feast and music tonight, but her father could not come as they had several guests.

'Also, his favourite mare is foaling,' explained Ardith, 'and you know how he loves his horses. He will not leave her.'

Merewyn strolled in the early evening air with Ardith to the Orchard to tell her the families' news in the village and share her thoughts and fears about Luc de Malvais and the incident at the river. They sat on the sun-dappled grass under the trees, the bees humming nearby on a carpet of wildflowers. Ardith laughed out loud as the scene was described, which exasperated Merewyn further.

'Tell me how, I can be so strongly attracted to someone I hate Ardith, you are more worldly than I am?' pleaded Merewyn, but she continued without waiting for an answer.

'He makes me feel things, physical things, that no man or boy has ever made me feel before,' Merewyn sighed. 'I often go weak at the knees when I see him, and I get these swirly sensations in my stomach.'

Ardith laughed at the fact that the fiery independent Merewyn was now so discomposed by a handsome man; she had turned down so many suitors in the past. 'That is love, Merewyn; you are falling in love; remember love and hate are two strong emotions, two sides of one coin. He is a very handsome and attractive man, a born leader and strong warrior that any women would find irresistible.' She said and smiled.

'Oh, I am sure he has had many women!' spat Merewyn, thinking of the practised way he had boldly handled her body and kissed her on that first night.

Ardith laughed, 'I find Lord Bodin more to my taste, more attractive in a cultured way, a polished courtier, so different from our sweaty uncouth Huscarls.'

Merewyn sat back and looked at her friend; she was so different from her with her very dark auburn hair and blue eyes. 'Have you fallen for him, Ardith?' she asked in a breathless whisper. Ardith nodded shyly 'maybe just a little.' Both laughed, 'time is a great healer, Merewyn, and hopefully, war is now behind us. It is time to forgive and forget, and maybe it is all right to fall in love with one of our conquerors. I do not doubt that Braxton is dead, and knowing my selfish, cruel brother, you should be glad; you should never have agreed to be hand-fasted to someone like him.' Merewyn looked at her friend in surprise; she usually said little about her older brother. She smiled wistfully, if only it were that easy to forget, she thought, as a picture of Garrett came to mind, riding off to the rebellion, battle-axe in hand, a boyish grin on his face.

She then shared with Ardith her father's latest surprise news that he may have found her a suitor. Ardith frowned, trying to think of anyone it could be.

'Several visitors from Denmark have arrived to speak with my father, Merewyn. Some of them were young men; it may be one of them. They were here to discuss buying some of our lands in Denmark; they seemed very wealthy and cultured but somewhat full of their own self-importance.'

Merewyn reacted with dismay. Denmark! That would mean leaving her family and Ravensworth. Is that what her father had in mind, to remove her from the dangers of Norman occupation and one Norman man, in particular, she wondered?

* * *

The atmosphere in the Hall that night was entirely different from the last time they had gathered, thought Luc as he made his way to the top table. The occupants of the Hall were now eighty per cent Norman, including his own Breton Horse Warrior contingent, who were delighted to see him, cheering and clapping him on the back as he arrived. What is more, Thorfinn was not here and, although Bodin was leaving tomorrow, there were not the same previous tensions and high-running emotions. As he approached the table, he noticed that Ardith was seated on Bodin's left hand and enjoying his company, her cheeks flushed, she looked charming. On her other side, Merewyn looked beautiful in a green overdress with her long hair flowing down her back. Then there was Arlo with a tall Saxon, a young man he had never seen before who sat beside Merewyn and Luc noticed that Father Giffard had wormed his way onto the end of the table beside two of Bodin's lesser knights. Luc bowed briefly to Bodin and the other guests at the table as he joined them,

'Always late to the party, Malvais,' joked Bodin as he sat down, although he knew perfectly well that Luc would have done a conscientious round of all the sentries before he joined them.

Luc replied quietly in French, 'You cannot be too careful,

Bodin, we received reports yesterday from De Brus that the large band of rebels which escaped to the coast were seen at the port of Hert-le-pool, and they were moving south. I will feel happier once the castle is finished, and we have managed to apprehend them.'

Bodin nodded, drained his cup of wine and clapped his hands for the musicians to appear. There were two musicians and a young French boy to sing and play the drum. The Hall quietened as he began with a plaintive French love song accompanied by the harp, which made it particularly haunting.

Merewyn stole a glance along at Luc but found he was listening. He seemed to be engrossed in the music with an intense but sad expression on his face. She felt that she had intruded on his thoughts and sat back instead to enjoy this rare occasion. She was also conscious of the young Danish man seated beside her.

She had been introduced to him tonight when her father arrived back home with this 'guest' and asked her to prepare a room for him. His name was Sigurd Sorenson. He had recently inherited his father's land in Denmark and was keen to extend it further.

He was wealthy and full of confidence, but he had said little to her when introduced in her father's Hall. She could see that he was pleased with her beauty, but she thought him arrogant; she had asked him several polite questions and received monosyllabic answers, while he talked mainly to her father. She had sat quietly on the wooden settle opposite and watched him. He was tall but thin, obviously a Dane, with his braided long blond hair. However, he had pale eyes and paler eyelashes that gave him a washed-out look. When the conversation waned, she had asked him a question about his family back in Denmark. He had turned a dismissive glance in her direction, obviously annoyed that she had addressed him directly, rather than being questioned by him or by asking the question through her father. She felt helpless. She could not marry this condescending, colourless man. She had leant back in her seat and pushed her shoulders against the comforting polished wood. She had closed her eyes momentarily, as the conversation continued in her home but what came to mind were a pair of black-lashed, steel-blue eyes and the dark, handsome, muscular frame of the man that unexpectedly seemed to haunt her thoughts.

As if on cue, Luc had come striding up the Hall to take his place at the table. She had surreptitiously observed him under slightly lowered lids. She watched the way he was constantly scanning the Hall, ever the warrior; she hungrily absorbed everything about him, from the way he moved his long muscular frame as he strode down the Hall to the way he delivered smiling nods to his laughing men. Then he was there, sitting at the table only yards away from her as he greeted the guests.

She was pulled out of this pleasant reverie by her father, insisting that she reply to Sigurd. She sighed and smiled at her father's unwelcome guest but did not speak to him.

'Do you enjoy such music, Ardith?' asked Bodin.

'Of course, my Lord, but our choices are minimal here and tend to be in the form of the skald's telling long sagas and tales of valour. We rarely have anything as beautiful to listen to as that young man,' she replied, gesturing towards the minstrel. Bodin smiled; he was pleased with her response and, clapping his hands, declared that they must dance. The musicians set up a lively beat with a small drum to accompany the cittern, and the harp and Bodin led Ardith onto the floor to form up for a circle dance. Luc watched with amusement as his Breton men almost fell over themselves to claim the hands of the Saxon serving-women for the dance, often to the dismay and anger of their menfolk. Father Gifford close beside him, looked amazed at what he was watching.

'Breton men do love their music, and they like to dance', he explained to the bemused priest.

Luc thought about asking Merewyn, but she was staring fixedly down at her trencher of uneaten food or talking to the young Dane on her left. As the circle dance progressed, he watched from the top table the dancers promenading to the left or the right and then encircling their partners.

'We need a second circle in the centre!' shouted Bodin looking up at Luc. 'Bring maid Eymer down.' Thus instructed by his friend, Luc stood and came over to stand behind Merewyn's, holding out his hand for hers.

Merewyn sat on the bench transfixed. She felt rather than saw him stand behind her. At first, she ignored the hand held out beside her, conscious of her father's glowering displeasure further down the table and frozen with embarrassment from the incident at the river. Then he moved closer, and she could feel the heat of his body against her back as he placed a hand on her shoulder. He whispered in her ear, 'Come Lord Bodin has ordered us to dance. Let us put this afternoon behind us; he is not one to be kept waiting.'

Merewyn stood, and stepping around the end of the bench; she rested her hand lightly on his powerful forearm. He immediately grasped her hand tightly and pulled her after him as he stepped down onto the boards of the Hall, pushing through to join a few others in the inner circle. There was not a great deal of room, and she found her body brushed continuously against his as they moved in and out of the other dancers, which had a disturbing effect on her. She was reasonably tall, but he towered over her and, when she looked up into his face, she found his blue eyes smiling down into hers in an intense way that made her feel slightly breathless.

She could feel the excitement building as the music got faster and the drumbeat more insistent. She knew what was coming; on the final beat, the men would lift their partners high in the air, twirl them around and place them gently on the floor, and everyone would applaud. The last beat sounded on the drum, the cittern strummed, and she felt herself swept off her feet. She could hear Ardith giggling somewhere close, but she was living in the moment, her hands on his broad shoulders, his arms pressing her body tightly to his as she gazed down into his laughing face.

He smiled up at her, and she closed her eyes, breathing in the masculine smell of him. She could feel the heat of his body on her thighs, his large hands on her waist and hips, and a warm, pleasing sensation spread up from her loins through her body. The moment seemed to last forever; she found she did not want him to let her go, and then, suddenly, she was back on the ground. He twirled her around, pulled her to him, and they both laughed.

A laughing Luc de Malvais was a joy to behold; his whole face lit up, so different from the stern Norman Knight and commanding Marechal she had seen before. She was aware other couples had left the floor. Still, she stood there, both of her hands in his, despite the displeasure of the Saxon men around them. She gazed shyly up at him. 'Thank you, my

Lord, but I think you should let me go now so we can return to our places.'

Just then, the young Danish suitor appeared at her side. He firmly pulled her backwards away from Malvais so that their hands separated. 'Your father has requested that you return to your seat beside me, Mistress Eymer, this behaviour is not seemly or acceptable,' he stated, in a disapproving voice, pushing her firmly in the direction of the benches while glaring at Luc. 'Especially with a Norman knight,' he added, as he turned away with a sneer.

At first, for a few seconds, Luc had been taken aback by the young man's blatant antipathy; was this young Dane a male relative of hers, he wondered, as he stood there bemused by what had just happened? Then a wave of cold anger descended as he made his way back to his chair beside Bodin.

'Who exactly is that man?' he asked him as he reached over to retrieve his eating knife, which was still embedded in the large joint of beef on the platter in front of them.

Bodin just shrugged. 'A guest who is staying with Arlo?' he queried. Ardith sat beside Bodin, quietly answered.

'He is a very wealthy Thegn, a second cousin of the King in Denmark, my Lord. His name is Sigurd Sorenson, and his first wife recently died. He has some interest in offering for the hand of Merewyn; he hopes to unite some of her father's extensive lands over there with his. He arrived today with a few of his Huscarls to stay with my father and now Arlo.'

This was unwelcome news to Luc; he may not consider marrying Merewyn, but he enjoyed his light flirtation with this fiery rebel. However, surprisingly, he had an unpleasant twisting knot in his stomach at the thought of her marrying and being bedded by this haughty Dane.

Arlo had watched all of this with concern, as he had brought this wealthy Danish suitor to meet his daughter tonight. What would this young Thegn think of her behaviour, to see her acting like this? He glanced at his guest as he sat back on the bench beside Merewyn. He could see the shocked, tight-lipped expression on the Dane's face. The young man turned to Arlo and angrily hissed, 'So, Thegn Eymer, do these Norman soldiers always make so loose with your girls and women folk? How do you tolerate this without killing them?' Arlo shook his head in exasperation, worried this inexperienced hothead might antagonise Lord Bodin and Malvais with his comments, notwithstanding what he had just witnessed on the dancefloor. Surely, this Dane was aware of the threat and danger they all lived under since the invasion, or did he think he was outside of their influence and reach because he lived in Denmark.

Hearing what was said, Luc stood up, his sharp eating knife in his hand, and he walked behind Bodin to where the young Dane was sitting. He grabbed the long braids in one quick movement and dragged the Dane backwards, pulling his feet off the floor and exposing his throat. In a flash, the sharp knife was held against the Dane's neck, pressing into the flesh and drawing blood, while his arms and legs were still flailing. Luc bent forward, so his face was only inches away from the terrified young man.

'I cannot remember inviting you to my Hall tonight; I cannot even remember giving you and your henchmen permission to enter my lands. Yet here you are, insulting me and treating the womenfolk with a lack of respect. I am Lord Luc De Malvais, the Marechal of these lands; you will not forget my name. I do not know or care who you are or where you are from, but you will leave early tomorrow morning. If I find you still on any of my lands, I promise that you will certainly never be able to father children again.' He suddenly released the Dane, who dropped to the floor with a thump gasping while holding a hand to his bleeding throat. Those sitting on the benches watched wide-eyed, all except Bodin, who had a broad grin on his face.

'Did he annoy you, Luc?' he asked with a shout of laughter, as the scared Dane picked himself up and, glancing apprehensively at Luc, marched swiftly down and out of the Hall, waving to his retainers to follow him.

Arlo was less shocked by the events than others at the table were; the priest was on his feet, mopping his brow and wringing his hands, but Arlo knew the reputation of Luc De Malvais. Even at Hastings when Malvais was a younger man, his name was uttered in awe by friend and foe alike; he knew what such a man was capable of doing. He glanced around at the girls. Ardith raised shocked eyes to him, her hand over her mouth, but Merewyn was calm beside him as he reached out and covered her hand with his, a small smile playing on her lips as if she had enjoyed the spectacle. She really was her mother's daughter, he thought, remembering his fearless Irish princess, who gave up everything to follow him first to Denmark and then to England.

It suddenly occurred to him for the first time, when watching them together in the dance, that Malvais might be more than just interested in a brief dalliance with his daughter, which was more worrying. As Luc stepped down to speak to a laughing Sir Gerard and his men, Arlo sent Merewyn to calm Father Gifford, and he took the opportunity to lean over to Bodin, 'Is Malvais married, my Lord?' Bodin shook his head while applying himself to the succulent joint of beef; he briefly related the tale of Luc's wife Heloise and his lost son to Arlo and Ardith before Luc and Merewyn returned to their seats.

'Oh, how sad, his heart must have been broken,' said Ardith.

'It was, and even after six years, he still mourns her; she was very lovely. He needs to marry again,' said Bodin.

Arlo excused himself and departed after his fleeing guest, who was staying in their home. He was not looking forward to the confrontation with the Dane, as he was tired after an eventful day. However, he was unwilling to halt the enjoyment of the two girls, or to take them back to suffer the further resentment of the Dane, so he asked Father Giffard to escort the girls to the door when the feast was over. The priest, drinking copious amounts of wine to deal with the shock of what he had witnessed, agreed to do so.

There was more dancing for the next few hours, and Luc danced with both Merewyn and Ardith several times, along with lively amusing banter at the table. With Arlo and the Dane gone, there was a more relaxed atmosphere at the table. Bodin was a natural raconteur when he had a charming audience, and he related a wealth of, often risqué, tales from life at the court, some positively shocking.

Luc watched Merewyn as she sat there with Ardith, the pair of them wide-eyed and taking it all in. In many ways, she was such an innocent; she knew little of the harsh world and life outside of this village. She caught his stare and smiled shyly at him; he had been pleasantly surprised by her reaction to his treatment of the Dane as although sitting beside the man, she had not flinched or recoiled just merely moved away along the bench. He felt his stomach tighten as he gazed into those huge green eyes. He looked away; this was no good; she was not for him, she was Saxon, and the rift was too great between them. He glanced away, round the Hall; it was now late, and many of the men slept, comatose on the benches, having consumed copious amounts of wine or ale. Father Giffard was now also snoring, head down, at the end of the table.

There was a lull in the conversation, and Luc stood up, 'It is late, and if you are ready to retire, I will escort you over to your abode, as your companion is not able to do so,' he said, gesturing at the sleeping priest.

He nodded to Bodin, who raised an eyebrow but waved him away, and Luc shepherded the girls to the porch. It was only across the village green, but there was just a sliver of moon, and it was very dark. He linked his arms and walked them to the door but, before Merewyn could stop her, Ardith bolted through it, leaving it just slightly ajar so that some light spilt out, where Luc and Merewyn faced each other outside.

He stood looking at her, and then he found that he could not help himself. He reached out, encircled her waist and pulled her close against him, burying his face in her hair. The thought of the young Dane coming to court her had lowered his guard, and he recognised how much he wanted to possess her. There was surprisingly little resistance from Merewyn; she initially put her hands on his chest as if to press him away, but then she left them there. Luc slid his hands slowly down her back and cupped her buttocks, pulling her body further into him. She shuddered at the delicious pleasure that coursed through her body. He kissed her deeply; his hands moved up to run his fingers through her hair on either side of her head. Then he ran his hands firmly down her arms to come round and cup and caress her breasts. Merewyn had never experienced anything like this before, and she moaned softly; she suddenly knew she wanted him with a force that astounded her.

This brought Luc back to his senses, and his lips reluctantly left hers. He gazed down at her parted lips. She was panting softly, and her skin was flushed pink. He gently kissed her again and drew back. She was looking up at Luc with genuine desire in her large green eyes, and he instantly knew he could pick her up and take her now if he wished to do so.

Somehow, though, it was not right. No matter how much he wanted her, this would never do, she was a Saxon, and he was a Breton Lord who had fought and defeated them. He cursed himself for being an honourable man. He gently leaned forward and kissed her lightly on the forehead. Merewyn looked at him in a puzzled way and gently reached up and ran her hand along his strong jawline; he took the hand and kissed it before stepping back. 'I bid you goodnight Merewyn Eymer. Make sure you bar the door, just in case I decide to come back and break it down,' he laughed as he guided her through the doorway and pulled it shut behind her.

He stood outside, alone, for a few moments to cool down and let his heart rate slow. He told himself this had to stop, and then he realised that something was disturbing the horses. He could hear them stamping and snorting, but the village dogs were quiet, so it was unlikely that it was wolves that were unsettling them. He headed off down to the horse lines to check what it was and see that his warhorse Espirit was settled before he went to bed. As he walked, he suddenly felt uneasy. He glanced over his shoulder several times, scanning the buildings and tree line, he stopped for a minute or two, but nothing stirred.

In the shadows, a watchful pair of eyes under a dark hood

followed his every move. The intruder was a tall, well-built individual dressed in dark clothes and fully armed; he had just walked around the outskirts of the village and cut the throat of the young sentry near the horse lines without a second thought. He had watched and taken in every detail of the two people embracing outside Arlo's house, and now he was shaking with rage, 'Your time will come, Norman!' he spat out. 'You will pay slowly and painfully with your last breath, for what I have just seen you do'. He swore.

He turned and leapt quickly over the village fence, making his way east through the forest and emerging a mile later on the lower banks of the Holme Beck where another man waited with two horses. The young man greeted him with noticeable relief. 'About time, I thought they had captured you. Have they taken the village, Braxton? He asked.

'It is taken Garret, taken and occupied by at least eighty troops. There are tents and horses everywhere,' he said, throwing back his hood to reveal his striking long blonde hair and beard. They had been back in the area for a few days, hiding on the outskirts of the villages, when he heard the news of a young Dane who was coming to court Merewyn. He had come tonight intending to dissuade or even kill this young man for daring to look at Merewyn, whom he still considered to be, his hand-fasted bride, but nothing had prepared Braxton for what he had just seen.

'The Normans have taken our village, our home and our women and probably killed or threatened our fathers.' he growled. He mounted his horse and splashed through the small river; he stopped for a moment on the other side and glared back in the direction of the village. 'But we will make them pay for this. Oh, how we will make them suffer for it!'

108

he shouted over his shoulder as he set off up the hill at a gallop to rejoin the rest of his men.

* * *

Luc was woken in the very early dawn by a knock on his door; he was only dozing, as sleep had eluded him since his passionate embrace with Merewyn. He swung his legs out of the temporary truckle bed and strode quickly to the door, glancing at Bodin on the other side of the room, who, as usual, could sleep through any noise. One of Bodin's Serjeants stood there, 'My Lord, your man Sir Gerard, he sent me to wake you. He thought you would want to know that one of our sentries is dead.'

Luc dressed quickly, strapped on his swords and followed the waiting man down to the camp, where he found Gerard in the dim light of dawn, standing over the body of one of Bodin's young men. The body was lying in the long scrub, just the other side of the horse lines and very close to the men's tented camp. The young man's throat had been viciously cut from ear to ear.

'When was the last seen alive, Gerard?' asked Luc.

'Just before midnight, Luc, he took over from Jean-Claud,' said Gerard.

Luc, looking down at the body of the young sentry, was thoughtful. He thought back to his movements last night; midnight would have been just about the time when he was walking Merewyn and Ardith home. He remembered that the horses were restless. He realised that the horses' sensitive noses would have picked up both the strong metallic scent of the blood and the sounds of a struggle, which had unsettled them.

'Send a patrol out round the wider perimeter of the camp, Gerard. I will take some men and search the village, but I imagine they will be long gone.' He said in a resigned tone.

An hour later, they had found nothing, and Luc returned to bed. He lay, wide-awake and angry that someone had breached the defences of the village. They would have to be more vigilant but was it a village man taking revenge for the recent events or an attack by one of the rebel bands still at large?

Bodin played it down, describing it as a one-off revenge attack, although he agreed to leave ten of his men behind for extra security. Luc hoped he was right as he walked him to the gate to wish him Godspeed. A group of villagers were there to watch Lord Bodin leave, and the Breton courtier did not disappoint with his troops lined up in military precision, his coloured pennants flying and his large gerfalcon on his wrist. He raised a hand in salute, and, twirling his showy grey mare around, he shouted to Luc, 'Good luck and don't forget my advice. Bed the Saxon wench and get her out of your system!'

Luc looked around in alarm at the crowd who were listening to this and then realised that Bodin had spoken in the Breton French that they used at home, and only a few of his Breton Horse warriors grinned and smirked. He shook his head in exasperation at his friend, lifted his raised fist in farewell, and watched the troop gallop away south on the road to Richmond in a cloud of dust.

Chapter Nine

L uc saw little of Merewyn in the following weeks. He realised that she was avoiding him and wondered why. Was she now betrothed to the young Dane, had it gone ahead, after all, he found the thought disturbing, but he also saw it as a solution, albeit an unpleasant one.

However, he was preoccupied as well; there had suddenly been several raids, by renegades or rebels, on the other villages, stealing animals and threatening village leaders, if they did not support them, or provide them with provisions. This meant that he now spent long hours in the saddle out on patrol, but they found no trace of the rebel group or those responsible, although they searched exhaustively. They seemed to have the ability to disappear into the forests, which suggested they knew the area well.

At first, he thought they were just an outlaw group, made up of runaway serfs and the odd rebel Saxon, or even the Border brigands, on raids down from Northumberland, but these attacks seemed to be more calculated. They seemed to take just what they needed; the grain store was broken into; they took chickens and small livestock. They were also actively recruiting as villagers reported that several of their young men had gone with them, which confirmed, in his mind, that this was a local rebel group. Two of his smaller patrols were attacked in the forests and men injured, and both reported the attackers had seemed to melt away into the trees. Arlo told Malvais that two ponies had gone from Thorfinn's Manor at Melsonby the previous night, including one of his best stallions, a distinctive light skewbald horse with a long flowing cream mane and tail.

However, he did not share with Malvais that this had been Braxton's horse or that Thorfinn, while annoyed at the theft, was not in the rage that he had expected. Arlo would not yet share all information with this Norman overlord, he may be a Breton, but he followed their orders and led their armies. He discovered that at Hastings, Malvais had been leading the Horse Warriors with Alain Rufus. Every Saxon on Senlac Hill remembered the fury of their charge, the trampling hooves and might of the Breton warhorses and the relentless slashing blades of their riders that had decimated and destroyed Harold's army. No, he may be working with them for the sake of the people and villages, but he was not prepared to forget yet.

They were into the hot sultry August days, and Luc was frustrated that the doubling of all sentries and patrols had brought the work on the motte and bailey castle almost to a standstill. He knew that they had constructed one in nine days at York, but here they were dealing with numerous small acts of sabotage, stolen tools, missing timber to the extent that he now had an extra patrol on a night. The dam and millpond not even started yet, and he was aware this had to be constructed while the water levels were low before the autumn and winter rains and snow brought the heavy run-off from the hills. The castle became even more of a priority; the massive mound of earth taken out by digging the encircling deep ditch had settled. Three-quarters of the surrounding palisade fence constructed. He hoped to get the gatehouse up this week, and then they could begin the work on the sturdy two-storey Donjon on the mound.

No trace had yet been found of the rebels, so he decided to drop the twice-daily patrols for the rest of the week and enlist Arlo's help to finish the palisade. The following day found Luc up early. Arlo came as promised with several men and worked alongside Luc, hammering wedges into the wood to split the huge logs into planks for the high fence. Arlo had been surprised to find Luc had again stripped down into serviceable clothes and was ready to work alongside them. His respect for him increased slightly. Luc was pleased with the men's attitude and the fact that the work proceeded at a good pace. They stopped for a quick nuncheon in the shade, and the women brought baskets of food and ale to the men.

Merewyn was with the village women; as she came over the meadow with two heavy baskets, she could see the two men, with their tunics off, sitting in the shade of a large oak, their backs against the tree. Arlo was only forty-three summers and was still a prime specimen; he was never still and kept himself in shape, training the village boys in fighting skills. However, he could not compare to Luc's long, imposing physique and Merewyn's eyes were immediately drawn to him.

Luc smiled as she put the baskets down on the grass. 'This is most welcome, Mistress Eymer,' he said as she poured cool ale into a tankard for them.

Arlo looked up surprised; it was their maidservant Helga, who usually brought refreshments. Merewyn smiled shyly back at Luc, her stomach tightening just looking at him and remembering what had happened the last time they had encountered each other. Their eyes met as he reached for the tankard, his full of amusement at seeing her discomfort. She watched him covertly through lowered lids; he was handsome even when hot and sweaty from manual labour, in fact, even more so. It made him more human somehow, and he was obviously more relaxed with Arlo, laughing at something her father said, how different he was when he laughed. Unlike the harsh Breton Lord, who would have cut an impudent Danes throat in an instance a few weeks before. Yet he had purposefully stepped in to stop the Norman Serjeant from killing Wiyot; she found him perplexing.

Luc also had the luxury of watching Merewyn in close proximity as she handed out the contents of the basket, fresh-baked bread, cheese and cold cooked chicken legs. She was truly lovely. Taller than average, she was slim and willowy but perfectly proportioned with wide hips and full breasts. She had a clear, unblemished complexion with no trace of smallpox and, of course, that long, fine, unusual silver-blonde hair, carefully braided and pinned on top of her head today. She had fine eyes, large and clear, a distinctive green, and now he had the leisure to look into them. He saw flecks of golden brown. He could imagine her sitting naked on his bed with that long hair hanging over her breasts, and he found his body responding to that thought. She leaned back; her glance flickered over to him. His heart missed a beat; she knew the effect she was having on him. She gave him the benefit of the innocent wide-open gaze of those large green eyes, she took her bottom lip between her teeth and he felt his heartbeat quicken again. He tried to calm his body down before it became apparent to everyone that she aroused him.

She turned away and talked to her father in a quiet voice, Luc gave a sigh of relief but found himself intrigued by the difference between this dutiful, respectful daughter in front of him and the passionate young woman he experienced in their last encounter.

Her father watched, in fascination, at the show Merewyn was putting on as she listened to his views with interest, nodding sagely at his advice. He realised quickly that this 'paragon of filial respect' was for the benefit of Malvais and a worried expression flitted across his face as he turned and frowned at her. He wondered what mischief she was up to; he hoped it was not about getting revenge for Garrett, something that would bring the Normans' hard hand down onto his house and the village. He needed to have a firm conversation with her; she was his daughter, and she needed to obey him. He had found himself forced to have a challenging interview with the young Danish Thegn, who was astonished that any woman could turn him down. Arlo loved his daughter dearly, but she was impetuous, downright stubborn at times and an absolute termagant when roused in anger, just as her beautiful Irish mother had been. Merewyn had a different type of loveliness, though, more celestial. She had inherited her silver-blonde hair from his mother, also a renowned beauty back in Denmark. If Malvais did have any interest in marrying her, then his life would never be the same again; of that, he was sure. He shook his head in denial; a Norman wedding a Saxon girl was almost unheard of in these parts. It would not go down well in the village; too many sons and husbands lost, too much pain.

'Well, back to it,' said Arlo draining his tankard and standing up. 'We will finish that gatehouse as well today with luck,' he said. Luc stood and handed the basket and leather tankard back to her. 'I hear that you turned down your Danish suitor. Do you have another man in mind,' he said with an amused smile.

She shook her head and glared at him, but as she found herself attracted to this Norman, she discovered that her guard was down. He had that perfect mix of looks, authority and a certain amount of menace. She could imagine what he would be like if anyone crossed him or if someone defied him. She found that thought quite unsettling as she looked up at him. As if he knew what she was thinking, he moved to stand close in front of her. She held her hands up as if to fend him off, a look of panic on her face that he might kiss her in public.

He laughed aloud, which made people turn and look at them. 'Mistress Eymer, come here; you have a horsefly trapped in your hair,' he said, moving even closer again.

She obediently stood still, inches from his bare chest, while he used both hands to remove the offending insect from under the braids on her head before it delivered a nasty bite. He pulled the front braid firmly to lift it, and she fell forward, putting her hands on his still bare chest to keep her balance. She stayed there, locked within his arms, as he finally ejected the insect. Her palms were still, against the crisp short black hairs on his chest; she breathed in the masculine smell of him and resisted the impulse to look up at his face… then, she found that she just had to look up…. and he was gazing down at her with amusement but with something else in those arresting blue eyes.

He laughed again and stepped back. 'You may have to re-braid that now,' he said as he stroked the hair back down into place.

Without warning, she gave him a smile that startled him and then she turned and began to gather up the rest of the food baskets and tankards as she made her way over to Helga, who was waiting patiently while shaking her head at them. He stood for a few moments watching her, and he found that it gave him a warm feeling as he watched her work; Luc recognised that feeling from the few years that he spent with his wife, Heloise, and he had never expected to feel it again. He shook his head in denial and set off to re-join Arlo and the men. Merewyn turned and watched him go, tunic still thrown carelessly over his shoulder, as he picked up two large planks, as if they were kindling, the muscles tensed and played in his muscular back and shoulders, his biceps bulging with the strain. She found she couldn't take her eyes off him. This will not do, she thought, shaking her head as she watched him; I promised I would make every Norman pay, but it is difficult when he comes down off his mighty step and acts like just another man. She laughed at herself for such a thought; the famous Luc De Malvais would never be just another man...

As she turned away to walk back into the village, she suddenly caught a flash of something from the trees in the north-west, almost like sunlight reflecting on metal. She glanced over at Luc, at her father, and then at Gerard and his men over at the other side, but they seemed unconcerned, standing, deep in conversations about the construction of the new gatehouse. It must have been nothing, she thought, but she shivered, even in the heat, and she could not resist giving another long hard stare, in that direction.

In the trees, two heavily armed men gazed down at the scene below.

'What did I tell you?' said Braxton as he stood, fists clenched with rage. 'She is bedding that Norman! Her hands were all over him, and no maiden would touch a man like that in public unless they were bedmates. She has become his whore!'

Garrett turned angrily to glare at Braxton for this slur on his beloved sister, but he had to admit that he was confused. He had watched, incredulously, the scene below for the last hour. Not only were his father and the village men working for this Norman Lord to build a castle on the common land outside the village, but his sister had so obviously given her virtue to him as well. They had all heard what had happened to Sweyn and his wife, so he looked for signs of threats and mistreatment to the Saxon men, but he saw none. He did not know what to think. His father fought at Hastings, alongside Thorfinn, against this enemy, his sister always espoused her hatred of the Normans, yet none of that seemed apparent today.

Even at a distance, he recognised that this Norman was a tall, well-muscled, good-looking man. Watching him directing the men, he admitted that he was a natural leader; Garrett thought he was older and far more experienced than they were, probably about 30 years old or more, in his prime. Their network of spies, one of whom was Wiyot, had told them Luc De Malvais was the new Marechal of the whole area, yet here he was doing manual work, alongside his men and the villagers. This was not how he expected Norman Lords to behave; Braxton repeatedly told him the Normans were murdering invaders, who raped and pillaged the English villages, not Manor Lords who planned to build mills on the river, for the benefit of the villagers.

However, he had seen Malvais out on patrol several times now, dressed in full chain mail. He wore two swords over his back like the foreign mercenaries he had seen in the past, and Garrett recognised a cold battle-hardened warrior when he saw one. After all, he could understand Braxton's anger, his sister had been hand-fasted to him before they left, and now he had lost everything, his home, his inheritance, and now his future bride. Garret stared down at the village below with sadness; he would love to go home, but there was no way back for them. They were rebel outlaws, hunted and living on their wits, and they would be put to the sword or worse if the Normans caught them.

'Well?' demanded Braxton breaking in on Garrett's thoughts.

'She certainly seemed friendly towards him and probably, thinking you were dead, she could be taken in by a handsome warrior like him, or he may not have given her any choice. It has been nearly ten months since the rebellion Braxton, and he was here while you were not,' said Garrett trying to defend what he had just seen.

Braxton stamped around, slashing viciously at the undergrowth and branches with his sword, as this statement enraged him even more. 'He won't want to be here when I have finished with him; I am going to make life a living hell for him and his men. We step up a campaign of attacks from every direction, at every hour of the day and night, especially now we have so many extra men and boys who have joined us; Luc De Malvais won't know in which direction to look for us or where we will strike next.'

'But Braxton, won't he just bring more troops from Richmond and punish the local people for hiding and feeding us?' said Garrett with concern.

'No. From what we have seen and heard from Wiyot and

the others, he is too proud to do that. He will want to catch us himself, and that is when we turn the tables; I want to capture him alive, and then I will enjoy making him beg for his life, over and over again.' He promised.

Garrett had never seen such hatred as he saw now in Braxton's face as his friend glowered down at Malvais and the scene below. He respected Braxton as a great fighter, but privately he thought it would be a fortunate man who could take or defeat Malvais if he had a sword in his hand. However, he kept these thoughts to himself; it was pointless antagonising his furious friend further.

'We start tonight with the castle they are building,' said Braxton with a wolfish grin at Garrett. 'There is a full moon and a clear sky, and we will ride out at midnight. Tell the men to be ready.'

* * *

Luc certainly had no problems sleeping after several days of satisfying manual labour. He considered himself to be in good shape and usually made sure to fit in an hour of sword practice each day with Gerard and his men. However, it had done him good to lift heavy logs and swing an axe, and they had made significant progress. The Donjon's palisade on the motte and the impressive gatehouse on the inner bailey was complete. Work could now start on the wooden Donjon inside and the considerable palisade fence around the outer bailey area.

He woke suddenly. The room was light. At first, he thought the sun was coming up and that he had overslept. He swung his legs out of bed; then, he realised the light was not natural; it was flickering on the walls. He strode over to the open shutters and saw the blaze outside the village. He swore as he realised it was the castle. He quickly pulled on his braies, grabbed one of his swords and ran, bare-chested into the night. Gerard and his men were already there, and Arlo had organised buckets of water from the pond close to the castle. It took them a good few hours to get it under control and, by that time, although they saved the palisade, one side of the new gatehouse was just a smouldering ruin. Gerard marched over to Luc with Arlo, 'It is definitely sabotage; Arlo found these pine pitch branches on the ground on the far side.'

Luc was white with anger, and he turned on Arlo, 'Do you know who was responsible for this?' Arlo grim-faced shook his head.

'I don't know the names. However, there are rumours of a rebel group, who are trying to prevent you from getting a foothold here,' he said. He swept his hand towards the assembled crowd of villagers, 'But I would swear that it is not in this village, Lord, I know these people.'

Luc frowned, 'Then how did they get in? How did they get past the sentries? Have we checked yet, Gerard?'

'Not yet, my lord, the priority was to douse the fire,' said Gerard. Luc nodded in understanding, his mouth a grim line.

Luc gazed at the smouldering and blackened ruins of three day's work. The dawn was breaking now, and he could clearly see the damage. Suddenly, he caught movement; a figure had appeared on the top of Kirby Hill against the tree line. As Luc watched, a striking skewbald horse emerged into the light; the rider stood in his stirrups, punched his spear into the air in triumph, then turned and was gone. Luc gazed at the space where he had been for a few minutes. 'Did you see that, Arlo?' he said with quiet fury.

Arlo nodded, 'I did, Malvais.'

'The horse was very distinctive,' said Luc, 'A fjord horse with striking brown and white markings and a long cream mane, just like one of Thorfinn's stolen stallions.'

Arlo nodded, 'I will ride over to Melsonby and make enquiries, my Lord. If Thorfinn knows anything, he will tell me.'

'Maybe I should ride over and do that, Arlo,' said Luc through gritted teeth.

Arlo looked at the tight-lipped angry face. 'No good would come of that, my Lord. Making accusations in your present mood would undo the work you have done to build a relationship with him. I swear that this is not the work of Thorfinn. He is committed to peace in this area. Please leave it to me.' He pleaded.

Luc knew that Arlo Eymer was right, but it did not make him feel any better; he wanted to find and kill the men responsible. He nodded curtly at Arlo and turned on his heel, heading swiftly back to the Hall, ready to dress and ride out to hunt them down. Merewyn watched him go; he strode straight past her without a glance, not even noticing she was there. Arlo followed, and Merewyn put a hand on her father's arm, 'Father did you see?' she said.

He abruptly turned and stopped her, 'Yes, I saw, but we do not mention it to anyone until I have talked to Thorfinn,' he muttered.

With that, he stalked off to the stables. Merewyn stared back up at Kirby Hill; she had recognised the distinctive skewbald stallion but could not quite make out the rider. A shudder went through her; everyone in the village knew that it was Braxton's horse. However, was it Braxton? Was he back? If so, was Garrett with him? Could he be alive? Had they both survived? She felt another shudder course through her body at the thought of Braxton back in the Ravensworth area and attacking the Normans. She picked up her skirts and ran after her father.

It took them a whole week to dig out the scorched timbers that had been so well embedded, then repair and rebuild the gatehouse. Luc worked like a man possessed, driving his men and the village labourers relentlessly. Merewyn saw very little of him; there were no more pleasant lunches in the shade. The laughing, genial Luc of the first few weeks had disappeared. In his place was a grim-faced, tight-lipped Norman Marechal. There were no more signs of the rebel group in Ravensworth, but reports came in daily of raids on surrounding villages. They were reportedly also recruiting the young and impressionable village youths to join them as their fame grew; they were thumbing their noses at the Normans. Gerard estimated that there must be over sixty of the rebel group now from sightings and reports.

Luc blamed himself and his brief flirtation with Merewyn. He had become distracted by her, he was caught napping, and he was determined that it would not happen again, so he avoided any contact with her and tried, unsuccessfully at times, to shut her out of his thoughts. Luc insisted on riding out on patrols himself, sometimes twice a day, and Gerard watched him becoming harder and more exhausted. He finally remonstrated with him, 'Luc, you are pushing yourself too hard. You have good men down there, so delegate; some of them are desperate for a chance to lead.' He insisted.

Luc nodded. He knew he was exhausted, but two sentries were killed on the night of the castle raid, not just stabbed but their bodies brutally desecrated, and he blamed himself for becoming complacent. 'I can't understand it, Gerard, these rebels, they disappear like ghosts. They melt into the countryside, and they are laughing at us. Someone must be hiding and helping them.' Gerard looked thoughtful. 'I heard a whisper or two amongst the villagers, Luc, that some of this group are local, they will know the area and its hiding places well, and of course, the villages will help their own kind.'

'What about the leader Gerard? Did you see him? That horse is distinctive; Arlo confirmed it was one of the two horses taken from Melsonby, the bigger stallion. What is more, Melsonby is one of the few villages that has not been raided again.' He said, raising a questioning eyebrow at his friend. Gerard looked thoughtful. 'That may be because they know Thorfinn is now living there, Luc, but I also think that Arlo Eymer knows more than he is letting on.'

'I know,' said Luc. 'I saw his face when he saw that horse and rider. I think it may be Braxton Le Gunn or his son, Garrett Eymer.' Gerard grim-faced nodded in agreement.

Luc took Gerard's advice and lay down on his bed to rest for an hour, but his mind would not let him sleep, and he knew he had to corner Arlo to get to the truth. He set off across the village green to the Steward's large house and found that the front door was unusually propped open with a bench. Luc knocked, but no one answered, so he went inside and stood in the ample cool space. He could hear voices, so he walked over to look at one of the impressive tapestries on the wall while he was waiting. It was a colourful hunting scene, and he noticed the dogs were the large, long-legged rough-coated dyer hounds that he had seen following Durkin; he heard they were bred in Ireland.

124

Merewyn and Helga entered the Hall laughing, their arms full of fresh, sweet-smelling rushes. They stopped in their tracks when they saw him and Helga quickly scurried backwards out of the room. Merewyn was taken aback. She had hardly spoken to him for weeks, and here he was, standing in her home. 'Can I help you, my Lord Marechal?' she said in her most confident voice, putting down the armful of fresh rushes while her heart was hammering.

Luc turned to look at her. He was struck again by her almost ethereal beauty. Even with her hair covered with a coif and in workday clothes, she would stand out anywhere. The silence hung in the Hall as he stared at her but did not speak.

'Are you well?' she asked in a puzzled voice.

'Yes, I am well, thank you,' he said, turning back to gaze at the tapestry. 'This is of an amazing quality with expensive silks, almost as good as any made by the nuns in Normandy,' he said.

Merewyn moved to stand beside him and smiled. 'Yes, it was made by my mother. The nuns taught her in Ireland, and she was highly skilled. She came from a wealthy family, and my father met her while trading in Dublin.'

This brought Luc's mind back to the task at hand. 'I need to speak to your father. Is he here?' said Luc.

'He is over in the south field, checking the wheat. We hope to harvest the crops next week, as you know,' she said.

'Thank you. I will go out and find him,' said Luc, but he stayed rooted to the spot, just gazing down at her. Having pushed her out of his mind on purpose, now he was here and so close, he was reluctant to leave her. His face softened for the first time, and he smiled down at her. He leant forward and tucked some stray strands of hair behind her ear, caressing her cheek as he did so.

'Would you like some refreshment, sir?' she said quietly as she glanced up at his face.

'No, thank you, but I am riding out to look at the Dam site early this evening; ride out with me if you will?' Merewyn was taken aback but considered the invitation for a few minutes, and the silence hung between them. Then she smiled shyly. 'I think I would like that,' she said.

'I will bring a horse here for you early in the evening. I look forward to it, Mistress Eymer,' Luc responded in a very formal, courtly way, and he bowed before turning on his heel to find her father.

Merewyn was left standing in the Hall perplexed; she found it difficult to believe that she had just said yes to a ride out with Luc De Malvais; she had no hesitation. What was she thinking? What would her father think? She took a deep breath and found she felt excited at the thought of riding out with him. Would he have a manservant or Sir Gerard with him, or would they be alone? The idea of being alone with Luc De Malvais for several hours filled her with apprehension; she felt she had no control over her body when he was near or even if he just touched her. She picked up the fresh rushes and tried to concentrate on the household tasks in hand.

Luc, meanwhile, found Arlo walking the strips of wheat, rubbing the husks between his fingers, testing the quality. 'Is it ready, Arlo?' he asked.

'It will be by next week if the weather holds. I will arrange for extra men from Melsonby and around to help us get it in and threshed,' he said. He looked at Luc under troubled brows because he knew he was not here to speak to him about the wheat.

However, Luc stood in silence, gazing out over the rippling golden wheat and barley fields. Finally, he spoke, 'I know there is something you are not telling me, Arlo, about these attacks, and I think I have worked out why.' Arlo stood grim-faced in silence while Luc continued.

'You now know that your son Garrett is alive and that he is leading the rebels,' said Luc, turning to look at him.

Arlo turned an earnest face up to Luc, 'Malvais, I swear on the Gods, I have not seen or heard from Garrett since the day he left. You have my word. I do believe he is dead, or he would have found a way to contact us. He is not like Braxton. However, I will tell you, from what I have seen and heard, that I believe Braxton Le Gunn is the leader of these rebels, although you also have my word that he has made no effort to contact either his father or me.'

Luc looked thoughtful. 'Thank you, Arlo. Therefore, Garrett could be with him. You know they will probably die if we catch them. They have attacked and killed Norman soldiers.'

'I am aware of that, and so is Thorfinn, but I swear Braxton is receiving no aid or information from us,' he said.

Luc nodded and introduced a different topic. 'I am riding up to the valley head this evening, and I have asked if Merewyn will ride out with me; she has agreed if I have your consent; it should be safe enough as there are several patrols around that area.'

Arlo gazed at Malvais for some time, his brow furrowed, a worried look on his face, and then he sighed and nodded reluctantly, as if resigned to the situation, and, bidding Luc farewell, he left to go back to his home.

Luc stayed for a while staring at the peaceful pastoral scene, which reminded him of his estates at home in Brittany, wheat fields reflecting the sun's deep glow, the ears of corn waving in the slight breeze. He was pleased Merewyn was coming with him this evening, but he still had no clear idea of what his intentions were towards her, an amusing dalliance as a mistress as Bodin suggested or was it something more. He had already crossed the line in the way he had previously handled her, but Luc had felt her passion when he kissed her; she had wanted more as well, which made him ask himself, had she lain with a man before? Was it Braxton? After all, she was hand-fasted to him, and they were to be married as soon as he returned. So how did she feel now? She must also know from her father that it was Braxton leading the rebels. Did she want to be with him? If so, why had she kissed him back a few weeks ago?

He would ask her tonight. He needed answers, to be clear in his mind how he felt about her, but, just as importantly, he needed to know how she felt about him, as a man and of course as a Breton Lord in patronage to the Normans. The thought of Braxton having her suddenly filled him with a disquiet that surprised him; he was not usually the jealous type. He had taken numerous women over the last few years, loved them and left them, but, although he had enjoyed his time with them, not one of them had tugged at his heart as Merewyn did. She was different, and he felt differently about her.

So, was this more than just passion and lust? Was he falling in love with her? Could he see her established as the Chatelaine of his castle in Brittany? Would his mother accept her? Probably, with time, after all, his mother just wanted him to be happy, and she wanted grandchildren. He imagined waking up with Merewyn every morning in his home, Merewyn as a wife, as a mother to his children, her tall, graceful form directing the servants and running the home farm. He could see her there; he felt happy at the thought of her in his home, walking and riding over his lands in Brittany, leaving war and rebellion behind them. Instead, they would be breeding the huge Destriers, the warhorses that every knight wanted, a string of horses descended from the bloodlines of Espirit and some spirited Arab mares.

It was a pleasant image, but he sighed as he returned to reality with a jolt, she was a Saxon, and he was perceived to be a Norman, the enemy, by the whole village. He needed to solve the problems here first; he decided to find Gerard and tell him what Arlo had disclosed about Thorfinn's son, Braxton, they needed to increase the guards around the village and the patrols. He wanted more information about Braxton; he needed to know just what kind of man he was dealing with and what he was capable of doing. He reluctantly turned away from the golden wheat fields, sighed and set off with determination to summon Gerard.

Chapter Ten

Merewyn waited for Luc in the sunshine outside the hall with an apprehensive Helga and a visibly excited Durkin, waiting to see Espirit. Although the sun was sinking, it was still amazingly warm, a perfect summers evening.

Luc arrived leading a pretty palfrey mare, much smaller than Espirit but still larger than the horses she was used to riding. Malvais had discarded the usual heavy chain mail, she noticed that he had not brought manservants, which meant they would be riding out on their own after all; her stomach knotted at the thought. He smiled as he saw Merewyn and Durkin waiting for him, and she responded while trying to restrain Durkin.

Luc dismounted, and within seconds, Durkin was off the bench and there, holding his hands up. Luc laughed and swung him up to sit on the enormous Destrier. 'Now you must sit there quietly, Durkin, and hold Espirit in place while I help your sister mount.' He said, giving the small boy the reins.

He beckoned Merewyn over to the Palfrey, who skittishly sidled away until Luc pulled her back. He held his knitted hands for her to mount, and he swept her up into the saddle like a feather. 'You will find she has a soft mouth but be careful; she can go like the wind when necessary,' he said, smiling up at her. His hand rested for a few moments on her upper thigh as he checked the girth; she could feel the heat of his palm through the linen tunic, and, at his touch, a wave of excitement coursed through her.

'Don't worry, my Lord, I have been riding horses since I was Durkin's age,' she said confidently.

Luc then thanked Durkin for holding his horse and lifted him down to Helga, promising the child he could give Espirit an apple tomorrow. Merewyn watched with an appreciative eye. He was very good with Durkin; she thought he would make a wonderful father. She blushed at the thought then sobered as she realised that he could already have several children. After all, she knew nothing about him really; it was very likely he had a wife back in Normandy; after all, he must be about thirty years old and would be wanting or already have several heirs. She knew that this was just a dalliance for him, a flirtation to keep him amused while he was away from his home and lands. It would mean nothing to a man like him.

They walked the horses slowly through the village so that Merewyn could get used to the Palfrey's pace. Merewyn noticed the smirks and the headshakes of the village women as they rode past. She turned and saw the men spitting on the ground in disgust at her; she felt her heart sink, an unmarried maiden, riding out alone with a man and not only a foreigner but a Norman at that. More gossip about her, and she thought guiltily, more disapproval for her father. When they reached the meadow, they broke into a steady canter, scattering the grazing sheep before them. The mare was skittish but delightful and Merewyn, her hair loosed by the breeze, gave a laugh of pure joy. Luc watched her and smiled, the troubles seeming to lift from his shoulders for a while. They slowed when they reached the top of the hill, and they gazed at their destination far up the valley.

Although he had provided a soft leather saddle for her, she noticed that he was again riding bareback, his long muscular legs wrapped around Espirit, his strong, tanned hands resting gently on the reins. He looked strikingly handsome; he wore a soft leather doublet over a white linen open-necked shirt, which revealed his muscular, tanned neck. The breeze ruffled his dark hair as he sat there, scanning the valley and hills ahead, his swords strapped across his back. He suddenly turned and gazed at her with those steel-blue eyes and smiled, and she felt her stomach flip. It suddenly came to her, almost reluctantly, as if it had crept up on her that she was in love with Luc De Malvais, breathtakingly in love with him. She felt helpless as she smiled back at him; this was never meant to happen; it could never work.

She knew now how her father had felt about her mother. She understood now why the French sang such poignant love songs. She now understood how love could be bittersweet, as she realised that to him, a wealthy Norman Lord, she was probably just a temporary amusement before he returned to Brittany. However, as her head struggled to get control over her wayward heart, she still found it difficult to tear her eyes away from him as he continued to stare into her eyes, and she tightened her reins and leant forward slightly. Luc misinterpreted the signs,

'Oh! You want a race, do you?' he laughed.

Merewyn nodded; finding herself unable to speak, without warning, she kicked the Palfrey on, and it shot across the hillside. She could hear Luc laughing behind her and the thunder of his Destriers large hooves as he caught up. She reached the riverbank ahead of him and splashed through the shallows, racing up the other side to reach the ponds and reed beds on the valley floor. Luc stayed on the southern side of the river, and, for a while, they raced, laughing, side by side, both of them determined to win. However, the big Destrier swallowed the softer ground with his long stride, and soon he was ahead of her and slowing at the small dam site.

Merewyn crossed the river to join him; she was breathless, her face flushed with colour and excitement, and Luc thought she had never looked so beautiful. He swung down quickly from Espirit's tall back and went to help her down. Luc gripped her by the waist, lifting her into his arms; he dropped a chaste kiss on her cheek as he put her on the ground. He tied up the reins and let the horses graze before they strolled over to the large pile of newly split logs. She scanned the valley floor and saw that work had already begun on the project.

Luc saw her interest and explained to Merewyn where these logs would go across the river and how they would pin them to create a barrier with wide culverts on either side. This would make a water reservoir up here in this boggy area, a large millpond fed by the numerous streams running off the hills; they could control the small gates to increase the water's volume and speed when the small mill was in use. He described the millrace and small water wheel built in the broader, deeper parts of the small river downstream.

Merewyn was impressed. She knew just how important this would be for the villagers. She watched him talking animatedly with his hands on the subject, explaining the engineering of it all to her as if she was his equal. Her eyes softened; he made her feel special and important as if her views and thoughts mattered to him. She needed to know more about him and his life before coming to England; she was not sure that he would tell her anything, but she had to try. She turned and led him over to sit on the logs in the sun. However, at first, he stood beside her, his foot on the logs, his knee bent as he scanned the hills and horizon around them, ever watchful, ever the warrior. 'Tell me about your home in Normandy, My Lord,' she said.

The question took him by surprise, and he gazed searchingly at her face as he knew she hated all things Norman. Seeing no guile there, he smiled down at her. 'Please call me Luc when we are alone, and I am not a Norman; I am a Breton,' he said. Then he took a deep breath, and he began to describe his home and land.

'My home is in Brittany, a large province to the west of Normandy, at present, the main Breton families are allied to King William. My Patron is Count Alain Le Roux, a Breton and a nephew to William; he is better known as Alain Rufus. My castles and estates surround the small port of Morlaix, which sits in an estuary on the northern coast. I have several estates at Malvais, which lies down in Vannes; this is where my family originated. It was my grandparent's home— however; my mother and my younger brother live in the castle at Morlaix. However, I also have extensive lands over in Burgundy that came as a dowry for my wife, Heloise.'

Time suddenly stopped for Merewyn, and she went stone cold, her stomach knotted. 'You have a wife in Brittany?' she said in a halting voice.

Luc took a long time to answer as hands clasped in front of him as he stared at the grass beneath his feet. Merewyn, believing that she had lost him now, felt her eyes fill with tears as pain pierced her breast. It was precisely as Merewyn had suspected, she was no more than a quick roll in the hay, and she felt her anger building. Oh, how naïve she had been to think he could be unmarried.

Luc, meanwhile, was struggling for the right words. 'She died in childbirth, Merewyn,' he said. 'Along with my infant son, Alain, he only survived for five days. I loved Heloise dearly. We were so happy and so in love. She was only nineteen years old when she died and full of life and laughter. I was also very young when the grief nearly broke me, but Gerard and Bodin pulled me through it with tough love. They turned me into a mercenary, taking me on raids against William's enemies in France, even further into several Italian wars and then, of course, we came over to Pevensey and Hastings five years ago. I was fearless and reckless, and I did things during that time in my life that I am not proud of, but there was so much anger inside me, and it took a long time for it to dissipate. I thought I would never love again.'

He raised his eyes to Merewyn at that point and looked in amazement to see her eyes filling with tears. He grasped her two hands. 'Don't be sad, Merewyn. I came to terms with it some time ago, and I have learnt to live again; I hope that someday I will love again,' he said, pulling her into his arms and nestling her head under his chin.

'I am falling in love with you, Luc De Malvais', she bravely whispered.' Luc held her close, and then lifting her face to him, he kissed her deeply.

'You have bewitched me too, my little Saxon rebel,' he said as he held her tightly.

That was the problem; she thought as she nestled in his

arms, that she was a Saxon, and to her father and brother, Luc De Malvais was the enemy; this made their love almost forbidden; Merewyn also knew that her people would revile her. Still, it was a price she would happily pay to be with him. The sun was now sinking behind the hill, and there was a slight chill in the air. He pulled Merewyn to her feet and lifted her into the saddle. They rode slowly down through the scrub to the edge of the forest, with Luc describing more of his life as a boy in Brittany on his father's estates, the verdant forests for hunting and the beautiful, endless beaches on which to gallop and train their horses. Merewyn was mesmerised; she just loved to hear him talk and describing his homeland; she could hear the passion for Brittany in his voice.

As they rode back down the valley, they cut across through the sun-dappled forest. Suddenly, Luc caught movement on his right; it was a man from the village walking through the trees, carrying a small hand-held scythe and a bundle of saplings. He had a large hunting dog with him. His path meant that he would intercept them ahead. As Luc watched, there seemed to be something unusual about the villager, and then he realised that the man was wearing a thick winter hooded tunic in summer, the hood pulled up to hide his face in shadow. Luc's first thought was that he was poaching deer, which was now against the King's new laws, hence the disguise, and he turned to Merewyn to ask if she recognised him. Merewyn, a perplexed expression on her face, shook her head; she did not know the man or his dog, and he was definitely a stranger, which was rare in these parts.

Luc signalled Merewyn to stop and gently pushed Espirit forward, intending to challenge the man. Without warning, two more men emerged from the scrub behind them, swords drawn. Merewyn cried out and quickly turned the Palfrey to face them, but one leapt towards her, grabbing the reins and pulling her out of the saddle. The other thickset man made for Luc.

Merewyn fought back, screaming, punching and kicking at her assailant, who put his left hand over her mouth and nose and tried to drag her away backwards. Shaking her head violently, she bit down hard on his hand, drawing blood and breaking free before he had a chance to use the sword. He swore loudly and then swung and hit her hard as she turned to run, knocking her to the ground. He moved to stand over her, sword drawn. Meanwhile, aware of what was happening behind, Luc tightened the reins and rode the big warhorse straight at the first hooded man who was now running towards him. Espirit, trained to fight, immediately reared up and struck out at the man's head with his heavy hooves, knocking him to the ground. In a second, Luc was off the horse's back. Sword drawn, he faced the second attacker behind him, an older man with a scarred face. The man laughed and came towards him. Luc could see that this was not just a villager; his stance and how he handled the weapon showed that he was a trained soldier or mercenary. Luc glanced behind him. The first man was still on the ground, the big warhorse stamping and snorting in front of him.

'You need to back off, Norman, if you know what's good for you,' the older man shouted. 'We only want the woman, but we will kill you if you try to stop us taking her,' he said.

Luc said nothing; he just smiled and threw his sword from hand to hand as he waited for the man to attack. The man, slightly apprehensive now, glanced behind for a second to see if his partner had secured Merewyn. That was his undoing.

When he looked back, Luc was only feet away, running straight at him. He managed to raise his sword in front of his face as a relentless flurry of blows rained down on him. He tried to dodge to the left or right as Luc forced him backwards, but none of his strategies worked against the relentless force and blows from Malvais. Within minutes, he was against the trees with no room to manoeuvre, and he held his hands up for quarter, his sword raised above his head at first until he dropped it. Luc did not hesitate, 'I am not a Norman, and Bretons do not back off,' he said with a grim smile before coldly running him through. As the man crumpled at his feet, he turned towards Merewyn's assailant, who, having watched the fate of his companions, turned and ran swiftly through the trees. Luc looked over to check that the third man was still unconscious as he raced towards Merewyn, who was pushing herself up off the ground; he gently pulled her to her feet and into his arms.

'Are you unharmed?' he asked, holding her at arm's length and then running a finger over her bruised cheek.

'I fought back, but he was too strong for me. He said he was taking me to Braxton,' she said, raising concerned eyes to Luc.

Luc nodded. 'Yes, you seemed to be their target. Stay here while I see to our third attacker.'

He walked over to where Espirit was standing, nostrils flaring. The man was still on the ground and out cold. He patted the big Destriers neck.

Just then, he heard horses and crossed quickly back towards Merewyn. Pulling her behind him, he stood sword drawn, expecting a further attack.

Both of them breathed a sigh of relief as a Norman patrol came into view on the path. Luc sheathed his sword, and stepping forward, he greeted his men, explaining what had happened to the young Serjeant. Within a short time, the assailant, hands bound, was tied across a horse and heading back to Ravensworth, and the rest of the patrol was riding to hunt down the man that escaped.

As the patrol left them, Luc helped Merewyn to mount and, bringing Espirit alongside her, they rode quietly through the forest, both of them aware of the danger they had just experienced and thinking their own thoughts. For Luc, it made him aware of just how much he cared about her. Merewyn, meanwhile, was shaken, not so much by the experience but by the fact that Braxton had attempted to kidnap her and that he had men who were obviously tracking her movements.

Before long, they had reached the edge of the vast, golden wheat field that was still basking in the last rays of the setting sun. Luc stopped. 'I am not letting you go this soon, Merewyn,' he said, and he swept her from the saddle into his arms. He tied the horses loosely to a nearby tree, and, taking her firmly by the hand, he strolled a few paces into the waist-high wheat and then sank to the ground, pulling her helplessly down on top of him. Merewyn laughed, wrapped in his arms, her palms on his chest, but the laughter slowly died as they gazed at each other. Luc kissed her long and hard, his tongue entering and possessing her mouth. She returned his kiss with equal passion, her fingers stroking and caressing his strong neck and running along his broad shoulders. He rolled over, so she was on her back, kissing her neck and face until he hungrily sought her mouth again.

Merewyn loved the feel of his body pressed against her, his hard manhood pressing and rubbing against her hip and stomach. She felt a quiver of excitement, some anticipation and a slight frisson of fear about what she thought might occur, but she knew she wanted it to happen with Luc, especially now that Braxton was back. She wanted to belong to this Breton knight, to live under his protection, she thought of Braxton possessing her with disgust.

They paused for breath, and he gazed down at her, his face a mask of passion. His hands moved over her breasts, caressing and squeezing them gently, then he moved lower, and she could feel his hands running down the outside of her thighs. Her heart started to beat faster as he gently pulled up her clothes and slid his hands underneath, stroking the top of her thighs and then he moved one hand up to caress the mound between her legs. She was now breathless with desire; there was no way she wanted him to stop. He brought his knee gently between her legs to allow him access, and this time, he slid his hands up the inside of her thighs, stroking her soft skin. He stopped kissing her for a moment, raised himself and looked down into her face.

'Do you want this, Merewyn?' He asked. 'I would not do anything you did not wish me to do; I care too much for you now.' He was gazing down into her eyes with a passionate intensity that left her breathless.

She nodded; she could not speak. She so wanted Luc to take her, to make love to her; he cared for her; the words reverberated through her. Did that mean he was in love with her? At that moment, she knew he could do with her as he wished, and she would not have called a halt. His fingers moved gently upwards, caressing and stroking her intimately, outside, then inside. She gasped with shock, and he stopped his face ablaze with passion but also with concern for her.

'I want to make love to you, Merewyn,' he said.

'Yes, Luc,' she said in a whisper, 'I want you too.'

He laughed joyfully and continued his exploration of her body while opening and unlacing her clothing, squeezing and kissing her breasts and gently biting her nipples. Merewyn felt taken to heights of pleasure she never knew existed as she exploded into her first orgasm. Luc watched her face as she writhed in joy, and he smiled.

'Now we do all that, over and over again,' he said. She looked at him in amazement. 'I am, of course assuming, that you have never done this before?' he said.

She shook her head in an emphatic no, and he smiled as he began stroking her down there again. This time he guided her hand down under his braies to his manhood and clasped her fingers around it; it was large and hard and easily filled her hand. He moved her hand gently, showing her how to please him. Her eyes widened as she gazed into his face; his eyes narrowed with passion and desire. She felt shocked at what they were doing but excited at the same time. It felt so intimate, him touching her in secret places and her holding him...

Merewyn lay mesmerised, floating on a wave of feelings and sensations as his fingers entered her again. This time, he guided her hand on his manhood simultaneously, which throbbed with a life of its own. He reached down, and she felt him undo the ties at the top of his linen braies so that he could bring his erect organ out. Bringing in his other knee, he gently spread her legs even further apart, and he lay back down on top of her, propped up by one elbow but totally pinning her beneath him. Her overgown was now pushed well above her waist; she could feel the flesh of his manhood

141

pressing, insistently hot, against her bare skin. He felt like heated velvet, and she was shocked that she loved the intimacy of being with him, naked like this.

He gazed intently down at her, his face full of passion; he began to kiss her deeply and caress her nipples, waves of pleasure travelled through her to pulse in her groin, her body rose to meet his...

'Please, Luc, please,' she heard herself moaning.

He positioned himself at the entrance to her body and just inserted the head of his manhood into her while he gazed down into her eyes. 'It may hurt for a few moments, Merewyn, but I promise you that after that, it will be pure pleasure,' he said.

Merewyn smiled and gazed up at him, awash in a sea of pleasure as Luc pushed forward and entered her. She looked up at him, astonished by the sensation of him being inside her. He felt hot and huge; he was a big man, and she had a moment of panic. She felt the pain as he pushed more insistently, his hands pinning her shoulders to the floor as the passion took him. Then he was through, and she could feel the whole length of him moving slowly and repeatedly inside her as he brought her again to orgasm. He continued moving more firmly and urgently for some time while caressing and kissing her body until he brought her to orgasm once again and, finally, he exploded inside her, his whole body shuddering with pleasure.

They lay entwined there for some time, sated by passion but unwilling to let each other go. She could feel the slight breeze now on her bare legs and hear the rustle of the leaves in the birch trees behind them. Then he withdrew slowly, rolled over onto his back and after a few minutes, he pulled up and refastened his braies. Merewyn lay watching him through eyes still lidded and heavy with passion. She recognised, at that moment, the power women have over men in both allowing and wanting them to do this. She closed her eyes. Nothing will ever be the same again, she thought. I am his mistress now.

To her dismay, she suddenly realised the implications of what she had done. She had bedded a Norman Lord, one who would never marry her, but her eyes softened as she watched him lying there, on his back, his eyes closed, his body relaxed, looking almost boyish and much younger than his 30 years. It was no good; she loved him, and she knew she would stay with him for as long as he wanted her or until he returned to his lands in Brittany.

Luc turned his head and looked at her. She smiled a slow, lazy, sensual smile at him, and he gazed at her, entranced. The sun was sinking fast, and he looked at her lying there in the light of the deepening golden dusk. She had taken to his lovemaking joyfully with no false modesty. Luc knew then, without doubt, that he was in love with her, and he would have to raise that with his Patron, Count Alain, when he visited Richmond in two weeks. He hoped it would not be a problem, as he knew Alain was encouraging intermarriage between Norman and Saxon families to heal the rifts in the north. Still, Alain was his Patron, his previous wife's uncle, and things needed presenting formally. He also had to speak to her father, who probably had his suspicions already. That would be his main obstacle. Would Arlo consent to his daughter marrying a Norman Marechal, a usurper, sent to rule over them? He had his doubts, not only about her father; he had seen the reaction of the villagers today would they influence Arlo Eymer's decision. He was slowly winning their respect

143

RAVENSWORTH

through patience and hard work but marrying their Saxon
Thegns beautiful daughter was a different matter.

The August sun was setting in a blaze of dark orange.
He pulled her to her feet, holding her tightly in his arms
for several minutes, just breathing in the smell of her. He
reluctantly let her go and collected the grazing horses. They
walked hand in hand through the wheat field back into the
village, leading their horses, totally wrapped up in each other
and not caring who saw them at that point. Merewyn guided
Luc to the rear of the house and noticed that her father's horse
was missing; he had still not returned from Melsonby. Luc
impetuously pulled her into his arms to say farewell, and she
blinked up at him, still glowing from the hour of lovemaking
they had enjoyed.

'I am in love with you, Merewyn Eymer,' he said. She
nodded, smiled at him and wordlessly reached a hand up
to place a finger on his lips. 'Until tomorrow,' he said, leaning
down and gently kissing her bruised lips.

She watched him turn and stride down through the kitchen
garden to the waiting horses, and she felt she could almost
burst with happiness. Merewyn was pleased her father had
not returned from Melsonby when she entered the coolness
of the house. He would only have had to look at her to know
what had happened; she was glowing with happiness, her
clothes were crumpled, her hair undone, and she needed time
to wash, change and compose herself; Helga came into the
bedroom and looking at her she shook her head. Helga had
been their maidservant for the whole of Merewyn's life; she
was a hard-working feisty woman who could hold her own
with any of the villagers; her husband had died at Hastings
riding to war with Arlo. Now she tutted as she regarded the

144

young woman in front of her. 'This will not end well; your father will not like it,' she warned, helping Merewyn pull her dress over her head.

The father in question was riding slowly home from Melsonby in the twilight, and he was a troubled man. His worst fears had come to fruition; not only was Braxton leading the rebel group attacking the villages as they had thought, but one of Thorfinn's Huscarls was in contact with them, and he confirmed that Arlo's son, Garrett, was with Braxton. Thorfinn had discussed different options at length, to try to save their sons, before finally deciding to contact them and persuade them to give up and throw themselves on Count Alain's mercy. A gold ransom was on offer to save their lives and, of course, a promise of surety for their future behaviour. This was the aspect that worried Arlo. He knew his son, and he would happily vouch for him, but Braxton could be unpredictable and thoughtless, a cruel and selfish man ruled by his emotions and his temper.

As he rode, he hoped Merewyn was home early from her ride to the dam with Malvais; he now had severe misgivings about letting her go in the first place. It was apparent to anyone who watched them together that she was falling in love with Luc De Malvais. No one was more surprised than Arlo at this turn of events, given her hatred and antipathy to the Normans. However, he recognised that she had fallen for the man, this Breton Lord, regardless of what he represented. He had to admit that Malvais was perplexing; Arlo found that he had more and more respect for the man and what he was trying to achieve as time went by.

However, he dreaded to think what Braxton would do if he saw her with the Norman. Arlo knew that Braxton, in a jealous rage, was quite capable of anything, even of killing them both in revenge.

Chapter Eleven

The following weeks passed in a haze of happiness for Luc, walking and talking with Merewyn on almost a daily basis, taking an occasional stolen kiss or embrace. He found her enchanting, learning more about her every day, and he could see a happy future ahead with her by his side.

At the same time, he threw himself into completing the tasks he had set. The strong, sizeable wooden Donjon was constructed on the Motte with sturdy parapets now built inside the surrounding palisade for sentries. The high outer palisade was also finished around the huge Bailey area and the ditch deepened outside it. They were now attaching the stables and the inner barracks for his men to the palisade, and, next week, the large, temporary tented camp would move in and take up residence. The outer Bailey would become almost another village in its own right with blacksmiths and dwellings built inside. Luc was not caught napping again, and the rebel attacks had lessened, thanks to regular patrols under newly promoted Serjeants.

Luc was due to go to Richmond later that morning to report to Count Alain, but, as usual, he took part in the early morning sword practice and training for his men. He was delighted to see some of the older village boys, encouraged by Arlo, taking part this time.

Gerard always trained the novices, but, as usual, he kept a critical eye on Luc. He had not seen his friend so light-hearted for many years. He stood and watched him parrying killer sword strokes from two or three young fit opponents at a time, driving them back against the fence with powerful blows until they called for quarter and leant exhausted on their swords. Gerard thought him one of the best and most dangerous swordsmen he had ever seen, years as a young man serving as a mercenary had seen to that, but now he was a large, powerful man in his prime, and few could ever stand against him, especially if he used his trademark two swords. Luc had always been able to fight as well with his left arm as his right; something, which gave him an untold advantage in combat, as he suddenly threw a sword to his other hand.

Garrett, who sat on his horse in the shade of the birch forest watching the training, agreed with Gerard; Malvais was probably the most formidable warrior he had ever seen, and it was hard not to admire his skill. Their rebel attacks had lessened of late. For the present, they were out gathering as much information as possible to be lethally effective when they did attack. His job was to watch the Norman Knight. As he knew the village well, he had volunteered mainly because he was worried that Braxton would be too volatile near Ravensworth in his present state of mind.

The rebel group had now established a more permanent camp further away from the villages, down inside an old quarry about seven miles to the east of Ravensworth. He knew that they were well hidden there, in the overgrown scrub and trees and off the beaten track. Hopefully, no one would come

148

near. They had also set up a valuable ring of paid informers in all of the villages, feeding them regular information.

They received the message from Thorfinn and Arlo for them to surrender to Alain Rufus. It was considered and discussed at length, but Braxton did not trust the Normans, and he had his own plans to put into place. He had decided that they would terrorise the area for a further month or two, and then they would take ship to Denmark before the winter gales set in. Both of their families had extensive lands over there, and they would be out of reach of these Norman Lords until they left England and returned to their lands in Normandy; only then would the rebels be able to return.

Garrett was in two minds. He honestly believed that the Normans were here to stay, but he was always more of a realist than Braxton. Part of their strategy was to go to Richmond for a few days to assess the Norman strength and fathom their intentions. However, it would be dangerous to go there, as they knew Count Alain Rufus had taken up residence there temporarily. Furthermore, Garrett had grown up, maturing quickly over the last year, and he felt he had been away from his family for far too long. His brother, Durkin was almost unrecognisable as the toddler he had left behind, so sometimes he thought he might take the chance of a pardon, bought with his father's gold. However, when Garrett felt like this, he also felt guilty; he owed his life to Braxton several times over, so he owed him allegiance and loyalty. However, Braxton had changed since they had been in hiding; he worried Garrett with his long brooding silences and his unhealthy obsession with Malvais and Merewyn. He had always had characteristic rages and a fierce temper, but now he seemed almost out of control, and he refused to listen to any advice Garrett tried to give.

Garrett watched in awe as Luc saw off yet another skilled opponent in minutes, and then he noticed Merewyn, watching at the side, holding an excited Durkin by the hand. He watched Malvais walk over to her and hold her hand to his lips while she gazed up at him. They were so obviously lovers that Garrett found he could understand Braxton's fury. Luc then reached down, and, picking Durkin up, he threw him in the air. Garrett could hear the child's gurgling laughter and squeals of delight. He gazed at his sister and his young brother and felt a poignant sadness for the life and family he had lost. His eyes pricked with tears as he turned his horse away, unable to watch anymore.

Later that morning, Luc bid a soft farewell to Merewyn and then rode out with an armed guard to travel to Richmond. He would be gone for a few days. She, of course, did not realise the significance of this trip for him. He was about to request permission from his Patron to marry a Saxon noblewoman. Therefore, Alain Le Roux could seal his happiness in one word or destroy it. If he refused to allow the marriage, Luc knew he could never consent to the shame of Merewyn becoming his mistress, and her father would never forgive him. He knew that he had gone too far already by making love to her, and she could even be carrying his child. His stomach clenched at the thought of Alain saying no and that it would probably mean the loss of Merewyn, married off to someone else in another Manor or even country, to keep the scandal at bay, the young Dane, Sigurdsson, rose unbidden to his mind.

It was only an hour and a half to Richmond along dusty dry roads, so Luc had time to prepare himself and get his words and arguments together for his audience with Alain Rufus.

Riding into Richmond, Luc saw that a bustling town had indeed grown up here, as Bodin had foretold. He rode through the crowds and market stalls, following the road around to the river; he found that Alain was constructing a vast castle. Predominantly of wood, Luc knew that it would all be replaced by a stone curtain wall and buildings once the ground had settled. He dismounted and sent his men to the stables while he went through the completed gatehouse into the large courtyard. There were many shouts of recognition and smiles as Luc entered. He had fought by the side of all of these Breton knights, and they were delighted to see him, clapping him on the back or clenching forearms. Entering the large and impressive Hall, he saw Alain at the far end on a large raised dais, deep in discussion with two what looked like merchants in their belted robes. He saw that Alain had seen and acknowledged him, so he made his way to a table at the far end of the Hall and stood quietly until he had finished.

'Malvais! It has been far too long since I clapped eyes on you,' he said, embracing Luc and patting him heartily on the back. 'Come into the solar where we can talk in private.' He led the way up the stairs to a richly decorated and comfortable room; Luc walked to the window and looked down the cliff towards the river below.

'A good, strategic spot, Patron,' he said. Alain smiled and nodded, handing Luc a cup of full-bodied Flemish wine to take the dust from his throat.

'Firstly, well done on cleaning up and capturing the remaining rebels in Northumberland; I know that was a hard six months for you,' he said. 'Bodin is, of course, singing your praises and tells me you are doing a good job in managing the manors and villages that belonged to Thorfinn of Austwicke.

We must build bridges with these people now and make the land productive. These dales are a rich area and especially for what I have in mind for the future. Wool production Malvais! Sheep seem to thrive on these wild northern hills,' he said.

Luc nodded, 'I understand. There is good arable land in the valleys, but the hills and moors are ideal for sheep. However, there are still some loose rebel ends I am tying up at the moment, Patron.' Alain studied him.

'Yes, I heard about the attacks on the castle and the villages. A similar situation erupted in the West Country, but William has acted with speed and punished them harshly. We need to do the same here. Our response needs to be swift and ruthless.'

They talked for some time of other matters, news from the court, the plans that William was making before he returned to Normandy to deal with problems on his borders. Alain had news and letters from Brittany and Luc relaxed as he updated him on issues and news from home, including a letter from his mother with news of his brother Morvan, who was managing Luc's estates. It was late, and the sun was setting as Alain called for dinner, and, as they ate, Luc tried to find a way of broaching the subject of Merewyn. Fortunately, Alain raised it.

'So Bodin tells me you have a Saxon beauty in Ravensworth.'

Luc smiled, 'Yes, Patron, she is the daughter of a wealthy Saxon Thegn, Merewyn is half Danish and half Irish and, yes, she is very beautiful.'

Alain laughed, 'has the cool and remote Malvais finally fallen for the wiles of a blonde Dane instead of a dark Breton beauty?' Luc frowned at first, wondering what Bodin had said but then realised that Alain was teasing him.

Alain studied the young warrior in front of him, one of his

most capable and bravest men. He had watched with concern as Luc gave in to his grief when Heloise died, and he was pleased that he was finally showing interest in another girl. 'Do not worry, Malvais, I am only joking. However, according to my source, which is my brother Bodin of course, I believe that you do like her' said Alain, raising a questioning eyebrow.

Luc took a deep breath. 'Yes, my Lord, for the first time since the death of Heloise, I am in love again; I am asking for your permission to marry her,'

Alain stared at Luc for some time with an enigmatic expression on his face and then pushed his dish away. He stood up, walked over to the window and stared down at the swirling River Swale below in the twilight. He remembered Heloise well; she had been a Breton beauty, a sweet girl who was a distant cousin. Still sitting at the table, Luc found the silence interminable and his stomach clenched, ready for what he assumed would be failure and disappointment.

Eventually, after what seemed an eternity, Alain turned from the window and spoke, 'Who are her family, Malvais?'

Luc described Arlo, a wealthy Thegn in his own right with extensive lands in Denmark. He did not hide Arlo's part in Hastings, or her brothers suspected inclusion in the rebel band with Braxton. However, he emphasised Arlo's help in building the castle and in forging links with Thorfinn and his offer of a ransom for his son.

Alain looked thoughtful, 'I cannot promise anything for these young Saxon men; they must be taken and must come to trial if they have attacked and killed our men. I need this group rounding up and capturing as soon as possible; they have thumbed their noses at us for far too long,' he said.

Luc bowed his head and nodded in agreement. 'I understand, Patron. I promise I will bring them to heel before the month is out.'

Alain walked forward and reached a hand up to pat Luc's shoulder. 'When that is accomplished, you may marry your Thegns daughter. You can even marry her here in the new Hall and chapel if you wish.'

Luc laughed with relief and thanked him profusely; Alain smiled, noticing the changes that love had wrought, in one of his most formidable knights. He knew how that felt; he found himself in love with Gunnhild, the youngest daughter of the Saxon King Harold killed at Hastings; she was in a nunnery at the moment, and he admitted to himself that this had probably influenced his decision to say yes.

Luc spent the next few days in the town ordering supplies for Ravensworth and, with Alain's permission, selecting further men to make up his depleted numbers. He knew they would have started the harvesting in the villages by now, and he longed to be back there to see Merewyn again. There would be a harvest feast, with dancing and music this coming Saturday; he would ask Arlo then, for his daughter's hand in marriage. He had a few nagging moments of doubt that Arlo might refuse or that Merewyn might even say no, but then he remembered those large green eyes gazing at him with such passion when he had made love to her in the wheat field which was reassuring.

He wandered through the stalls and the traders inside the large Bailey area of the castle to find her a present and finally found a decorated Venetian glass loving cup with a silver stand and handle; he knew she would like it. He went on to buy Arlo a Toledo steel dagger with a decorated sheath and a fabulous wooden horse for Durkin, so cleverly carved that the arching mane and tail looked almost real. He set off back to the castle to pack his saddlebags, ready to leave the following day.

With a few bedraggled sheep grazing on the Bailey grass, two hooded shepherds watched him go through narrowed eyes. Braxton had insisted on accompanying Garrett to Richmond. What they found dismayed them both, the size and extent of the new castle was overwhelming for the young Saxons. There were hundreds of Norman troops here. This was no mere temporary incursion into the north. There was no doubt that the Normans were here to stay, and both men were plunged into despair and anger at the thought.

Luc set off for Ravensworth at sunrise the following day. He was full of good cheer, bringing ten extra men allocated by his Patron to replenish the contingent at Ravensworth. In his mind, he had a clear strategy for catching the rebels using his Breton Horse Warriors, and he hoped to marry Merewyn on All Hallows Day, as Count Alain had suggested. Espirit, alert to Luc's light mood and enthusiasm, pranced sideways out of the castle gates and down the road before breaking into a gallop. Luc's entourage followed on behind with wagons full of supplies.

Leaning against the gatepost, Garrett watched them go in a state of hopelessness. 'We have to leave, Braxton; we must sail for Denmark. It is pointless staying here and fighting against the Normans or the Horse Warriors at Ravensworth. It is an impossible task.'

Braxton scowled and kicked the mangy sheep they had stolen out of the way. 'We will, Garrett, we will, but I have some unfinished business first. I need to make that Norman suffer as he never has before, and I intend to take Merewyn with me to Denmark when we leave.'

Garrett looked at him in alarm, his thoughts in turmoil. He still loved his sister dearly for all her faults and betrayal. Although he hated the idea of her with the Norman, he didn't want her with Braxton either. However, he pressed his lips firmly together and said nothing; Braxton's temper was unpredictable at the best of times these days.

* * *

Merewyn's heart missed a beat when she saw Luc cantering back into the village earlier than expected; he sat astride his striking dark grey dappled horse, riding at the head of his Horse Warriors; they were an impressive sight. He was so handsome, so upright in the saddle, his longer dark hair ruffled by the slight breeze. Gerard was waiting for him as he vaulted effortlessly from the saddle, slapping his friend on the back and laughing as they made their way to the Hearth Hall.

He paused for a few seconds on the step before entering the Hall and scanned the village and the women on the green until he found where she was, and he turned a gaze onto her face that spoke volumes, the love just blazed from his face, and he beamed with joy. Some of the other women saw this too, and, shaking their heads, they turned and looked at her. Had she no shame, their glances said.

Merewyn, overcome with emotion at seeing him openly acknowledging her, looked away first. Her stomach was in knots of desire and love for this man, and she ran towards the house, knowing that she would see him tonight. On her way across the green, she spotted an unkempt youth leaning on one of the barn doors. He looked about fifteen summers old and in dire need of a meal. He belonged with one of the more impoverished villein families, here to help with the harvest; this was one of the few times of the year, when the villeins could hire themselves out to earn a little more money.

She smiled at him, 'What's your name, boy?' she asked. His eyes opened wide, surprised that she would speak with him.

'It's Rolf, Mistress,' he said.

'Well, Rolf, would you like some pottage?'

'Yes, please,' he mumbled, tugging at his forelock. Rolf gazed hungrily after her.

Braxton had said nothing about taking food from her. He watched and reported her every move to him; the boy grinned at this opportunity for a good meal as he followed her to her house. He had watched the shameless interaction between her and the Norman, and he knew Braxton Le Gunn would want to hear of it.

It was several hours later when Luc knocked on the door of the Eymer household. Merewyn answered, looking as lovely as ever, and he noticed Arlo sitting in the Great Hall beyond. He smiled down at her and handed her a large apple. She looked bemused. 'Is that for my father or me?' she said.

Luc laughed. 'Neither. It's for Durkin; I promised him he could give Espirit an apple on my return, so please walk him down to the paddock while I talk to your father so that I have fulfilled at least one promise to that little boy.' She laughed and showed Luc to a seat on the wooden settle next to Arlo, pouring them both some ale.

'So! What news from Richmond, my lord?' said Arlo, looking astutely at Luc from under frowning brows.

'I have much to tell you, but you may not want to hear it,' warned Luc. He explained what Count Alain had decided regarding the rebels and their two sons in particular.

157

Arlo shook his head. 'They have brought it on themselves by this campaign of attacks and deaths. Mark my words, Malvais; it will be Braxton behind this. He is a nasty piece of work.'

Before he could stop himself, Luc blurted out, 'Yet you were happy to marry your daughter to this man.' He regretted it as soon as the words left his lips; Arlo was out of his seat, glaring down at him.

'You know little of our ways, Malvais. I owe Thorfinn. He is my friend and my liege lord, and he has saved my life on many occasions when we were fighting, side by side, in the shield wall. Thorfinn requested that they be hand-fasted before the boys went North to the rebellion. He thought she would tame and steady his reckless son, and it would give him something to stay alive and come back for.'

Luc sighed. He had hoped to ask Arlo for his daughter's hand, but in his carelessness, he had angered him. He felt very frustrated, but he would have to leave it for another day.

'I am sorry I could not bring you better tidings from Richmond, but much depends on Garrett's role in these attacks, Arlo, whether he is a leader or a follower? If we capture him alive, I promise I will do what I can for him.'

Arlo nodded and thanked him. Luc had no choice now but to go, and he took his leave, with Arlo gazing thoughtfully after him. They had still heard nothing back from the message they sent to the rebel group about the possibility of surrendering and paying a hefty ransom, so it did not bode well for his rebel son. Perhaps Malvais may facilitate the surrender, but if Garrett had indeed killed the Norman sentries, then Arlo knew there was no hope for him.

The last day of the wheat harvest arrived, and there was a buzz of excitement in the village. There had been ten days of backbreaking work, from dawn to sunset most days, as they tried to get the harvest in before the weather broke and damaged the crop. It had been a glorious late summer, and the sheaves were now stacked in stooks in the fields waiting to be loaded onto carts and stored in the barns, ready for threshing and winnowing.

Luc had been up since dawn, ensuring with Gerard that all the preparations were in place for the harvest feast. He was determined to win the villagers over and show them a positive side of Norman rule. They were feeding the whole village and the harvest labourers from other villages, nearly a hundred people. He ensured that the fire pits were being dug and lit for roasting a whole ox and several pigs. Large butts of ale, flagons of mead and wineskins hung in a cool room in one of the big barns. He smiled as he knew there would be some sore heads tomorrow.

He saw Merewyn fleetingly as she went with the other women to get the wheat straw and corn heads from the final bundle. They would spend the next hour making the traditional corn dollies that were to encapsulate the spirit of the corn, and they would be placing them on the fronts of all of the houses in the village. In the spring, he knew that they would be ploughed back into the soil, as the dollies' seeds were sown as an offering for good crops. Having slept on Luc's news from Count Alain, Arlo seemed resigned to the fate of Garrett. Now Luc just needed the opportunity to raise the subject closest to his heart, that of marrying his daughter. Finally, there came an opportunity.

'Arlo, walk with me to the church. I need to ask Father Giffard to bless the stooks and give thanks for this bumper crop.' Arlo nodded; the pagan and Christian festivals and ceremonies ran side by side; when they reached the church, there was no sign of the priest, so a servant went to fetch him. The two men moved through the large wooden door into the cool of the only stone building in the village; the walls whitewashed with small, religious scenes painted directly onto the walls.

Luc took a deep breath and began, 'Arlo, I received some good news from Count Alain that I would like to share with you.'

Arlo turned piercing eyes onto Luc, 'You are leaving us, going home to Normandy Malvais?'

Luc laughed. 'No, you are stuck with me for a few years yet, and my home is in Brittany, not Normandy. However, he gave me leave to marry your daughter if you will agree to that. I love her dearly, and I believe she loves me too.' Luc held his breath and waited, hopefully, for a positive response.

Arlo sighed and stared at the stone-flagged floor for what seemed like an eternity to Luc. 'I am not blind, Malvais. I have seen the way you look at each other, and so has most of the village. The talk is that you will make her your mistress and abandon her when you leave; her reputation is in tatters; I will be lucky to find any Saxon man willing to take her.'

Luc was shocked. 'I thought you knew me well enough by now to know that I would not do that, Arlo.'

Arlo shrugged, 'Many before you have done exactly that in these situations, and in some places, Norman knights and soldiers just take what they want from our womenfolk.' Luc shook his head in exasperation, 'That happens in many wars, but we are not all like that, Arlo.'

Arlo looked searchingly into Luc's face, frowned and continued. 'Such a betrothal will not be popular at first. You are a Norman invader marrying a renowned local Saxon girl. You will face difficulties, and even more, families may shun Merewyn in the villages.'

'Merewyn and I have talked about our love for each other and the problems it raises; we are aware of the difficulties and will work to overcome them. In all events, I could not mention marriage to her until I had spoken to Alain Rufus and then to you to get your permission and blessing.'

This admission somewhat mollified Arlo. However, on a more serious note, he had to warn Malvais of a more dangerous threat. 'I presume you have also worked out that there may be retaliation for all of us from Braxton. Thorfinn tells me his Huscarls have been in touch with the rebel group, and Braxton still thinks of Merewyn as his property, his hand-fasted bride.'

Luc went stone cold at the thought of Braxton ever laying a finger on Merewyn. He would make sure that Braxton came nowhere near her ever again.

'As you know, I am aware of that; we questioned the man we captured in the forest; at first, he would tell us nothing, but Sir Gerard persuaded him otherwise. He admitted that they had been brought in and paid by Braxton to kidnap Merewyn and that they had been watching her for days.'

'You have my promise that as my wife, I will cherish and protect her, Arlo.'

Arlo looked sceptical, aware of Braxton's long reach. But Luc continued regardless,

'I will also do my utmost to catch this group of rebels and protect you and your family from them. I am aware that this may be bittersweet, as Garrett may be with them.'

Arlo nodded. 'If that is the case, and of course, if she is

agreeable, I will not stand in your way. Unfortunately, my son chose his path and must pay the price,' he said.

Luc breathed a sigh of relief, and his eyes lit with joy at the thought of Merewyn as his wife. 'With your permission, I will ask her tonight during the feast.'

Arlo smiled for the first time. He had a lot of respect for Luc, even though he was a Norman. He just hoped that she would accept him; she turned down so many as not worthy of her respect. However, Luc De Malvais was a different proposition from her usual suitors. He was a grown man, not only wealthy but with a fearsome reputation. Just as importantly, it was evident that he loved her.

By early evening, the sheaves were all in the barns, the carts put away, and the smell of roast meats spread tantalisingly around the village. Several children were chased away from the spits, fingers burnt from the hot fats streaming down the beef and dripping into the fires below. Benches and tables pulled out into the cool of the evening were filling up where the villagers were now gathering to celebrate a bumper harvest. Luc had ordered large, round, flat loaves baked with a sheaf imprinted on the top, as they did in Normandy. They were handed to each table, which drew appreciative sounds, not least from Luc's thirty-plus Breton men, who were already tearing chunks out, ready to dip in the meat juices when the trenchers arrived.

Merewyn was disappointed to find that Luc had gone when she returned home, so she dressed with care for her time with him tonight. Her body ached to be near him. She had chosen a white linen under-tunic and a deep green over-tunic embroidered around the hem and neck with white flowers. On her long, silver-blonde hair, she wore a headband woven with freshly picked wildflowers. Like the other maidens of the village, she wore bracelets of long coloured ribbons and woven wheat. Merewyn took a washed and combed Durkin by the hand; she walked out across the green to join the festivities. However, within minutes he was gone, running and playing with the rest of the village children.

Luc was standing talking to her father, Sir Gerard and Father Giffard. He was wearing the midnight blue tunic embroidered with a silver thread that she loved, and he looked breathtakingly handsome as he threw his dark head back and laughed at something Gerard had said. His face lit up at the sight of her as she headed to her place at the table. He walked forward and took both of her hands in his.

'I love you, Merewyn Eymer,' he said in a voice loud enough to be heard several tables away. She looked up into those clear blue eyes, and she melted inside.

'I love you too, my Lord,' she whispered in a breathless, husky voice, her eyes wide with astonishment that he had shown this open display of affection in public. She looked over at her father, but he just gave her an enigmatic smile.

The celebrations were now in full swing, helped by copious amounts of drink and food. The musicians had started to play, and people clapped along to the lutes, horns and drums. Merewyn smiled; she loved Harvest Home nights because everyone was usually so happy with the gathered crops. Luc was holding her hand under the table and refusing to let it go, his thumb stroking the inside of her wrist, sending sensations of longing through her body. Then he moved his hand down to stroke her thigh, and she gasped, which made him smile.

The horns blew, and Merewyn saw her father stand to give his usual harvest home speech of thanks for all of the summer's hard work. There were several toasts and jokes about individual villagers. He thanked the gods of the land for their bounty and the gods of the sky for sending good weather. The people clapped and cheered, and Merewyn expected him to sit down. However, with a serious face, he went on to say that the war was in the past. He hoped that the people of Ravensworth and this area would now have peace and prosperity, and he raised his cup high.

'To that end, I have today, given the hand of my daughter, Merewyn Eymer, to our Marechal, 'Luc de Malvais', and they will be married in Richmond at Samhain or, as Father Giffard and our Christian friends know it, All Souls Day.' At first, there was a stunned silence.

Not least from Luc, who realised that Arlo had pre-empted him before he had a chance to ask Merewyn for her hand. However, he need not have worried. Merewyn turned huge, tear-filled eyes to a grinning Luc. He pulled her into his arms, and Luc's Breton men went wild, cheering, clapping and banging on the tables. After a moment or two, not to be outdone by the foreigners, most of the villagers joined in, although there was still head shaking and spitting amongst some.

Luc was overjoyed at the response from Merewyn, and the crowds began celebrating the end of the harvest. He pulled Merewyn onto his lap, and he held her tight, dropping kisses on her face. Merewyn could hardly breathe. She was so overwhelmed with happiness; she could not believe that Luc De Malvais would marry her. She shyly looked up at the dark, handsome knight that she loved so dearly. The light from the large flickering fires played on his firm jaw as he gazed out at the happy village scene. His eyes were creased in smiles as

164

he watched some of the dancing and antics of his men; she thought she would never tire of gazing at her lover, her future husband, the love of her life. She wanted to spend the rest of her life with him, even though that meant that she must leave Ravensworth and her family and travel to his estates in Brittany.

Rolf, the underfed gangling youth, watched the lovers with interest through the fires' smoke and sparks while sat on one of the far tables. As Luc kissed Merewyn, he sighed. Well, he thought, this would probably mean a trip back to the quarry tonight with this vital information. They would pay him well for this news. Then he thought for a moment, not a little worried, at just how Braxton might receive this news. He had been bullied and beaten by Braxton into carrying information for him; he still had the bruises, and, like most people, he was frightened of Braxton and tried to stay out of his way. Instead, he decided to stay here, enjoy the free food and drink tonight, and take the news to Garrett in the morning. Garrett could have the unenviable task of telling Braxton Le Gunn that his hand-fasted Saxon bride was marrying a Norman Lord. Rolf shook his head as he thought of the impact and fall out of that news, and he promised himself he would keep well out of the way when Garrett delivered it.

Chapter Twelve

For days after the announcement of their forthcoming marriage, Merewyn felt as if she was walking two feet above the ground, she loved Luc De Malvais, and now it was in the open. They took every chance to be together, to touch, kiss or hold hands. They sat in the orchard and talked, long into the warm late summer evenings, about their plans for the future. Luc intended to stay in the north of England for the next few years until Bardolf, Alain's half-brother, arrived from Europe, but they would visit his mother in Brittany during this time. He shared his dreams with her about breeding huge part Breton-part Arab Destriers like Espirit when they returned to his estates in Brittany, intelligent, resilient, brave warhorses for the future. Merewyn shared her wish for lots of children; she could see a large, happy family, and Luc watched her blush delightfully, as she said it. He laughed, pulling her into his arms. 'I promise I will work hard every night to fulfil that wish, my lady.

Merewyn laughed with him but then became serious for a moment and gazed at him in a perplexed way. 'What would you have done, Luc, if your Patron said no,' she asked, raising her large deep green eyes to his.

Luc paused and stared off into the distance taking several minutes before answering. 'You have to understand, Merewyn, I am a Norman knight first and foremost, we have a code of honour, and no matter how much I love you, I owe allegiance and loyalty to my Patron, I have to defer to his decisions in all things. I would have been devastated if he had refused my request, but I am sure I could have talked him round eventually. Let us not think about things that did not happen; let us look to our future instead;' he then set about kissing away her concerns, leaving her breathless and happy.

They had not made love again, as Luc wished them to wait for their wedding night; however, they kissed and caressed constantly. Merewyn, who was new to lovemaking, had loved every minute of their time in the wheat field, and she longed to be with him again. She imagined them at night, lying fully naked in bed, his muscular body covering hers. She smiled with delight at the thought of their entwined bodies, with him deep inside her. Then she blushed again when he asked her why she was smiling. However, the amused look in his eyes told her that he knew just what she was thinking, and she shyly laughed as well.

There had not been a sound or sighting of the rebel group for several weeks, and Luc began to wonder if the extra patrols had worked, that the rebels had left the area because things had become too difficult for them. He had ensured that things were more secure at Ravensworth; the Motte and Bailey castle finished, and Gerard had taken up residence on the top floor of the impressively sizeable wooden Donjon. The tented camp was gone, and his men were now rehomed in the long, dry, wooden barracks in the Bailey area, ready for the change in the autumn weather. He had smiled to see that some of his single Breton men were courting Saxon girls after the harvest home feast, and he smiled at them for following his example.

It was now September, early morning in Ravensworth but still warm and Luc stood bare-chested in just his linen braies at the open window of his solar. Today, they were constructing the sides of the millrace at the village end of the river. The dam and millponds were in place further upstream; with these projects completed, he felt as if everything in his life was coming together. The early morning mist was sitting on the fields, and the countryside looked lush and green. As he breathed in the early morning air and stretched his powerful shoulders, he saw Merewyn leaving her home, with Durkin running behind her. It was Friday, so, of course, she would be heading to the hives in the orchard. Every week without fail, Merewyn would collect the honey; she had some cycle set up to move around the dozens of hives, taking honey from only three or four at a time. As he watched her, she looked up for him, smiled and waved. He was overwhelmed by the love he felt for this beautiful but feisty young woman, and he couldn't quite believe that soon she would be all his, sleeping in his bed, wrapping her long lovely legs around him.

Once in the orchard, Merewyn quickly set about her tasks. Durkin was running through and around the trees, galloping with that carved wooden horse in his hand. He had barely put it down since Luc brought it back for him. She had pulled the thin linen veil over her head, and she was carefully extracting the honeycombs to place in the pot when she heard him talking to someone. She was at a crucial point in the manoeuvre, and the veil limited her vision, so she could not see who it was, but she thought it might be Helga, who had promised to come and help. As it was the end of the season, more hives needed emptying to make the spiced honey mead for the colder autumn months ahead.

As she placed the combs carefully into the pot, a man's hands came round her and slowly fondled her breasts. She laughed as she knew it would be Luc; she had seen him wistfully watching them from his window. She could feel the heat of his body and his swelling manhood pressed against her back as the fondling became more insistent. He reached up and undid her shoulder broach so that her tunic came down, exposing the lacings underneath. She still had hold of the honeycombs but could not release them into the pots as his actions were holding her against him. Within seconds, he had harshly pulled the lacing apart, and his rough hands were squeezing her breasts, unusually hard.

Merewyn became alarmed. 'Luc, stop, not here, someone might see us, Durkin could be watching as well,' she said. She heard his breathing become more ragged as he continued to hurt her, then she realised… this was not Luc, he would never do this to her, especially not in front of Durkin. Merewyn then became aware that there was a powerful, unpleasant, rancid, animal smell about this man. 'Let me go!' she shouted, trying to extract herself and dropping the dripping honeycombs.

Instead, he ripped off her linen veil and forced her head back. A hard, bearded mouth came down on hers, biting her lips and forcing his tongue into her mouth. She tried to wriggle free, but he was too powerful. His knee was between her legs from behind, and his powerful arms and hands clamped around her were still kneading and bruising her breasts. With a start, she suddenly knew who it was. She wrenched her mouth free and shouted,

'Braxton! Stop it! Let me go!' He whirled her round to face him, gripping her upper arms so hard it hurt.

She stared at the huge man in front of her. He was like a stranger, not the young boasting Braxton who had left for the north. In the past, she found she could handle him, but this man was a stranger. She had not seen him for well over a year, and this Braxton was almost unrecognisable. He had filled out in his time on the run and had put on a lot of muscle, now nearly matching his father's impressive build. He looked hard, cold and unforgiving and what she saw in his face was anger, hatred and contempt for her. For the first time in her life, she was afraid. She knew, however, that if she gave a hint of it, she would be lost. Braxton was a sadist and a bully, and she knew first-hand from the past how he enjoyed inflicting fear, pain and punishment on others, especially if they showed fear.

'Let me go now, Braxton or your father and mine will hear of this,' she said, in what she hoped was a confident voice. He stared back at her and snorted in contempt and derision, 'What will those two worn-out warriors do? They are too busy bowing down to their new Norman masters.'

He stared down at her; she was more beautiful than ever, even more so than he remembered. He hated her for what she had done with this Norman, but he still desired her with every bone in his body. She should have been his, and she would be again from now on. He would make sure of it.

When Rolf had brought the news to the quarry about the forthcoming wedding and shared it with Garrett, Braxton thought he might lose his mind. He had never felt rage and anger like it. He punched through several walls of the huts they were living in, and he raged and ranted, inconsolable, for hours, about what he would do to both of them. He, then, spent several days locked away, drinking himself into oblivion, eventually emerging yesterday with a wave of stone-cold, tight-lipped anger that burnt within him. He would make them pay. He had lost everything. He was now almost penniless, living like some outlaw because of this Norman, Luc De Malvais, who had taken all of his father's lands. Well, he was determined to show him and his woman the meaning of the words pain and suffering.

Now, she was here, standing in front of him... looking down on him again with disdain, as she did when they were hand-fasted. He was sure she had hoped he was dead, but he had escaped, and now he intended to take back what was his. 'So I hear that you have become a Norman whore!' he said, glaring into her face and pulling her tightly against him, his arms pinioning her against him and bruising her arms.

Recognising the hatred in his eyes, Merewyn thought it best not to answer. She could not hold his gaze because, in some ways, he was right; she had given herself to Luc, her Norman overlord. She dropped her eyes, but not before Braxton had recognised the guilt and shame; he felt a surge of triumph.

'Well, seeing as you are giving out your favours so freely to the Norman army, you can accommodate me now, here on the grass,' he said.

She gasped out a 'No!' and desperately looked around for an escape or help, but what she saw filled her with horror. Her young brother Durkin was tied up and gagged. They had placed a noose around his neck, thrown it over a branch and the Saxon youth, Rolf, now held it. 'No, Braxton, do not do this. He is only a little boy,' she sobbed.

Braxton was becoming even more aroused by the apparent fear on her face, and he began to enjoy himself. She could feel his large erection rubbing against her body.

'I tell you what you will do for me, Merewyn: you will go

today and find out the details of every Norman patrol for the next three days. I want to know where and when they are going, and you will give that information to Rolf in the village tonight. He will be outside your back door near the kitchen garden. If the information is correct, then Durkin will remain unharmed. If it is not... then he may begin to have a series of harrowing accidents, losing a hand or a foot, or an eye.'

Merewyn closed her eyes in shock, and she felt her legs begin to shake.

'You will go back to your Norman lover and tell him you now realise you cannot bring yourself to marry a Norman after all, that you cannot cope with the shame of it, and you intend to marry a Saxon. You will not touch him again, I will be watching, and he will not touch you at all. You are now completely mine, Merewyn Eymer, body and soul, to do with as and when I please. Tell anyone what has happened here today, and I promise you will find Durkin's body swinging from a branch. Rolf and several others I have planted in the village will be watching your every move.' Braxton turned his head and gave a signal to Rolf.

The youth nodded and tightened the noose so that Durkin writhed and shrieked in dismay, his little boots almost off the ground.

Merewyn watched, sobbing. 'No, put him down. Please don't hurt him, please Braxton!' she cried.

He narrowed his eyes, 'I know how much you love your brothers, Merewyn, and for the last year, Garrett has also been like a brother to me. I have protected him on the raids we have carried out, keeping him in the background, but I promise you that if you do not do everything I say, I will make sure that Garrett leads those raids from the front every time

172

we attack the Norman patrols.' Braxton grinned in pleasure. 'Do we understand each other, Merewyn?' he asked, cruelly grabbing her hair and forcing her mouth to his, bruising her lips again and thrusting his tongue into her mouth. 'Now I want you to start saying, 'Please Braxton' for another reason,' he said with a wolfish grin that chilled her to the core.

He suddenly threw her forcefully back onto the grass where she lay slightly winded. Then he came down on top of her, pinning her to the ground. He was a large, heavy, powerful man, and a wave of revulsion swept over Merewyn as he pushed her clothes up around her waist and roughly forced her legs apart with his knees, bruising her thighs. He pushed himself up onto his knees between her legs, staring hungrily down at her semi-naked body, and began to undo his heavy linen braies to release his manhood. She wanted to die. He could not do this. He moved forward and roughly pushed his fingers inside her to guide himself in.

Suddenly, she could visualise Luc's dark blue eyes gazing down, as he had gently made love to her, and she screamed, twisting her body and fighting back as hard as she could. Braxton swore and clamped a hand over her mouth. Suddenly, in the distance, Merewyn heard someone shout her name. She writhed in fury, managed to dislodge his hand and screamed. Someone called her name again, and she realised it was Helga, coming to find them.

Braxton glared down at her. 'I need to teach you a lesson in obedience; I promise I will punish you for this. We will continue this pleasure another day and every night and day afterwards. I know where you sleep; I can get into any house in this village. You are mine, Merewyn and I will take you again and again.'

He laughed as he stood up, slowly refastening his braies. Helga coming through the trees, stopped dead, her hand to her mouth, then taking in the situation at a glance, she started forward at a run. Braxton, still standing between Merewyn's bare legs, barely glanced at her. He just waved Rolf away from Durkin, and they both disappeared back towards the forest.

Merewyn lay on the ground sobbing in shock, the tears coursing down her cheeks, as Helga came running over to help her up from the grass, pulling her clothes down. Helga's shocked face said it all.

Merewyn gave her a tight smile. 'I am alright,' she gasped. 'You arrived just in time, but please see to Durkin.' Merewyn watched as Helga untied and wrapped Durkin in her shawl; picking him up, she began crooning to him, wiping away his tears.

Merewyn found she could hardly walk; her legs were shaking so much, it was the helplessness, which overwhelmed her; she had never felt so vulnerable and alone in her life. Braxton would be back to take her whenever he wished, to hurt the ones she loved, and she had no defence against him. On the way back home, she told Helga what had happened and swore her to secrecy.

'What are you going to do, Merewyn?' whispered a horrified but angry Helga.

'There is nothing I can do, Helga. If I tell my father or Luc, then Braxton's men will snatch and harm Durkin. They have several men in the village watching our every move. Luc and my father would not be able to prevent it.'

At the thought of Luc, Merewyn dissolved into tears again. She felt defiled by Braxton even though he had not succeeded in taking her, and now, she was about to lose the love of her life. She could not stay with Luc if Braxton were coming to her bed every night. Luc was not a man to take someone's leftovers and, because of Durkin, she would not be able to say no to Braxton whenever, or wherever, he wanted her.

She felt physically ill at the thought of Braxton using her body as he wished, and she went through to the back of the house to scrub every inch of herself with lye soap to remove the acrid smell of him. Afterwards, she lay down on her bed in a state of abject misery. She could see no way out of this situation, and she sobbed convulsively at the thought of losing the man she truly loved.

Chapter Thirteen

Luc was riding back from the millrace when he saw one of his men carrying a large honey pot. Luc made a joke about the man's many talents, but he told Luc he had found it lying in the orchard. Luc dismounted and led Espirit back through the orchard to the hives. There was no sign of Merewyn, but her linen veil and gloves were on the ground. He picked them up, noticing the rip in the veil. Maybe she was stung by a bee, and she is coming back, he thought, glancing around, and then he noticed that the meadow grass was flattened and Durkin's wooden horse was lying close by. He picked everything up and headed over to the house.

Helga answered the door with Durkin clinging tearfully to her skirt. Luc held out the much-loved horse to the boy, but he cowered back behind Helga. 'Is Merewyn here, Helga?' he asked, puzzled by the boy's behaviour; Durkin usually rushed to him.

Helga could not meet his eyes. 'Yes, my lord, but she is not well; a summer ague,' He nodded, handed the items to Helga and said he would call later to see if she had recovered.

Merewyn heard Luc's voice, the pain, and the tears welled again. She had never felt such despair or anger. She realised that she now had to get the information about the patrols to

176

Rolf this evening, so she forced herself to dress and then see Gerard in the Donjon. He would have information about the patrols, but she needed an excuse to ask him.

She covered herself in a large hooded cloak despite the warmth of the day as her arms and neck were covered in bruises, and, picking up the pot of honey, she headed for the large wooden Donjon where Luc's right-hand man had taken up residence. Gerard was surprised to see her but invited her to sit. Merewyn explained that she had brought some honey for his men, who were doing such an excellent job of protecting the villages. She then talked animatedly about admiring the new castle and the large solid Donjon. Gerard eyed her critically; she looked ill, pale, with huge dark smudges under her eyes. She told him that there was a rumour in the village he should hear and that the rebels would attack the village of Layton in the next few days. She then expressed an interest in how he would prevent that from happening and protect them all. Gerard happily took her through his patrols and rotas, and he felt appreciated when she praised his organisation and skill. She told him Luc was lucky to have him, gave him a winning smile, handed over the honey and was gone, leaving a bemused Gerard.

Luc was surprised and disappointed when he was turned away from Merewyn's house that evening. He walked down to the river in the twilight afterwards on his own. On his way back, he saw a cloaked woman talking to the Saxon youth, Rolf. They saw him coming, and both melted down the side ginnels into the shadows. He gave chase. The boy had disappeared, but he quickly caught up with the woman, grabbed her arm, and he saw her wince and fall. As he helped her to her feet, he realised it was Merewyn. She clutched the cloak tightly around herself and gazed dully up at him. She was almost unrecognisable.

She looked away from him. 'I am not well, my lord, please leave me,' she muttered.

'Merewyn, what is it? I will bring a physician or healer to you,' Luc said with concern. However, she shook her head and stared at the ground. Then she turned and was gone into the shadows leaving him standing alone and perplexed.

* * *

Merewyn went home in a wave of misery, seeing Luc had been torture. She retired to her room, and before long, Helga joined her after locking all of the doors. Merewyn's room was on the ground floor at the back of the house, so Helga had insisted on bringing a pallet bed into the room and sleeping with her. Despite the warm night, they closed and barred the heavy wooden shutters before blowing out the candles. Nearly an hour later, both women heard the shutters repeatedly pushed from the outside, insistently at first and then banged with force. Helga put her finger to her lips and walked over to them as she heard Braxton's voice.

'Open these now, Merewyn; I have come to finish what we started.'

Helga answered back just loud enough for him to hear. 'This is the servants' room; my lady is upstairs near her father. Go away, or I will call the Normans.'

Braxton swore loudly and punched the outside wall, which set the dogs to barking; soon afterwards, they heard him move away. Both women let out the breath they had been holding and wrapped their arms around each other in relief, tears streaming down Merewyn's face. Would he come every night looking for her? How would she fight him off?

* * *

Luc did not sleep well that night, and more trouble was to come. Gerrard came to see him just after he dressed. 'The early morning patrol to the village of Layton has been ambushed and attacked, one man dead and two men injured. It was as if they knew we were coming,' said Gerard. 'They all described the leader, a huge blonde man armed with an axe, on the back of a skewbald stallion. They said he fought like a demon, and they couldn't stand against him.' Gerard looked troubled.

'Braxton!' spat Luc, 'It's time we brought him to heel Gerard.'

Arlo was anxious about Merewyn. Helga told him that his daughter was ill, and he could see himself that she was not well, but it was more than that. The light and life had gone out of her eyes. He saw some of the bruises on her arms and was perplexed. Surely, Malvais would not have done that to her. He questioned Helga, but she just shrugged, but he noticed that she could not meet his eyes, and he felt that he was missing something. He insisted that Merewyn come out into the hall and have dinner with him. She drank several glasses of mead but just picked at her food.

Finally, he could not take any more. 'Has Malvais done something to you, or has something happened?' he asked.

Merewyn just stared at her trencher and sighed. 'No father, but I wish you to tell him that I cannot in all conscience marry a Norman. I want a Saxon husband. I do not want to see him again.' She quietly stood, refused to meet his questioning stare and went back to her room.

Arlo was taken aback. Only days ago, everyone could see how much in love they both were. He walked over to the Hearth Hall to have it out with Luc, who was coming over to see them.

'How is Merewyn? She is not well, I believe?' he asked.

Arlo looked up at Luc, 'What has gone on here between you, Malvais?'

Luc looked confused, 'Why… nothing has changed or happened. I love her more than ever.'

Arlo frowned. 'She tells me that she no longer wishes to marry a Norman, and I have to keep you from the house.'

Luc felt himself go stone cold. 'I don't understand. Two nights ago, we were talking happily about our future. What has changed her mind?'

Arlo was pensive. 'Something is not right, Malvais, and it's not only her. Helga and Durkin are subdued as well. It is like all the happiness has suddenly gone from my house. Stay away, Malvais and I will try to find the underlying cause of this.' He turned on his heel, and, shaking his head, he walked back through the gloaming to his house to question Helga again.

Luc paced the solar room for most of the night. He could not begin to understand what had happened between Merewyn and himself, but he had a tight knot in his stomach at the thought of losing her; he loved her with all of his heart and soul. Could this possibly have to do with Alain's insistence that Garrett will be brought to trial? He turned over every conversation with her repeatedly in his mind but could find nothing. He finally fell into an exhausted sleep but was up at dawn to meet Gerard. The plan to stop Braxton and his rebel group began today. He and Gerard would lead a group of crack Breton Horse Warriors out to follow the two routine patrols this morning, and he prayed that Braxton would be found and caught.

Luc led Espirit out of the paddock and tacked him up. The horse, spirited and fresh, was dancing on the spot. Luc noticed Rolf, the gangling Saxon youth Merewyn had been talking to, leaning on the fence, watching him intently, and he felt uneasy; there was something about this boy. Luc vaulted up into the saddle with ease and spun round to question the young Saxon, but he was gone. It came to him then that he was likely one of Braxton's spies; if that was the case, what did he want with Merewyn last night? Arlo was right. Something was amiss.

Merewyn felt unbelievable guilt that men had been killed and injured on the previous day because of her. She had to stop this somehow. She stepped out into the stable to find Rolf; she needed to send a message to Garrett. Her father had told her he was with Braxton. However, Rolf was nowhere to be seen. He was, in fact, on the back of a fleet-footed pony, racing through the forest towards Melsonby with important news.

Merewyn walked to the front of the house and scanned the green for any sign of him, but instead, she saw Luc and Gerard both mounted, with dozens of the mounted Breton Horse Warriors. As she watched, they split into two groups, ready to canter off into different directions. Luc was leading his patrol north over the river.

Merewyn was frozen to the spot at first. 'No!' she shouted at him, and she ran out as they raced across the village green and down the bank to cross the river, but it was no good. Over the thunder of the hooves, he had not seen and could not hear her. She stood there, clutching her hands to her face. Luc had not led patrols for weeks. She knew, instinctively, that Braxton would be waiting for him. Luc was in grave danger if he fell into Braxton's hands, and Merewyn had no way of warning him or stopping this. She turned and saw Gerard watching her, but before she could beckon him, he had turned his horse, and they galloped off in a different direction to the south-west. She dropped to her knees, sobbing uncontrollably.

Then she pulled herself together. She had to find a horse and go after Luc. She raced around to the stables, but they were empty, her father had ridden up to the top meadow, and their manservant had gone to Melsonby on the other horse. She whirled around desperate to find a solution and then remembered the Norman horse lines. The young grooms were surprised when she ran up, demanding a horse; she grabbed at the halter of one of the big destriers and pulled it towards them. The boys were reluctant to let her take one of the big warhorses, but she was Saxon nobility and betrothed to Malvais, so they followed her orders with reservations. She seemed frantic. As Merewyn cantered the huge horse out of the village, she realised almost immediately that she was having trouble controlling him. He was a Breton stallion and far too strong for her. Within minutes of entering the wood, she was on the ground, having swerved to avoid trees and branches but thankfully, as she fell, she held on to the reins. She lay there winded for a few minutes while the horse cropped grass and realised she could never catch Luc and his patrol, but she knew that she could find her father; only he, with Thorfinn's help, could stop this.

* * *

Rolf galloped into the clearing in the woods just as Braxton and his men were mounting up. They were heading south that morning to attack Gerard's patrol on the moors, but once he listened to Rolf's news, Braxton crowed with triumph. 'I've got him!' he shouted, punching the air. He pointed at Garrett. 'Bring those ropes, all of them; I know just the place to bring him down, but we must be quick. We need to be there before him.'

The rebel band headed north at a gallop until they came to a heavily forested ravine, with a broad valley floor that narrowed at one end. Braxton instructed his men to stretch several of the ropes across the narrower end of the valley floor with a horse's length between them, putting two men at either end, and they covered them with moss, bracken and grass. The men mounted on the sturdy ponies, hid either side of the ravine, in the bushes, close to the cliff face, from here they would attack. Braxton, then, rode down to the ravine's broadest part where the path went into the trees. The undergrowth was low and less dense here so that you could see some way ahead. He positioned 'Flame', his skewbald stallion, exactly where he thought Malvais would get a good look at him. He smiled to himself. He knew from instinct that Luc De Malvais would be leading from the front, and he intended to capture him alive if the Norman didn't break his neck first.

Luc was preoccupied. He was hurt and angry at Merewyn's refusal to see him, and he was bewildered by her declaration that he no longer wanted to marry him. He had never felt such loss or desolation since the death of Heloise. It filled his thoughts to the exclusion of all else as they cantered along the forest path, weaving in and out of the trees. It was barely wide enough for two or three men to ride side by side, but he was confident that his ten Breton Horse Warriors could outfight and outride any outlaw rebel. This preoccupation with Merewyn's decision not to marry him and his overconfidence was his downfall.

It was shaded and dappled in the forest, and he could see the cliffs ahead of him in the distance. Suddenly, Espirit snorted, and Luc could not believe his luck. There ahead of him, disappearing into the trees, was a large bearded blonde warrior on a striking skewbald stallion; it could not be anyone other than Braxton Le Gunn. He reached up for one of the swords in the crossed scabbard across his back and yelled, 'To me, Bretons!'

He kicked Espirit into a gallop, ducking to avoid low branches as he and his men went thundering into and down the ravine. What happened next was a blur of chaos and confusion; he saw Braxton suddenly stop ahead, swiftly turn his stallion and yell, 'Now!' and then all hell broke loose.

He felt Espirit go down with a thump, and he was flying over his mount's head through the air into the clearing. He was conscious other horses had come down beside him, and now, the rebels were attacking his men from both sides of the ravine. He had landed on his back, totally winded and his sword gone. He could not believe he had allowed himself to be thrown from his horse, but Luc knew he had to get up if he wanted to live. He was still winded, but he managed to get over onto all fours, he was reaching for his sword when a foot stamped heavily down onto his wrist, and a shadow fell over him. He looked up into Braxton's grinning face,

'Well, well, Norman! Not so clever now, are we? Not so great a leader either, your men mostly dead and injured and you disarmed and on the ground.'

He laughed, swung back and delivered a vicious and powerful kick to Luc's ribs, which rolled Luc over onto his back, his knees raised in agony. Luc opened his eyes and looked up to see another three or four Saxon rebels now standing around him. Luc knew what was coming, and he tried to roll into a ball to protect himself. Braxton was smiling in anticipation. At first, the rebel leader stood back to watch, but he stepped forward again to join in. As the kicks and blows continually rained down on Luc's body and head, he lost consciousness and sank into oblivion.

Braxton's eyes gleamed with victory as they made their way back to the camp in the quarry. They had stripped the injured and dead Normans of their mail hauberks and weapons, and they had taken some of the larger Norman warhorses, which would fetch a pretty penny. However, the greatest prize was strapped across one of those horses behind him, stripped of his mail and doublet, his head dangling and blood dripping from a gash on his brow. Braxton laughed and grinned with pleasure at what lay ahead for this Norman; he would ensure that Luc De Malvais would wish he had died when his horse came down on its knees. What a horse, but unfortunately, his men were unable to catch the big Destrier as it snapped and struck out at them before galloping away.

Behind Braxton, Garrett sat quietly on his brown mare; he was not as euphoric about the victory. Too many had died. He had to stop Braxton from killing any more Normans, and, more importantly, he had to try to keep this one alive. This was the man his sister loved and wanted to marry. However,

Garrett was just as concerned at the retribution that Alain Rufus would visit on the area if Malvais died at their hands. This knight was his champion, and he would not take this attack on one of his lords lightly.

Garrett had seen the remains of the burnt-out villages in other areas that had suffered in revenge attacks. However, he knew it would be difficult, if not impossible, to protect Malvais; he saw the all-consuming hatred in Braxton; he wanted revenge on this man, who he blamed for all of his misfortunes. Garrett shuddered at the thought of what this knight had coming to him, no matter how strong and courageous he was. Braxton was one of the cruellest men he knew, so, somehow, he had to try to keep Malvais alive while persuading Braxton to flee to Denmark as soon as possible.

Chapter Fourteen

L uc woke slowly. He was conscious of a pounding pain in his head and an even sharper one in his side, but he could not work out why. He tried opening his eyes, but only the left one would open fully; the right one felt caked in something. He glanced around the limited area he could see, took stock, and realised he was lying on his back in a large barn with massive beams above his head. It was empty and, as he looked around, he realised that it had a deserted air about it. It took him a moment to work out why he was here, and then it all came flooding back. He cursed himself for his stupidity at riding into such an ambush like a novice; Gerard would be furious. He tried to roll over and sit up but soon realised he couldn't; his arms were spread-eagled and tied to the ends of a solid pole across his shoulders.

He managed to wedge one end of the pole on the ground to push himself into a sitting position. As he moved, he was aware of sharp pain in several areas. He looked down and saw that he had been stripped of his mail and shirt down to only his thin, linen braies tied loosely on his hips. This was an old ploy, obviously used by Braxton to make him feel vulnerable and defenceless. However, the braies were filthy and splashed in blood, his blood, he asked himself? He quickly looked around his body and arms for sword wounds but found none, although much of his body was turning black and blue from the beating and kicking they had given him in the clearing. He realised that he must have a head wound. They usually bleed copiously, and that might explain the reluctance of his right eye to open. He was desperate for water but could see nothing around him. Then, he heard voices outside, and he tensed. He was not naive, and, as an ex-mercenary, he knew he was in for a rough time with Braxton. However, he was tough; he would survive this; he would escape and go back to Ravensworth and find out why Merewyn had rejected him.

The large barn door was dragged open, and what looked like evening sunshine flooded in; he must have been out for some time. He blinked rapidly, and his right eye finally opened through crusted blood. He saw three men outlined in the doorway. As they came towards him, he recognised the rider of the skewbald. Braxton was undoubtedly a big, imposing Saxon with his father's huge build and blond good looks, but there the resemblance ended. Luc had led and fought with many men, and he recognised the cruelty and arrogance in the face in front of him.

The second man was a good-looking young warrior, with dark auburn hair cut much shorter than Braxton's long locks and not braided. Luc took a sharp intake of breath, for Merewyn's green eyes stared back at him. This young man was undoubtedly Garrett; he looked stern but somewhat unsure of himself in this situation as his glance darted around the barn. The third individual was the gangly Saxon youth, Rolf, who looked exceptionally nervous. *I was right about him,* thought Luc; *he is one of Braxton's spies, feeding information about the village and Norman movements back to the rebels.*

Braxton smiled down at Luc, but it was not a pleasant smile. 'So, our guest is awake. Have you enjoyed our hospitality so far?' He walked over and looked down at Luc, standing so close, Luc could smell the rancid odour of his stale sweat. Luc glared back at him and said nothing.

'Oh, you won't be this quiet for long, I have plans for you, Norman, and you are mine for as long as I want to keep you here. No one knows where you are. I will make you pay for what you have done to both my people and me. String him up, Rolf.' He shouted as he turned away.

Luc tried to appear unconcerned, but in reality, he watched apprehensively as the youth untied a rope and hook from one of the posts and attached it to the pole across his shoulder blades. He then waved to Garrett to give him a hand to hoist Luc upright in the centre of the barn. Luc felt himself being dragged forward across the floor and then upright, the strain on his arms and shoulders beginning to tell and the pain in his right side increasing. Braxton watched with a smile as the rope was tied off so that the balls of Luc's feet were only just on the ground.

Braxton took out his dagger and walked close to Luc. He placed the tip of the weapon on Luc's shoulder, slowly piercing the skin with the point while staring into Luc's eyes with utter hatred as he drew it in a sharp line from one side of Luc's chest across and down to the other, just deep and painful enough to cause droplets of blood to run down Luc's chest. He then did the same across the other side and then along the front of both of Luc's biceps. Garrett became more concerned as he watched; Braxton had a cold rage tonight, which he had never seen before. It worried him, as he knew he had to keep Malvais alive, which would be difficult as Braxton wanted

189

revenge. Luc never flinched as the knife moved back and forwards across his body again, and the blood began to run down his chest. He gazed back, calmly, into Braxton's face, which, of course, enraged the large Saxon even more. He turned slightly away, putting the dagger back into his belt and then, without warning, he swung a violent punch into Luc's middle, which forced Luc to bring his knees up in agony, lifting his legs off the ground as he curled up and putting more strain on his shoulders and arms.

'Bring two of the men in Garrett,' said Braxton in an icy cold voice as he stepped back to look with satisfaction at his captive.

Luc knew what would happen next, and he thought back to everything that Gerard had taught him to do, if, or when, enemy troops captured him. He could almost hear Gerard's voice: 'Remove yourself from what is happening and go into your mind. Think of a pleasant memory and focus on it. Do not ever give them the satisfaction of seeing you beg for mercy. Think about what you are, 'You are a Breton Horse warrior.'

Garrett did not return with the two men. He stayed outside, gazing down into the old quarry, where they hid their horses from sight. He could hear the blows and punches inflicted on Luc, but he did not want to watch such punishment. He knew, however, that he had to keep Braxton from killing him, so he shook his head, took a deep breath and went back through the doors. Luc hung there, blood trickling from the corner of his mouth and nose, purpling bruises appearing everywhere on his face and body, but still with defiance in those steel-blue eyes.

Braxton walked up to Luc again, 'This is only the beginning, Malvais. We have days of this, and I *will* break you.' He swung another solid punch into Luc's side, and Garrett saw Luc wince and grit his teeth as he heard another rib crack. Braxton smiled and went to swing in the same place again, but Garrett jumped in between them. 'That's enough for now, Braxton; we need him alive. You will kill him if you keep this up; remember that we want a huge ransom for him.'

Luc lifted his head and smiled at Braxton, who was patently unhappy that he had to stop, but he was weighing Garrett's words as were the group of men standing watching this spectacle.

He was almost spitting with rage, his face inches away from Luc's. 'Oh, you will still live, Malvais, but you will be in pain and maimed for the rest of your life when I have finished with you.' He promised.

Luc laughed in his face, which earned him a punishing blow to the head, rendering him unconscious again. Garrett just shook his head in disbelief at the foolishness and bravery of the man hanging in front of him, this Norman, this man that his sister loved.

Braxton stormed out into the dusk, and Garrett ordered some water brought. Rolf came back with two buckets and a cloth. Garrett threw one bucket directly at Luc, washing away some of the dried blood from his face and head and bringing him around slowly.

'Merewyn,' whispered Luc in an agonised voice as he slowly came back to consciousness and looked into Garrett's green eyes. Garrett and Rolf looked at each other, they were both afraid or wary of Braxton in their own way, but they both admired how a bound and beaten prisoner had stood up to him.

Rolf shook his head. 'He'll get himself kilt,' he said, turning

191

a concerned face to Garrett, who was beginning to clean the encrusted blood from Luc's eye with a dirty damp cloth. There was a deep gash above the eyebrow, but the eye itself looked fine.

Luc lifted his head further and looked at Garrett with those piercing blue eyes, and then he gave a lop-sided smile. 'Thank you,' he said.

Garrett used a dipper to pour some water down Luc's throat, which Luc gulped noisily. 'Are you mad, Malvais? Is your pride so important that you will die for it? Give him what he wants – beg for your life and go back and save my sister.'

Luc smiled. 'I am a Breton Horse Warrior, Garrett, we don't beg, on our knees, to anyone and do you honestly believe he will just let me go if I do. How did you get involved in this, Garrett? You are nothing like him, and your family miss you. They thought you were dead.'

Garrett shrugged. 'It just all went too far, but now I am involved, and it's impossible, we can't just go back to our homes,' he said sadly.

'There is always a possible way back, Garrett,' said Luc in a breaking voice.

Garrett sighed, 'Let him down to the ground, Rolf. He is not going anywhere.'

Rolf slowly let Luc sink to the ground where he lay, groaning and trying to move his pain-wracked body, almost impossible while still strapped to the pole. He heard them leave and bar the barn door, and then the pain became too much as he slipped back into semi-consciousness.

* * *

In Ravensworth, Merewyn had wrestled the plunging horse up the hill to find her father. Arlo was in the top meadow checking on the sheep when he saw his daughter on a huge Norman Destrier racing up the hill towards him. She threw herself off the horse and fell sobbing into his arms. At first, all he could get from her was that Braxton would kill Luc, and it was her fault.

Arlo held her at arm's length and gave her a good shake. 'Calm down, Merewyn and tell me, from the beginning, what has happened.' She was still distraught, but she tried to control the racking waves of tears and hysteria to explain to her father why he had to come with her now.

Arlo listened in mounting horror to the tale she told. He felt a wave of all-consuming anger that his family had been threatened and vowed to kill Braxton himself when he found him. However, he immediately realised the implications of the capture and possible death of Malvais. He knew what Alain Rufus would do to the villages if his favourite champion and knight were killed or maimed. He needed to find out what was happening and get to Thorfinn immediately. He glanced at the wild-eyed warhorse and decided against taking it as he grabbed his distressed daughter by the hand and set off at a run down through the meadow, heading back to where his horse was tethered under the trees.

* * *

There was absolute panic and shock when Luc's famous horse came galloping riderless into the village. Gerard had been back for some time, and he was concerned when there was still no sign or word of Luc's patrol. When he saw Espirit cantering down the village lane without his master, Gerard went stone cold; he had never known anyone to unseat Luc in an attack. He reached up, grabbed the bridle and hung on tightly, pulling the frightened horse to a stop. He looked wildly around, as if he expected Luc to come running into the village after him, then he looked down and saw the rope-burn marks on the fetlocks and the badly cut knees of Espirit.

'So it was an ambush, and that's how they brought him down. Please, God, let him still be alive,' he said. He handed Espirit over to the stable hands, with instructions to put poultices on those swollen knees immediately, and shouted to the men to mount up. By this time, a crowd of villagers and Normans had gathered as word spread that Malvais was missing or dead. As Gerard gathered the remainder of the Horse Warriors together to begin the search for Luc, Arlo reined his horse in beside him. 'What can we do to help, Gerard?' he shouted down from his horse.

'We need information, Arlo. Where will they have taken him? Go to Thorfinn and see what he knows? If we find the ambush site and there are no obvious clues, we will join you at Melsonby. This must be the work of Braxton?' he declared.

Arlo nodded, and pulling his horse sharply round; he headed off to Melsonby at a gallop. Someone in Thorfinn's household must know where they were hiding; he thought as he splashed through the ford and on up the hill. He remembered the rebels had been communicating through some of Thorfinn's Saxon Huscarls – they must know something about the hidden rebel camp. He was sure that was where they would take Malvais, and God help him in the hands of Braxton, they had to find him sooner rather than later, or they would be looking for a body.

Merewyn heard the shouts and commotion, and Helga came rushing in to tell her what had happened; his horse had returned, but Malvais was missing. Merewyn went stone cold. It was her worst nightmare. She had seen the hatred in Braxton's eyes and the idea of Luc, helpless in the hands of such an unpredictable and cruel man who was after revenge, filled her with horror. If he had taken him alive, and part of her knew that this would be his aim, he would take delight in torturing and, finally, killing Luc. The worst part of it, though, was that it was her fault. She had betrayed him and handed him to Braxton; if he survived, which was doubtful, he would never understand the position she was in, and he would never forgive her. She fell into Helga's arms, sobbing and praying that Gerard or her father would find him in time.

* * *

Luc woke to waves of searing pain; everything had stiffened during what little sleep he had managed to get. He had tried, repeatedly, to loosen the bonds on his wrists and arms but to no avail. They put the ropes on his arms and wrists wet, and they had now tightened as they dried, digging into his flesh. He knew it was on purpose, and it could do significant damage if he did not manage to escape soon. He scanned around the barn, looking for any chances, or possibilities of escape, any old tools he could use. He pushed himself upright. He had to stand and try to move around if he hoped to tense his muscles during any further beatings today.

Despite what he told Garrett, he wanted to survive this, and one sentence used by Garrett kept coming back to him: 'Go back and save my sister.' He meant from Braxton. What did

Braxton have planned for her?

The pain was fogging his brain. His body was now a sea of black, purple and yellow bruising, but still, in his mind, he kept returning to Merewyn; something was not right. What had happened to make her suddenly refuse to marry him? Was this the fault of Braxton? Could she possibly have decided that she should honour the pledge she made at the hand-fast ceremony to marry him? He tortured himself with this thought for several minutes, dismissed it, but then in his weakened state, it returned to haunt him.

Luc heard the sound of the bar on the substantial barn doors lifting and, taking a deep breath, braced himself for what was to come. He knew that Gerard and his men would be searching for him, and he prayed they would find him soon as he was not sure how many more days of Braxton's punishment and revenge his body could take or survive. He had seen the hatred and stone-cold anger in the Saxon rebel's eyes, and he knew how dangerous that was.

Chapter Fifteen

Gerard, riding out to search for Luc, met up with the first wounded Horse Warriors limping back through the forest. The rebels had stolen their horses, and two of their number killed; this was so rare for the Horse Warriors, they were shamefaced, but Gerard brushed it off and reassured them. They told him what had happened—describing rows of their horses being brought down on top of each other by ropes raised in sequence, impossible to avoid.

'Do we know which way they went, which way they took him?' Gerard asked in a strained voice. The trooper pointed vaguely to the north-west.

'And Malvais was he still alive?

The soldier found it challenging to meet Gerard's concerned eyes, and he looked away as he replied.

'They beat him very badly, about six of them. There were far too many of them for me to be of any help, so I pretended to be dead. The big, blonde leader kicked him unconscious, and they stripped him and tied him over a horse. He was bleeding badly from a head wound,' he said, now gazing at the ground.

Gerard nodded his understanding of the situation and put a reassuring hand on the man's shoulder before turning away.

Then he stood and clenched his fists in rage. Luc was like a son to him; he had taught him to ride his first stallion, hold his first sword. He had to be alive. However, he knew that he had taught Luc to be tough; he had managed to get him through the death of his wife and son, although it had taken time. He knew Luc was resilient and had a vast store of courage, but they needed to find him soon, tonight if possible, before Braxton and his men killed him.

Minutes later, he rode into the clearing at the end of the ravine. He scanned the area for any clues, looking at the rows of discarded ropes. He acknowledged that it had been a well thought out ambush. However, he was perplexed about how they knew that Luc was leading this patrol; Braxton must have had spies in the village feeding him information. Or had they just got lucky, he wondered as he mounted up and, waving his troop on, they would go back to Ravensworth to see if there was any news and then head towards Melsonby; Thorfinn must know something, he reasoned.

* * *

Luc was strung back up from the beam in the middle of the barn. Braxton was pacing backwards and forwards in front of him. He was furious that Luc showed no signs of being cowed by the situation he was in, and Braxton was now working himself into yet another rage.

He spat furiously at Luc. 'I have lost my home and my inheritance. My father, the renowned warrior Thorfinn reduced to living on a paltry little manor, and I am penniless, without the lands and rents that were ours, while you Normans, you treat us like cottars and villeins.' The large group standing at the barn's sides voiced and mumbled their agreement, many spitting on the ground to show their contempt for this Norman.

Luc watched Braxton warily, waiting for the blows to come and getting ready to tense his muscles.

' Then,' Braxton almost screeched at him, his voice rising, 'you take my woman, Merewyn, my hand-fasted virgin bride, that I have patiently waited years for, while her father kept her at home to raise her mewling brother. I know you have swived her, I have my spies, and everyone tells me she is your whore now.'

Braxton stood inches away from Luc, physically shaking with rage. His breath was ragged and coming in snorts and grunts. Luc noticed Garrett in the background, looking very concerned. Garrett met Luc's eyes, and he shook his head at him to prevent Luc from making any comments.

Braxton launched a tirade of hammer-like blows into Luc's stomach that left Luc grunting with pain and gasping for breath, but through gritted teeth, he managed to mutter,

'Maybe that is because she prefers a real man, Braxton, one who doesn't run and hide in the woods each time a patrol appears.'

Behind Braxton, Luc saw Garrett groan and put his head down in his hands. Luc thought, yes, Merewyn's brother was right; I should not goad Braxton. However, he could not help himself; he despised this Saxon bully, and he wanted to push Braxton over the edge, so he lost control and possibly, knocked him unconscious again. It was a dangerous strategy; Braxton might kill him, but if not, if he was rendered unconscious, it might buy more time for Gerard to find him.

However, regretfully, the strategy did not seem to work;

Braxton had turned away and calmed, now he just stood there, icily cold, staring at Luc through narrowed, pale blue eyes. He suddenly seemed entirely in control, and Luc realised his gamble had failed. Without warning, Braxton punched Luc in the side where the rib had broken. This time, Luc could not stop himself, and he cried out in agony, doubling his knees up to try to reduce the pain.

Braxton gave a smile of satisfaction that he had broken through Luc's defences. Most of the rebels who stood around watching the punishment laughed and cheered Braxton on. Braxton gave a smile of satisfaction that the Norman had shown reactions and pain for the first time. He turned and walked to the barn's far side, and reaching up, he took something down from the wall. Luc saw that it was a long flat leather drover's lash with a hard leather-wrapped handle, not as lethal or sharp as an ox whip, which would flay a man, but it would still do considerable damage.

'We are going to show you, Malvais, what it feels like to be one of those serfs you flog on your estates in Normandy; we are going to punish you for what you have done here to us in our lands, in the North.' The dozen or so men behind Braxton cheered and stamped again, raising their clenched fists in the air.

He walked behind Luc and roughly ripped his linen braies down, leaving him hanging naked, unravelling the lash; he held it high, stepping back he brought it down viciously with substantial force onto Luc's back. Slowly at first, then gathering momentum, he administered blows, from Luc's shoulders down the length of his back, across his buttocks and thighs to his calves, and then he started again, building in force. Luc gritted his teeth and clamped his mouth shut as each lash bit into his skin, determined not to make a sound. At first, the Drover's lash did not cut the skin being of broad, flat, woven leather; it just delivered deep red raised weals, but repeated blows made them split. Braxton called the next man over with a grin and handed him the whip.

'Cross them,' he said while he came round to sit on an old bench and stare at Luc's face, enjoying the pain inflicted on his enemy. The man continued with zeal, the raised weals now started to bleed, and before long, through the pain, Luc could feel the blood beginning to run down his back.

'This can stop Malvais as soon as you beg me on your knees for your life,' said Braxton.

'Bretons don't beg Braxton, especially not Horse Warriors, you should know that,' hissed Luc through clenched teeth.

Braxton just smiled, cruelly, and waved the next man over to take his turn. Luc saw that it was one of the massive Saxon Huscarls, who brought the lash down with such force on Luc's back, that his feet swung forward off the floor and despite gritting his teeth; Luc cried aloud in agony. Braxton grinned at the blonde Huscarl, nodding with satisfaction. As similar blows followed, Luc doubted if he would survive this. The pain reached the point where it was almost beyond bearable, but he was determined not to give Braxton the satisfaction of hearing him cry out again.

However, when Braxton turned and looked away, Luc turned his head and looked desperately over at Garrett, who watched in mounting horror as the blood began to spray with each lash. Luc saw some sympathy there, and he mouthed the words, 'Au Secour,' at him. At first, nothing happened, and the whip continued to lash, savagely moving down across the back of Luc's thighs.

Luc had remembered that Garrett had learnt French along-side Merewyn, but he could see that his loyalty to Braxton tore the young Saxon. Luc closed his eyes, tried to focus on pleasant memories and silently began to pray, something he had not done much of since his son and Heloise had died. Then suddenly, Garrett intervened, 'That's enough, Braxton, he can't take much more and live,' he said.

'Oh, I think he can,' said Braxton, taking back the blood-stained lash, 'he has spirit and fire in his belly. I want to find out exactly how much he can take before he gets down on his knees and begs me to stop.'

'I know when I am watching a man being flogged to death in front of me, Braxton. They will take this out on our families, our villages as well if you continue,' said Garrett. There were mutters and murmurs of concern from the other rebel group members as they realised the sense of what Garrett was saying.

Braxton sighed, 'Very well, we will have a few hours of ale, food and sleep, and then we will come back and start again.' Suddenly, he turned back to face Luc. 'Shall I give you something to fire up that hate, Malvais, so that it will burn brighter and you will last longer?' he said with a lascivious grin.

'Did Merewyn tell you I swived her on the grass in the orchard on Friday? Shall I tell you how white and pale the skin on the inside of her thighs looked? Shall I describe how she screamed and squealed in pleasure when I was deep inside her? She is coming with me, Malvais, to Denmark; Merewyn has decided that she can no longer stay in England under Norman rule, and she wants a real Saxon man.'

Garrett got to his feet in confusion. He knew nothing about this. He looked at Luc, and he saw that the eyes that had been clouded and dull with pain were now wide open with hurt, of a different kind, gazing at Braxton. Luc painfully turned his head and saw Garrett give a questioning look at Rolf, who nodded and shrugged.

'No! I don't believe you,' gasped Luc through dry, cracked lips. 'Merewyn loves me; she would not lay with you.'

Braxton laughed aloud and continued to boast, 'Why do you think it was so easy to capture you? We knew exactly where you would be; she has been working with us. Merewyn set you up for the ambush. She hates the Normans. It's all been an act she has put on to get you here, and now she wants me to make you suffer.' Garrett saw the shock and disbelief on Luc's face, and then he watched every spark of fire slowly go out of him.

'Leave him strung up, and no water this time,' said Braxton as he turned and left the barn, the rest of the group following him.

Rolf followed and left Garrett standing in front of Luc. He had never seen so much pain and confusion in a man's eyes. 'I am sorry,' he said, and he slowly made his way out, closing the barn door behind him.

Luc hung there, his feet just touching the ground. Every part of his body seemed to be on fire or in agony, but it was nothing to the pain of the betrayal he now felt. It could not be true; Merewyn was the love of his life, his soulmate. Yet it must be true if she gave them all this information. How could he not have known this, seen this? How could she have tricked him so easily, was it all an act, he asked himself?

As he had looked down at Garrett, he could feel the raw emotion surging up inside him. He knew he could not contain it and mentally willed Garrett to go and leave him. The quiet 'Sorry' from Garrett opened the floodgates. It was now apparent to him that Garrett had known about the ruse, if not the tryst in the orchard, and he was apologising for his sister's duplicity. Luc watched him walk to the door, and then he gulped huge ragged mouthfuls of air as the door closed, he sobbed loudly, tears raining down his cheeks, and he gave a loud cry of pure anguish, not only at the loss but also at the betrayal of him, by the woman he loved.

Standing just outside the barn, leaning against the doors, Garrett and Rolf heard it all. It was heart-rending to listen to this agony from such an awe-inspiring warrior. Especially for Malvais, who had fought and resisted all the physical punishment that Braxton had thrown at him over the last days. They felt for this brave man, who had only broken at the end because of the betrayal of Merewyn.

Rolf shuffled his feet nervously. He was unexpectedly consumed with guilt at what he had just witnessed, and he was pleased that Braxton had not heard it. He turned to Garrett. 'It wasn't how Braxton told it, the meeting in the orchard,' he said. Garrett turned a questioning glance on him. 'So what did happen?' he asked impatiently.

Rolf sighed, shuffled his feet and related to Garrett what had happened that morning in the orchard. Garrett filled with a cold fury at what Braxton had done to his family; he came to a sudden decision and narrowed his eyes at Rolf. 'We need to act quickly. I have to get to the horses and leave,' he said.

Rolf looked alarmed at being left alone in this situation with Braxton, but Garrett reassured him that he needed his help and that for this, he would be pardoned and rewarded.

'This is what I want you to do,'... he said.

* * *

Merewyn sat outside her father's house on a wooden bench and shaded her eyes as she watched the search parties come back in, dispirited and empty-handed. The patrols had been out all day, searching every village and barn, but had found nothing. Gerard glanced at Merewyn as he rode back in and came over. 'Any news from your father?' he asked in a hopeful tone.

Merewyn shook her head and gazed at the ground as she spoke. She found it difficult to meet Gerard's eyes, this man that cared so profoundly for Luc. She had betrayed them all. 'No, he is still at Melsonby working with Thorfinn to try and find them. He is doing everything he can. He has a lot of respect for Luc.'

Gerard nodded and then shook his head in sorrow. He was confounded that they had found no trail to follow at the ambush site, and she could see that he was exhausted. More importantly, though, he knew the horses needed rest. 'We will ride over to Melsonby this afternoon to extend the search.' He said, turning away.

* * *

In Melsonby, Arlo and Thorfinn were losing patience and becoming as equally frustrated as Gerard was. The new Steward at Melsonby admitted that two of Thorfinn's huge Saxon Huscarls had left the previous day left to join Braxton and the rebels. They had been the only link with the group, and no one else knew how to contact them. There was some indication that they were far to the east. This information came from a groom who had overheard them talking, but nothing concrete enough to send out more pointless search parties. Arlo watched Gerard and his horse warriors ride in to join them that afternoon with a sense of relief. However, this significant Norman presence added to the tension at Melsonby as the Saxon Thegns felt the finger of blame pointed in their direction. As if they had been complicit in this ambush.

There was no doubt that they felt responsible for the actions of their sons. Thorfinn now knew that Braxton and his rebels had crossed the line. The murder of Norman sentries, the beating of villagers who did not fall into line and the capture of Malvais had gone too far. He knew just as well as Arlo what the repercussions would be if the rebels killed the Norman Marechal, and he cursed the rebel group's recklessness for putting them in this danger. Arlo did not doubt that this recent brutality was all down to Braxton, but at present, he kept his thoughts to himself.

They stood outside the small manor Hall with Gerard, discussing other possible places to search when suddenly a horse appeared at a gallop, racing through the village of Melsonby and up towards the Manor Hall. The horse was pulled up abruptly and reared when the rider saw the Normans, but then the man seemed to recognise Arlo, and he came on at full pelt before pulling harshly on the reins to skid and stop in front of the three men, sending up a cloud of dust.

'That is one of our stolen warhorses. I would recognise our destriers anywhere,' said Gerard, stepping forward angrily. Arlo looked at the horse through narrowed eyes and then recognised the strapping rider. 'That is my son, Garrett', he said, and he ran forward to meet him.

Garrett sat spent with exertion on the exhausted horse, trying to catch his breath. The horse was lathered up and foaming at the mouth, its sides heaving.

'We have to go if you want to save Malvais!' Garrett shouted at the group.

Arlo reached up and clasped an arm with his son in greeting. 'You cannot go anywhere on this horse, my son; it is spent', said Arlo.

Garrett slumped forward. 'Well, get me a fresh one quickly.' Gerrard had now seen enough, and he grabbed Garrett by the arm, pulling him roughly out of the saddle onto the ground and shaking him. 'Where is he?' he yelled into Garrett's face. Garrett looked defiantly back at this seasoned older warrior. 'They have him in the old barn just near the old stone quarry, but we have to go now.' He shouted bravely.

'He's still alive then?' questioned Gerard, hope filling his eyes.

Garrett took a long drink of the water his father offered and found it difficult to meet Gerard's eyes. 'They beat him very badly yesterday, and he was bleeding from a dozen dagger scores Braxton made across his chest and arms, but he survived that and still taunted him to do more. I couldn't understand it,' he cried.

Gerard smiled grimly at the thought of a bound and beaten Luc, still showing defiance and contempt for his captors, but his smile faded as he heard Garrett's following words. 'But now, Braxton is even more out of control. This morning he had Malvais flogged. He has had at least thirty lashes, and I honestly don't think he can take much more of that on top of his broken ribs and other injuries. He has had no water since yesterday. I tried to stop Braxton, but he wouldn't listen. He hates this Norman so much.'

Pure fury flared in Gerard's face as he shouted to his men to mount up. 'Tell me how to get to this barn,' he yelled at Garrett.

'I will have to show you. It's taken an hour of hard galloping to get here, and we only have another hour, at most, before he starts on Malvais again.' Garrett looked meaningfully at Arlo and Thorfinn. 'Braxton has the Huscarls flogging him; you understand why we have to go now.'

Arlo and Thorfin stood with grim faces, and Gerard paled as he realised what that meant. With their strength, they could kill a man in an hour easily. 'We leave now!' Gerard shouted at his men, vaulting into the saddle and turning for the road to the east, the Horse Warriors and the Saxon Thegns following after him as Garrett, remounted on a fresh horse galloped to catch up and show them the way.

* * *

Luc only just registered the barn door opening again as he hung in a sea of pain and anguish, his arms, now throbbing in agony, still strapped to the pole. He vaguely recognised that the boy Rolf was in the doorway and was trying to keep someone out. He heard Braxton's voice yelling at Rolf, 'So where is Garrett? Where has he gone?'

'Something spooked the horses, so he has gone down to the quarry to check on them. He will be back soon; he said to wait for him,' lied Rolf, nervously twisting his hands but wedging his scrawny frame across the doorway.

'So we start again, without him, he won't be missed', laughed Braxton, looking at his men. He was quietly pleased that

Garrett was not there. His friend was now trying to water down their actions and even stop him from maiming this Norman Marechal, this enemy who had destroyed their lives. However, Garrett was not here, and he intended to break the Norman this afternoon without any interference this time. He smiled at the thought as he walked towards the doorway.

Rolf stepped forward, 'He said you had to wait,' he said in a frightened voice while trying to stand in Braxton's way. He received a punch in the face that sent him flying backwards into the wooden doorframe and brought blood pouring from his nose as he slid down onto the ground. Braxton walked into the barn and stood in front of Luc. He stood in silence, staring with hate and venom at this man who had stolen his woman, but he was pleased by what he saw as his eyes travelled over his captive.

'You don't look so pretty now, Malvais,' he laughed as he stared at Luc's bruised and bloodied face and body. He stepped closer, 'We can stop this,' he loudly whispered. 'As soon as you go down on your knees and beg me for your life.'

Luc tried to gather every bit of saliva he could from his dry mouth, and he spat into Braxton's face. As expected, Braxton responded with fury. He had the long-handled lash in his hands, and he slashed the long leather handle harshly across Luc's face, leaving a large, red wheal that began to bleed, but Luc still grinned defiantly down at him. Braxton shook with fury, 'I think we will manage to wipe that smile off your face now, Malvais,' he said, running the handle of the whip down the centre of Luc's bruised and bloodied chest to his groin before handing the whip to the grinning Huscarls. 'There won't be an inch of your body that is not in pain for daring to touch Merewyn,' he boasted as he moved back to sit on the wooden bench, stretching his long legs out, ready to enjoy the sight of the man he hated breaking in front of him. Moreover, break he would, in the shortest possible time; he would make sure of it.

The first lashes came down hard across Luc's throat and shoulders. Then the Huscarl began to work down Luc's chest, methodically, inch-by-inch. Luc gritted his teeth as he tensed his muscles and tried miserably to blank out the pain, but, through narrowed eyes, he could see the sadistic pleasure on Braxton's face as the lash moved lower. Soon the pain became too much, it occupied every waking second, and as he rasped air through his bruised mouth into his aching lungs, he could feel himself blacking out. He thought he could hear shouts of triumph, and Luc hoped and prayed that he had not cried out for mercy or begged for his life, but then it was too late; his body could take no more, as he floated into pain-filled oblivion.

Chapter Sixteen

G arrett had led the Normans into the quarry floor, so they could leave their horses and come quietly up the path to the top of the cliff, to the barn. Once at the top, Gerard split his forces into two, with over half heading with Thorfinn and Arlo to attack any rebels in the huts, while Gerard, Garrett and fifteen men tackled whoever was in the barn with Luc. They crept along the front of the barn to where the door stood partly open. Gerard could hear laughter and the steady constant thwack of a lash on flesh. He could not contain himself and full of fury, he burst into the barn sword drawn. There were a group of Saxons, one of which, a tall blond Huscarl, was holding the whip. He backed away when he saw Gerard advancing towards him and lost his life in seconds as Gerard running forward, plunged his sword into his chest. Gerard let the Horse Warriors deal with the others and turned to Luc, just as Garrett came running into the barn behind him with a blood-spattered but highly relieved Rolf.

Gerard stood there in shock, looking at what they had done to Luc. This was not just a beating; this was unbelievable punishment. Braxton had undoubtedly taken his revenge out on Luc. His young friend hung suspended from a beam; his arms cruelly lashed to a pole, his naked body was black and blue, crisscrossed with dozens of red bleeding wheals and cuts. His head hung forward on his chest, his dark hair caked in dried blood. Gerard roared with rage, and Garrett stepped back in alarm, unsure what to say or do.

'Is he alive?' asked Arlo in a whisper as he stepped into the barn behind them.

Gerard had to look away and take a deep breath before he stepped forward. He shook his head in dismay, then reaching up, he checked for a pulse at Luc's throat. He breathed a sigh of relief and nodded to Arlo. He was still alive. There was a faint pulse.

Gerard turned and told Garrett to undo the rope, and he caught Luc as he was lowered, folding him gently to the floor. He growled with rage as he saw the sadistic lattice of dozens of raised welts and deep cuts down Luc's back and legs. Yet, he had not given in to them. He could not imagine the pain Luc must have gone through for the past two days, yet Garrett told him that he had not surrendered or begged for his life. Any lesser man would have begged for mercy after hours of this, never mind days.

'I couldn't understand it,' said Garrett. 'He kept taunting Braxton, who then retaliated with more brutal punishments. I tried to stop him, but it was like they were both involved in a personal war; they wouldn't listen to anyone else.'

Gerard nodded; he understood perfectly, proud and re- silient but bound and helpless. This was the only way Luc could have shown that he was still the stronger of the two, pushing Braxton to do his worst and then surviving it. Therefore, it had become a competition, but a deadly one for Luc; the pulse was so faint that Gerard doubted if he would survive it.

Using his dagger, he sawed through the thick ropes that bound Luc to the pole across his biceps and wrists. They had cut deeply into the flesh of his arms, they were so tight, almost cutting off the blood supply, and although Luc was breathing, it was very shallowly. He was unconscious; at that point, Gerard honestly thought they were too late as he threw the pole across the floor. He could not see how Luc could survive such a beating. There was hardly a spot on his body that was not black, purple or yellow; blood still oozed or ran from dozens of deep cuts, and a fresh welt bled across Luc's face as Gerard tried to trickle some water down his throat.

'Arlo, find me a cart or a travois,' he said, as he laid Luc gently on his side on the barn floor. 'We need to get him back to Ravensworth as quickly but as gently as possible to try and save his life. Tell the Serjeants to help Thorfinn rope the prisoners together; they can walk back to Melsonby.' Then he stood, drawing his sword.

'Garrett, which one is Braxton?' he asked, striding towards the group of captives, sword in hand ready to kill him outright for what he had done to Luc. Garrett scanned the group of bound prisoners in the barn, some subdued, some not, and many glared back or spat at Garrett as a traitor, but he knew Braxton was not there, and he shook his head at Gerard, who swore long and loudly while re-sheathing his sword.

The Serjeant came forward, 'Two of them escaped up that ladder and out of the thatch in the barn while you were dealing with the Huscarls, sir,' he said, pointing to a raised platform at the back, with an old ladder leaning against it. 'We gave chase for about half a mile, but they had raced down into the quarry, and they galloped off on those skewbald horses.' Thorfinn had stood quietly during all of this; Gerard could see how shocked he was by what his son Braxton had done to Malvais.

However, as he heard the Serjeants words, it spurred him into action, 'I promise I will find him for this, be assured even if he has boarded a ship for Denmark, I will personally drag him off it and bring him back to hand him over. He has disgraced my family name by his actions, this is not the mark of a warrior, and he is now no longer my son,' he declared, standing proudly and beating his chest in anguish, his eyes full of unshed tears as he turned and left the barn.

Arlo had found a wooden cart, they put layers of straw pallets and blankets from the huts into the back of the cart, and they laid Luc on his left-hand side. Luc had groaned in agony as they lifted him in, and Gerard suspected several broken ribs. It felt like one of the longest journeys of Gerard's life until they were finally pulling into Ravensworth several hours later. Riders had gone ahead, and the Norman camp physician was waiting for them together with the village healer. The Norman soldiers unloaded Luc, carried him carefully up to his room, and laid him on the bed. He was still unconscious but groaned loudly throughout, and the healer, with a nod from the Norman physician, poured a potent tincture of poppy down his throat to try to dull the pain. They worked slowly but methodically for the next few hours, carefully washing and treating the dozens of wounds and cuts across his body. They strapped up his side, where swelling indicated broken ribs, and stitched the open gash above his left eye. They laid strips of linen, soaked in herbal salve and honey, onto the open bleeding welts left by the lash that covered most of his body. Arlo and Gerard stood watching.

'If he survives the night, it will be a miracle,' said the

214

physician,

'I hope for all our sakes he does,' said Arlo.

Gerard looked long and hard at Arlo, understanding what he meant. It brought his mind back to Arlo's son Garrett, and he came to a decision. 'I am leaving Garrett in your custody at present. He was responsible for possibly saving Luc's life by coming to find us and leading us back to the quarry, so I am reluctant to put him in bonds yet,' said Gerard.

'You will stand surety for him?' he asked, although he already knew the answer.

Arlo nodded in gratitude, although he knew Garrett would be taken to Richmond sooner rather than later. He would have to stand trial for his role in the attacks on the castle and villages.

Merewyn had watched from the Hall steps as they brought Luc back to Ravensworth, her eyes wide, her hands pressed against her mouth. She had gazed in horror as they lifted his beaten and bloodied body out of the cart. The words 'this is my fault' went round in her head repeatedly. In her mind, she conjured the vision of his beautiful, long, hard-muscled body as he had emerged from the river, but all she could see now was his bruised, swollen flesh, crisscrossed with dozens of bleeding wounds. He looked barely alive. She heard him groan in agony as they lifted him out of the cart. At that point, although she wanted to run to him, she could watch no more, and she fled back to the house. What had she done? Her father's words did not help. He had been furious that she had agreed to Braxton's demands rather than coming straight to himself or Luc to sort it out. He did not hold back on the accusation that she had caused this, and if Luc died, it would be on her head. Since then, he had barely spoken to her or given her a further chance to explain. She sank to her knees in the Hall and broke her heart, crying for the man she loved, praying that he would survive.

This was where Garrett found her. She was overjoyed to see her brother alive and well but inconsolable about what she had done to Luc. He told her everything that had happened in the barn. She listened in horror, but she was not at all surprised at Braxton's cruelty. She was relieved that Garrett knew how Braxton held her in his power, with threats to Durkin, but her nightmare began again when Garrett related what Braxton had told Luc.

'So, he thinks I have truly betrayed him and that I wanted him to be captured and beaten,' she said. Garrett nodded.

'He also thinks that you have been lying with Braxton as well, during all of his courtship of you, that everything you felt for him was a sham; this is what Braxton told him.'

'How could he believe that of me?' she gasped, shaking her head in disbelief. Garrett sighed.

'Malvais was at a very low ebb by then, Merewyn, beaten for days, deprived of water, he wasn't thinking straight. He must have been in so much pain he could not see through it, and Braxton was clever. He just mixed lies with the truth, made it all sound plausible; he made it all fall into place when he mentioned the ambush. I saw what that news did to Malvais; he gave up at that point. It is a good thing we got him out of there when we did. All of the fire and spirit had gone out of him. He truly loved you, Merewyn; he mentioned your name over and over again during the worst pain that Braxton could inflict.'

Merewyn sat on the wooden settle, the silent tears streaming down her face, an expression of such loss and bleak hopelessness that Garrett walked over and wrapped his arms around his sister. 'He will survive, Merewyn; he is unbelievably tough. Tell him the truth when he recovers and then let him judge you.' Merewyn nodded, cold anger beginning to fill her when she thought of what Braxton had said and done. Her heart ached for Luc and for the love they had shared, but she had no idea where she would get the courage from to face him with the truth if he lived.

Luc hung in a twilight world between life and death for several days. Gerard hardly left his side, watching as the healer came and replaced the dressings on his badly lacerated body each day. They dosed him continually with the poppy juice and feverfew to try to keep the pain and infection at bay, but several times, while asleep, he screamed out and writhed in agony or shouted Merewyn's name in the dark hours of the night. Gerard thought it likely that he was reliving what they did to him in nightmares. On the third day, his eyes cleared, he recognised Gerard sat beside him, and he lightly gripped his hand. Gerard spoke softly, reassuring him that he was safe, and Luc slipped back into delirium.

While Luc fought for his life, Gerard sent dozens of patrols to search for Braxton Le Gunn. Count Alain, who asked for regular reports on Luc's condition, sent twenty more men to Ravensworth and offered a considerable reward for Braxton's capture alive. Arlo and Garrett were constant visitors, sitting with Luc when Gerard was away.

Arlo was horrified to hear the truth of what Merewyn had been through, and he was angry that she had not told him of threats to Durkin's life; like Garrett, he believed that Luc needed to know all this if he recovered. He had shared the tale with Gerard, who became understandably angry that someone, to whom Luc had so obviously given his heart, could betray him in this way. He could not even look at Merewyn without glaring in a fury at her, and he was determined to keep her away from Luc; she had turned up at the Hall day after day asking about Luc, but he told her to go home, she had done enough damage.

Merewyn was heartbroken and continuously questioned her father and brother for details on Luc; she was terrified he would not recover from his injuries or be maimed for life because of her.

On the fourth day, despite being occasionally conscious, Luc's condition deteriorated. An infection had taken hold, and he was running a raging fever. The physician, a man, experienced in numerous battle wounds, shook his head at Gerard.

'If the fever breaks, he may live, but it's more than that; the pain is still unremitting, and it's as if he doesn't want to live. He is giving up. He needs something to live for.'

Gerard gazed down at the writhing figure on the bed, his eyes full of tears for the young man whom he loved as a son, and he turned on his heel and marched out of the Hall. He crossed the green, kicked the door of Arlo's house open and grabbed Merewyn by the arm. Arlo and Garrett leapt to their feet, but Gerard ignored them. 'You!' he said with suppressed fury into her surprised face. 'You come with me and see if you can undo the damage you have done and give him some hope, something to live for.'

He pulled Merewyn out of the door and dragged her across the green to the Hall. Once in the bedroom, he pushed her into a chair beside Luc, handing her a cold, wet cloth. Merewyn sat and gazed down on the broken body of the man she loved more than life itself, and the tears streamed down her face.

'I don't know how he can possibly survive this, but we need to help him,' growled Gerrard. 'We need to get his temperature down; he needs to hear your voice telling him the truth, over and over again, so it penetrates past the fog of pain into his mind'.

Merewyn took Luc's hand. It was very hot and dry. His face looked gaunt, the swelling around his jaw had reduced, but the yellow and purple bruising was evident everywhere on his body and still livid. The beautiful body that she remembered so well almost wholly encased in linen bandages; a thin sheet covered him up to his waist as he lay on his side, his hair dark and tousled against the pillow. He looked so vulnerable and so much younger than the warrior commander who strode, battle-ready and fearless, round the castle compound. She did not know how he was still alive while in so much pain. She remembered what Garrett had told her and the effect that Braxton's words had on Luc. "The light just seemed to go out of his eyes," he had said.

She could not bear to think about what they had done to him. Garrett had told her everything. This handsome warrior knight had been almost beaten to death, cruelly punished because he dared to fall in love with her and make her his own. She clenched her fists; this was her fault; this had happened because she had set up the capture of his patrol. He was lying here because of her betrayal. When Alain Rufus found out, she was sure to be executed alongside Garrett and other rebels for crimes against his Marechal and her overlord, and she knew that she deserved it.

Luc groaned in his sleep and clutched tightly at her hand. She kissed his forehead and spoke softly to him, telling him she was there. He cried out several times, calling her name as he thrashed around in the throes of a high fever. She repeatedly wiped him down with damp cloths, soaking the bandages; Gerard did the same on the other side of the bed. His skin was burning hot to the touch, and her eyes frequently met Gerard's as they both realised that he would probably not last the night. She poured feverfew tonic down his parched throat, encouraging him to swallow.

As they watched over him into the early hours, Merewyn talked to Luc constantly, reliving their times together, speaking of their future on his estates in Brittany. Gerard watched her, his eyes softening as he listened. He could see that she loved Luc, but he did not believe her betrayal would ever be forgiven by him, even when he knew she was being threatened and manipulated by Braxton. After all, she had still allowed him to ride into an ambush, set up purely for his capture.

As she talked, she watched Luc's face and saw tears sliding from under his closed eyelids and down his cheeks. It was too much; she wiped them away and collapsed on her knees on the floor, put arms gently around his waist and sobbed for the loss of this man she loved so much. The fever raged for hours, with Luc's pulse and breathing becoming faint and erratic. Several times, they thought they had lost him. He weakly cried out for Merewyn repeatedly, and she hung onto his hand, telling him she was there while sponging down his burning body.

Luc lay in a world of pain. For a while, the poppy juice dulled his senses, and he floated in a sea of nightmares. He found himself hung back on the beam again, but this time he was screaming for mercy from Braxton. He emerged from these dreams in a state of torment, thrashing around in the bed and reopening wounds. He could hear the voices of people around him, but he could not make it to the surface to reach out for them. In the worst nightmare, he found himself forced to watch while Braxton made love to Merewyn, and she was enjoying it while laughing up at Luc. Other times she was running terrified from Braxton, but he was helpless and unable to save her. He could feel the tears streaming down his face; inside, his heart was breaking.

Finally, he quieted, and the fever broke as the first light of dawn showed through the window. Merewyn opened her eyes and realised she had fallen asleep with her head on the bed. It was tranquil apart from the gentle snoring from Gerard, sleeping in the chair opposite. Her eyes flew to Luc. He was deathly pale and still. She felt for a pulse and breathed a sigh of relief; it was slow and steady. She felt his forehead, which was cool and damp, although she could see that the pillow and bedding were soaked with sweat. She stroked the side of his face, and he leaned his head on her hand and sighed. She did not dare move, but then he opened his eyes. Those beautiful steel blue eyes focussed on her face, and she saw them fill with joy. 'Merewyn,' he said and gripped her hand.

'I am here,' she said.

'I dreamt that I had lost you,' he said.

She reassured him that she loved him and would always love him, and then he drifted back off into an exhausted sleep. She saw that Gerard had woken and watched that interplay. 'I think he is going to be all right, Gerard; the fever has broken.'

He nodded, too full of emotion to speak, and he leant forward, putting his face in his hands, 'I will go and get us some breakfast,' he said, standing up and heading for the door, not wanting her to see the tears of relief that were now running down his cheeks.

Merewyn stayed for several hours more, watching over the sleeping Luc, as he continued in a deep tranquil sleep, while Gerard saw to neglected duties around the camp. Luc still looked so pale laying there, his arms and torso encased in linen bandages. She held his hand and gazed at the final few swallows swooping and dipping outside the window. A few weeks earlier, she had sat with Luc in the meadow, watching these beautiful birds and making plans for the future. Now they had no future, she thought. Suddenly, she realised the deep, regular breathing had changed, and she turned in alarm to find his eyes were open again, and he was staring at her. However, this was a robust and unforgiving gaze, followed by confusion, doubt and pain.

'Have some water,' she said, bringing a cup to his lips and holding his head. He drank greedily and then lay back on the pillow staring at the rafters.

'Where is Gerard?' he said in a low gravelly voice.

'He has gone for food. He will be back shortly. He has slept in that chair by your side for days.'

He nodded and turned his head away from her. How long he had lain here, and why was she here? Was she still pretending that she loved him? He found he could not cope with all the questions now. His head ached, and he was conscious of the soreness and throbbing pain all over his body when he moved even slightly. Minutes later, Gerard returned. He was delighted to find Luc awake.

He took both of Luc's hands. 'Welcome back. I really thought we had lost you, but you have always been a fighter,' he said.

Luc smiled weakly at him, thinking how drawn and haggard

his friend looked. Then he frowned; Merewyn was talking in a low voice to Gerard, and he knew then that he could not have her there in the same room. He couldn't cope with being this close to her, knowing that she had lain with Braxton, knowing that she had set him up to be captured and beaten.

'Send her away,' he said to Gerard through gritted teeth.

Merewyn looked at Gerard in dismay, who nodded at her; she turned and quietly left, stopping only for a sad, longing glance at Luc from the doorway. Gerard, watching this, was saddened by what seemed an impossible situation for these two lovers. He squeezed Luc's hand.

'Get yourself stronger, Luc, and I will tell you what really happened before and after your capture,' he said. Luc nodded, let out a deep sigh, and again, Gerard saw that silent tears ran down his face as he drifted back off into sleep.

Chapter Seventeen

T he next day, Luc came round more quickly and seemed stronger. He survived the painful changing of the dressings on his back, chest and thighs with groans and grunts of pain. The herbal salves mixed with honey were working their magic on the front of his body, which had taken slightly less punishment, and now the long broken weals were raised angry scabbed red marks and cuts, some of which would fade. However, his back, from his shoulders down to his calves, had taken the brunt of dozens of crossed lashes and had left searing open wounds; while watching the healers work, Gerard knew that Luc would probably always bear the marks from it.

He shook his head; God only knew how Luc had survived such a beating. Only his irrepressible uncompromising spirit and character had brought him through this ordeal. However, although the physical scars would eventually heal, he was worried about Luc's mental state – not just the pain of the ordeal but also the betrayal of everything he believed in and wanted a betrayal by the woman he had loved.

He gently propped Luc up on the pillows so he could get some gruel down him. Luc turned his nose up in disgust but eventually gave in, knowing it would build his strength up. As

Luc finished, Gerard found his direct piercing stare on him. 'So tell me of my rescue from the hands of Braxton.' Gerard frowned and sat heavily in the chair; he had hoped to delay relating Merewyn's betrayal.

He was not sure that Luc was well enough to hear all of the details yet, but he recognised that impatient look in his eyes. Therefore, he hunted for the words to describe those frantic days after the ambush. He took a deep breath and described in detail the days of fruitless searches until Garrett had suddenly appeared at Melsonby.

Luc nodded. 'He managed to stop Braxton killing me or doing worse when he had a knife in his hand on several occasions.'

Gerard described what they had found at the rebel hideout and how many had been killed and captured, as he knew Luc would want the strategic details. Then, he took a deep breath and told him that, despite their efforts, Braxton had escaped. Luc closed his eyes and clenched his fists at that news.

Then, he turned a blazing stare on Gerard. 'I will find him, Gerard, I will hunt him down, and I will kill him.'

Gerard nodded. 'Yes, and I will help you, but let us make sure you can recover first. You must rest.'

Luc nodded. He knew how weak he was, and he was totally frustrated. 'Yes, Gerard, but please bring me some decent food and some wine.'

Gerard laughed and left him alone. He was thoughtful as he descended the stairs. He had purposefully left any mention of Merewyn out of his accounts to Luc, but he noticed that Luc had not asked about, or even mentioned, her name.

Over the next few days, Luc refused any more of the poppy tincture for the pain. He found it clouded his thoughts and produced vivid dark dreams and memories that he did not want. Instead, Luc gritted his teeth at the agony he suffered every time he moved. As for Merewyn, he may not have mentioned her name to Gerard, but he thought of her constantly, of the first time he saw her in the meadow, of the happy times that they had enjoyed together after their betrothal.

He had so many questions. Why had she let him make love to her in the wheat field if she hated Normans so much? Obviously, it was her first time with a man, and she seemed to love him, yet she had then gone on to lie with Braxton in the orchard. Luc had seen the boy Rolf nod his head when Garrett had questioned if what Braxton was saying was true. The thought of Braxton swiving her filled him with fury and heart-rending pain.

'Why hadn't she run and gone with Braxton when he escaped if she loved him? Was she waiting for him now?' he asked aloud.

Why had she sat up with him, night after night, during the fever, if she hated him so much? What did she hope to gain from it when everyone now knew the part that she had played? His head ached as the questions went round and round. He needed answers, and he needed them now.

He propped himself up with some difficulty and agonising pain as his back touched the pillows, and he gently swung his lacerated and bandaged legs out of bed. He clung to the stout short end bedpost while the room swam, but he was determined to stand and find Gerard, despite the pain, the waves of nausea and dizziness. He closed his eyes, and, gritting his teeth, he took a few steps forward. He immediately broke out into a cold sweat and collapsed on the floor as his legs gave

226

way. He laid his head on the rug, seething with exasperation as he drifted into oblivion.

Gerard found him there and managed to get him back onto the bed. 'Are you trying to put yourself back a week?' he asked angrily.

Luc's skin was now a shade of grey and covered in a thin sheen of sweat; he leaned back with difficulty on the pillows and had the grace to look sheepish. 'I am sorry, Gerard, but I need to talk to Garrett.'

Gerard looked at him and sighed. 'Luc, you nearly died, and you are certainly not out of the woods yet. You have several broken ribs and dozens of deep lacerations and wounds that could become infected. You need to rest and allow your body time to heal. I know you are impatient and that there are things that only Garrett can tell you, but give it a few days, and I promise I will bring Garrett to you myself.'

Luc nodded and closed his eyes; he knew he had to be satisfied with that for now.

Each day after, he saw an improvement, and Gerard watched as Luc purposefully ate and drank everything put in front of him to build up his strength. Finally, on Friday, Gerard appeared at the door with Garrett. The young man was unsure of his welcome, and he hung back near the doorway. Immediately again, Luc was struck by how much he resembled his sister. He was a good-looking boy, with his father's auburn hair and an open, agreeable expression. He was still at an impressionable age, only a year or so older than Merewyn, and Luc could see how he could be taken in at first by Braxton's bold and brash personality.

'I believe I owe you my life Garrett Eymer,' said Luc. 'If you had not brought Gerard to the rebel camp, I know I would

227

not be here today; Braxton was determined to flog and beat me to death.'

Garrett, with a severe and concerned expression in his eyes, nodded. 'Yes, Malvais, but I realised there came the point where I could not stop him anymore, and I had to get help.' He grinned, and his young face lit up. 'It's the first time I have been pleased to see a full cohort of Norman soldiers waiting for me.'

Luc smiled and gestured him to sit in the chair by the bed, where he could clearly see his face in the light from the window. Luc gestured at his faithful retainer. 'Pour us some wine, Sir Gerard, and then leave us be, as we have several things to discuss.'

Garrett felt apprehensive now he was in the room alone with Malvais. His eyes ranged over Luc, still a formidable figure with his broad, powerful shoulders leaning back on the pillows. Wounded and bandaged as he was, the considerable strength and presence of this man were still palpable. However, Luc certainly looked better than the last time he had seen him, he had colour in his face now, and his eyes were clear, instead of clouded with pain. The ragged scar over his eyebrow was stitched and healing. The huge red welts and cuts across the front of his shoulders and upper chest were prominent but healing. He could see the tightly bound ribs and the dressings on his back. Garrett suddenly felt ashamed that he had been a party to the capture and beating of this man, and he dropped his eyes to the floor. Luc could see his embarrassment and led him in gently.

'How is Espirit? Gerard tells me you have the magic touch with horses and hounds.'

He could not have chosen a better subject as the boy talked

228

at length of what he had done to prevent scarring on the horse's knees. Luc watched him speak, and he saw that his mannerisms were just like Merewyn's; it was how his green eyes lit up and how he used his hands when enthusiastic about a subject. A bolt of pain shot through Luc as he watched her brother talk. He had loved her so much. They spoke of Destrier bloodlines for a while, but Luc knew he had more pressing questions to ask him.

'So Garrett, tell me about this group of rebels and what you know about how my capture came about,' said Luc, pinning him with that steel-blue piercing stare. Garrett shifted uncomfortably in the chair. Luc wondered if he would tell the truth. Would he incriminate his sister, or would he cover up her deceit and betrayal of him?

Garrett spoke from the heart. He told the story of their escape from the failed rebellion in Northumberland, then he described their journey on the run, hiding in fishing villages on the east coast as they gradually made their way south. Once they came within range of home, they set up camp in the disused quarry, hoping they could return home and get a pardon, but Braxton had become more and more unpredictable and unstable. When he discovered his father's fate, the loss of his lands and of his prestige, Braxton raged for days. However, it was nothing compared to when he found that Malvais was openly courting Merewyn.

'She obviously thought we were both dead, but we knew we could do nothing to let them know otherwise, or we would give ourselves away, and it pushed him over the edge,' said Garrett. He would not listen to me when I suggested we hand ourselves in and ask to be ransomed. Instead, he launched a series of raids on your patrols, each more violent than the last.' He paused, looked up and met Luc's eyes. 'I was there on those raids, Malvais, but I swear I did not kill any of your men.'

Luc looked into the eyes of this earnest young man and believed that he told the truth. If that was the case, he might just be able to save him from execution with the others. 'So what led to my capture?' said Luc. 'Did he just get lucky with one of the patrols he was planning to ambush?'

'In a way, yes,' said Garrett. He took a deep breath and went on to tell the tale that Rolf told him about what really happened in the orchard that Friday morning with Merewyn and Durkin. As he spoke, Luc could see the truth in this, her abandoning her belongings, the ripped veil, Durkin cowering in the house for days, a changed nervous child.

However, Rolf had never mentioned to Garrett that Helga had actually interrupted Braxton in the orchard, so the story was only part told. Luc was still under the impression that Merewyn had lain with Braxton, albeit unwillingly, in order to save Durkin's life.

Even so, Luc's hands clenched into fists, and the veins stood out in his neck as he listened, and he thought about what Braxton had done to her. 'Leave me for now, Garrett,' he said through gritted teeth. 'Come back tomorrow. I need to consider what you have told me so far.'

Garrett pushed his chair back and headed for the door, where he turned. 'Don't be too hard on her, Luc; she was terrified and feared for both mine and Durkin's life, Braxton came to my father's house night after night to take her, but with Helga's help, she managed to keep him out.'

Luc listened to him clattering down the stairs, and then he let out a roar of rage and swept everything off the table beside the bed. Gerard came running, thinking he had hurt himself, but he saw the white-hot fury on Luc's face and the clenched fists. He had not seen Luc so out of control since the death of Heloise. He stepped quietly back out of the room again and closed the door; experience had taught him to leave Luc alone at times like this. A few hours later, he returned, bringing a skin of good, strong, red wine, some roast chicken and fresh chunks of bread.

'Can I put this down in safety?' he said, picking up the overturned table. Luc stared at him and nodded tight-lipped. 'You must eat Luc,' he said.

'I know, but I will find him Gerard, and I will tear him limb from limb,' said Luc in a quiet, ice-cold voice.

'Yes, but only when you have recovered and built your strength up. Your body and muscles need time to repair, especially those broken ribs.'

Gerard sat down, and the silence built until he poured a large cup of wine, which Luc downed in one and held out for a refill. He looked up and met Gerard's eyes with a searching glare. 'Did you know?' he asked.

Gerard sighed. He knew what Luc meant but had tried to avoid the topic. 'I had my suspicions when I saw where the ambush had taken place and how they brought you down. I wondered how they knew which route you would take, and then I remembered Merewyn coming to the Donjon days before and showing an interest in the rotas.' Gerard shook his head in disbelief. 'It didn't raise any suspicion in me at the time because I saw how much she loved you.'

Luc gave a harsh humourless laugh. 'Not enough apparently, to give me any sort of warning.' Gerard shrugged, unsure what to say.

Luc stared stonily ahead for some time. 'Do you think he has gone? Taken ship for Denmark as Garrett thinks?'

Gerard shrugged again. 'Possibly, it is difficult to know when a man has that much hate in his heart. He is a wanted outlaw; Alain has put a huge bounty on his head and has said he will execute anyone who hides him.'

* * *

Garrett came again the next day, and Luc asked him to continue from where he left off. Garrett nodded and described Rolf acting as a go-between for Merewyn and Braxton.

'She provided the information, and we set out to ambush the patrols. Then we received the info about you leading the northern patrol that morning, and Braxton was elated; he was determined to take you alive, to make you pay.'

Luc held up a hand for Garrett to stop. 'So, they were told that I would be leading it?' he asked.

Garret nodded and then continued with the description of the ambush and capture. Luc barely heard him. There was a rushing sound in his ears. All he could think was that Merewyn had handed him over to Braxton on purpose. How could she ever have loved me? He asked himself.

He realised Garrett had stopped. 'Thank you, Garrett. Obviously, I know what happened after he had me strung up in the barn,' Luc said in a harsh voice.

'You didn't help,' blurted Garrett, 'You constantly goaded him and encouraged him to hurt you more. I could not understand that. I was trying to save your life, and you were making it impossible.'

Luc gave a wry smile. 'I hope you never find yourself in that situation, Garrett, but if you do, then the only thing that keeps the flame burning within you is your pride and self-respect. You have no other weapons to fight with and, yes, you may infuriate your enemy, antagonise him even, but it keeps your spirit alive that you still have the power to do that.'

Garrett just shook his head, staring in amazement at the strength and resilience of this astounding Breton. He stood up to leave, and then he paused. 'Malvais, you are twice the man that Braxton is, no wonder my sister loves you so much.'

Luc layback on the pillows as Garrett closed the door behind him, his thoughts in turmoil at what he had heard. If she loved him so much, why had she given him so calmly into the hands of Braxton? She knew Braxton well, knew his cruelty and his lust for vengeance, yet she had handed him over without a backward glance while knowing what Braxton would do to him if he captured him alive. However, he was determined to find out why she had done this, and he swore he would hunt down and kill Braxton, no matter how far he had to travel to do so.

Every day after that, Luc was up for an hour, painfully stretching his damaged body, walking around the room and bending, trying to prevent scar tissue from tightening on his back and legs. Gerard watched him occasionally. He was evidently still in agony at times as the wounds constantly reopened and bled, but Gerard knew that once Luc was determined, nothing would stop him. Luc also insisted on his wounds being washed with salted water every day, no matter how painful. As a Breton, he knew the benefits of salt-water on his horses' injured legs, and he had reasoned that it must also work on human wounds.

At the end of the week, Gerard came in to find Luc

dressed and in a chair having his breakfast. Gerard raised his eyebrows. 'I am walking up to the Bailey stables to look at Espirit, and nothing you can say or do will stop me,' Luc said with a challenging stare.

Gerard nodded sagely. 'I will walk two steps behind you to catch you when you collapse. You are still much weaker than you think, and your wounds are still open and healing. I will go to the stables and gently lead Espirit down here.'

Luc stared back at him, tight-lipped in defiance for several minutes, and then gave a bark of laughter. 'I will surprise you, Gerard; I will walk up there, albeit slowly and with care,' he said.

Luc took it very slowly and painfully down the stairs and out onto the steps of the Hall. He leaned against the doorpost for some time, surveying the village green to get his breath and then, gritting his teeth, he walked slowly and painfully up the slight incline towards the castle and the stables. The cheering began as soon as his men saw him approaching, and by the time he reached the gate, all of his men were stamping on the ground and clashing their swords against anything they could find.

Merewyn and Garrett heard the noise and came out of the house to look, as did many villagers. They were just in time to see Luc hold his arms up in salute to his men, and they watched him walk through into the Bailey area of the castle, followed by his cheering troops. Merewyn turned tear-filled eyes to Garrett, who put an arm around her and pulled her close.

'He is an amazing man, Merewyn. Many men would not have survived what he suffered at the hands of Braxton and yet look at him, no wonder his name is spoken in awe.'

Merewyn looked and felt as if her heart were breaking. She loved him so much, but she knew he would never forgive her; he was a proud and stubborn man. Besides, there was another complication she had not shared with anyone yet. Although she had only given herself to him the once, she was now sure she was carrying his child.

* * *

Luc bent slowly and carefully to run his hands down Espirit's front legs and over his horse's knees. Garrett had done an amazing job, the swelling was gone, and the hair was growing back over the rope burns. He leaned his head against his horse's neck for support, and Espirit turned his head and nuzzled him. Luc smiled. At least he was getting unconditional love from somewhere, he thought. He gazed out into the sun-drenched Bailey where several sheep and goats were now grazing.

'I am going to sit out there in the sun, Gerard, on that bench while you are going to bring me up to date on the progress of the castle and the mill.'

Gerard smiled. He knew the walk had tested all of Luc's strength and resources, but he would never admit it, and he knew he would sit, letting the pain subside to gather his strength for the walk back. After all, he was 'Luc de Malvais', a legend in his own right with the Breton and Norman men, and now more so, since they saw his unbelievable recovery. They had all seen his condition, as he was unloaded from the cart, barely breathing and beaten almost to death, and yet here he was walking and laughing amongst them, scarcely three weeks later. He was their Malvais, their Breton hero and one of the most formidable fighters in Europe. They all knew that only an underhand trick had allowed his capture, but he had survived everything the Saxon rebel had thrown at him.

Luc walked slowly down to the river for the next few days to swim gently back and forth in the deeper areas. He knew this would help his injured body recover and he could feel himself gradually getting more robust. He saw Merewyn at a distance, several times, each time his stomach knotting, but he pushed her resolutely to the back of his mind until he could deal with the pain he felt every time he saw her.

However, on Friday, he saw her heading to the orchard; he wondered if every time she went there to collect the honey that she thought about what had happened there. He felt the anger building inside him at the thought of Braxton taking her, and, picking up his sword, he headed to the Bailey training ground where Gerard was training the new men. Gerard was surprised to see him and privately thought this was a mistake, but then he noticed the pinched nostrils and steady glare, and he knew Luc needed to let some of that anger out.

Luc stepped into the ring with Gerard and launched a flurry of attacks on one of the young Norman soldiers, forcing him back until the man dropped to one knee and begged for quarter. Gerard smiled; even so severely injured, Malvais was a terrifying fighter, so he let him continue to destroy another few novices for a short while and then sent him away.

As he walked back to the Hearth Hall, Luc tried to tell himself he felt better for that physical exertion, but he still experienced significant pain from his ribs and badly scarred back, and he knew that the same white-hot anger was burning within him. He had loved Merewyn more than life itself. Since the death of Heloise, it had been the first time that he had given himself, body and soul, to any woman. However, look at how she had repaid him, giving herself to Braxton and then giving in to the Saxon's demands for information, instead of trusting Luc or her father to deal with it. The rage and anger in him bubbled just below the surface, and he knew he had to lay it to rest.

That afternoon he sent for Merewyn.

Chapter Eighteen

Merewyn received the summons with apprehension. On the one hand, she longed, with every bone in her body, to see him, to explain what had happened and ask him to understand. However, on the other, she was terrified that she had probably lost him forever, and anguish filled her at the thought of facing him.

She dressed with care and walked across the village green, her mind in turmoil and her legs trembling. She had to stand and wait downstairs in the Hearth Hall for some time, and she could feel the waves of panic rising in her chest. Then Gerard appeared. Staring at her coldly, he announced that the Marechal would see her now. As she ascended the stairs to the solar, she thought, so this is how it would be, a formal interrogation by her Norman overlord, not a conversation with the man she had been about to marry. She felt the pain course through her for the Luc she had loved and lost. Did she expect anything else after such a betrayal of him, one that had almost cost him his life?

She entered the large solar, and Gerard followed her; she looked across at Luc, who was standing, staring out of the window, his hands gripping either side of the window frame. He did not even turn and look at her as she entered the room behind him. Luc wore his full regalia as a Norman Marechal, with his long chain mail hauberk and sleeveless leather tunic, although his face was still pale against the shock of dark hair and the pale red welt was still visible across his face. He always looked unbelievably handsome and commanding, and her heart went out to him. She just wanted to run to him, to be enfolded again in those strong arms. However, he was now every inch a Norman Lord; his stern profile and rigid stance told her everything she needed to know, and she felt a shiver of fear go through her. He turned and pinned her with that cold, steel glare she remembered from the first time he saw her in the meadow.

'Sit down, Mistress Eymer,' he said in a chilling, unemotional voice.

She made her way to the chair he indicated, and, deciding to show her courage in the face of fear, she sat defiantly on the edge, her head held high. The silence that followed seemed interminable to Merewyn as Luc's gaze returned to the view out of the window, and Gerard stood behind her, arms folded, leaning against the door.

Then Luc turned and carefully and painfully lowered himself into the seat on the other side of the table, facing her. He put his elbows on the table, and, lacing his fingers, he regarded her in stony silence for some minutes before he spoke.

'I have heard various accounts of the circumstances that led to my capture and imprisonment. I would now like to hear your version of events.' He leaned forward, his face a mask of discipline, his steel-blue eyes that had once shone with love for her were now cold, and his mouth a stern line. 'I expect the truth. If, as other people believe, you aided and abetted in the attacks on myself and my men, you will go to Richmond for trial, Count Alain Rufus will decide your fate.' He sat back cold and distant. 'Let's begin in the Orchard, shall we, unless you were secretly meeting up with Braxton before that, as he suggested.'

Merewyn shook her head. She was dying inside. He undoubtedly despised her now, but she was not going to show fear; she lifted her chin higher and began. She spared him nothing; she described the attack on her by Braxton in graphic detail and how, at first, she had thought it was Luc behind her. She told of Durkin's terror at being held up with a noose around his neck. She described her horror at the fear of being violated by another man and her relief when Helga arrived. She noticed Luc's whole attitude and posture change at that point.

He stopped her. 'Are you saying you did not lie with Braxton in the orchard?'

She looked at him directly in the eyes as she said, 'No. He was disturbed by Helga's arrival.' She said, her eyes brimming with tears. 'I have only ever lain with one man, and that is you, Luc.' He sat back, frowning at her as if unsure to believe it. 'Continue,' he said.

She described Braxton's threats and attempts to enter her home and take her while her father slept, the threats to Durkin to maim or kill him. She admitted that she had gathered the information about the patrols and passed it on to Rolf, who was outside her house, watching her movements. The silence that followed was damning. She had admitted treason to her Norman overlords. Luc gazed down at the table in front of him, then he raised his eyes and looked at her.

'Why did you not come to your father or me for help? We

could have protected you and Durkin,' he said in a more reasoned but questioning voice.

Merewyn explained that Braxton could easily have whisked Durkin away. She had no one to turn to, or he would carry out the threats he had made. She was terrified for her family and Luc as Braxton had numerous men in the village acting as harvest workers who could enter any building on a night.

She saw Luc give a shake of his head. 'I could have sent you both to Richmond until we caught him and his followers. It would help if you trusted me. Did you think so little of my ability to protect you and your family?' He sat back and laughed harshly as he delivered the last sentence.

Merewyn just shook her head, gazed at the floor and explained that she had been too frightened and desperate.

Luc pushed his chair back violently and went back to stand at the window. Merewyn gazed after him. It broke her heart to know that he now despised her, this beautiful man, who was once going to be her future, the father of the child she was carrying. He turned suddenly and met her anguished gaze; she could see the anger and hurt in his eyes.

'So then, without a second thought, you just handed both the men in the patrols and me over to Braxton', he said in a quiet but deadly voice.

The tears spilt over from Merewyn's brimming eyes as she looked up at him. 'He promised me that no Normans would be killed; he just wanted to drive you away from his father's lands!' she cried.

Luc looked at her incredulously. 'And you honestly believed him, two of my Horse Warriors were slain, men who have been with me for over five years, men whose families are waiting for them back in Brittany! He turned away in anger,

241

then instantly turned back to her with a sneer.

'Oh well, I suppose he did not quite succeed in killing me, that is true.' He looked at Merewyn coldly, walked over and abruptly grabbed both her wrists, pulling her out of the chair to her feet.

'You told me you loved me Merewyn, did that mean nothing?' He asked as he glared down at her, showing the hurt and confusion in his wide, grey eyes. 'You knew all about Braxton and how cruel and pitiless he can be. You knew what he would do to me if he captured me, and you just handed me over to him,' he cried in frustration.

She watched as his eyes narrowed in anger. 'Shall I take these clothes off and show you my scarred back and thighs, or the knife and lash scars on my chest, shall I show you the result of a few days left in Braxton's hands, that I will probably carry for the rest of my life.' He dropped her wrists, and, flinging her away from him; he turned away in disgust at what she had done to him and to their relationship.

Merewyn collapsed back into the chair and sobbed out loudly. 'No, you don't understand. You were not leading patrols anymore. I never meant to put you in danger; you have to believe that I love you, Luc. When I saw you riding out that morning with your men, I ran out and tried to stop you. You didn't see me, but Gerard did.' She turned in mute appeal to Gerard, and Luc turned questioningly to him. Gerard looked thoughtful, and then he remembered seeing Merewyn running after Luc, waving her arms at him; on that morning, he nodded. Luc looked over at him and then at her, confusion in his eyes. Then suddenly, as if he still could not look at her, he turned away as she continued.

'I also ran down and took a horse from the lines to try and

ride to catch you, but it was too strong, and it threw me in the woods, so I went to my father for help,' she cried plaintively. However, she knew it was to no avail; she could see from his face that he had shut himself away from her and nothing she said now would make any difference. He did not even look at her as he said coldly…

'You may go. I will investigate further, then I will have to take this case to Count Alain, and honestly, I do not know what decision he will reach. King William's stance is unforgiving against rebels who attack and kill his troops. I will put forward some mitigating evidence for you and Garrett that you acted under duress, but I am not sure how much sway that will have, particularly as Braxton Le Gunn is still free and so many men died.'

Merewyn stood and made for the door. She stopped and turned, 'I never stopped loving you Luc, I am sorry for what happened, but I honestly believed that I had no choice; he was moving freely everywhere in the village on a night,' she said.

She received no response from the unsmiling, stern figure that was stood again at the window and made her way down the wooden stairs, following Gerard; her heart was breaking, not only for the love she had lost but also for the anguished man that she still loved.

Luc stood in the room alone, in torment. He had barely been able to contain his anger and fury as she described what Braxton had done to her, clenching his fists and muscles under the table as she faltered through the tale. He felt a conflicting range of emotions, guilt that he had been unable to protect her. Braxton had once again infiltrated his village unseen night after night. He felt anger at her lack of trust in not telling him about the threats that ultimately resulted in his

243

capture. However, he felt some relief; she had not deliberately handed him over to Braxton, although her information was responsible for Norman soldiers and Horse Warriors' death and injuries.

He gripped the window frame until his knuckles were white as he watched her walk back across the village green, her head bowed. She was still breathtakingly lovely, and he knew that he still loved her, but his loyalty was to his Patron, Alain Rufus and his King. How could he betray that loyalty for a Saxon girl who had worked with the rebels to undermine her Norman Lords? He had to go to Richmond as soon as possible and put this into someone else's hands, he was too involved, and this was too serious, or he would find his own allegiance in question. The thought of Merewyn in the hands of the Norman gaolers at Richmond, especially if she was found guilty, made his blood run cold, but he knew he had little choice in the matter.

Chapter Nineteen

T wo days later, Luc De Malvais, Norman Marechal of Ravensworth, set off with his cavalcade south to Richmond. It was only five miles or so, but Luc was taking no chances with Braxton still on the loose, and he took twenty of his Breton cavalry, leaving Gerard to oversee Ravensworth. They would only travel as fast as the wagons carrying the wheat tithes they were escorting; however, Garrett and Merewyn, their hands bound, were in one of the covered wagons. Arlo had requested to accompany them, as two of his children were to go on trial. He had insisted on being there when they were handed over to Count Alain Rufus to ensure they would be treated as befitted their station, and he rode, grim-faced, behind their wagon with some of his Huscarls.

For the first time, the enormity of her crime became apparent to Merewyn, and she was distraught that she was carrying a child, who would die with her if she was to be executed, as seemed likely. She felt that Luc had abandoned her. She did not blame him; she knew he had no choice. These crimes were far too severe for the Marechal to deal with, they were crimes against Alain Rufus, against King William himself, and she knew that they usually gave no quarter in these circumstances.

Garrett was also resigned to his fate; he had rebelled against their Norman overlords, been an active member of a rebel group that had attacked and killed Norman soldiers and sentries, and he expected to be put to death. The two of them leant against each other in the hot, dusty wagon as it bounced over the dry, rutted road. The swaying of the wagon began to affect Merewyn, who was already experiencing morning sickness. She had confided in Garrett about her child, and he had begged her to tell Malvais, but her pride refused to let her in case he doubted the paternity or felt it pushed him to intervene, which could damage his position as Marechal.

Luc had watched with a heavy heart as Garrett and Merewyn were loaded, hands bound, into the covered wagon. As he watched her, he knew he loved her as much as ever, but he could not ignore the fact that she had betrayed him, even though it was under duress. He still struggled to understand why she had not come to him or her father for help. It rankled that she did not seem to have the faith in him he expected; did she think he was no match for Braxton? Alternatively, was she trying to protect him as well as her family? Did she think he needed protecting? The only reason he had been captured was because of her perfidy and betrayal. The questions went round and round in his head as he led the cavalcade to Richmond, the Horse Warriors in perfect formation behind him and several outriders scanning and patrolling the wooded hills on either side. Braxton was still at large, and he was taking no chances.

He knew he was doing the right thing in handing her over to Alain, but it meant he also handed over any decisions about her fate. He knew Alain was fair, but he also knew that William influenced him; they would be judged with Norman laws, establishing a just system was a priority, and Luc felt helpless. He could do nothing at this stage to help them until he made a case for leniency to his Patron. In the interim, they would be incarcerated, treated as prisoners. He would try to protect her and Garrett as much as possible until their fate was decided. He had sent a brief report of all the recent events to Alain over a week ago, so his Patron would be aware of the background. Still, Luc knew this would carry little weight if Alain were following William's decrees of ruthless subjugation.

As he rode through the newly built stone Barbican into the large and impressive Bailey of Richmond Castle, he could see the progress that Alain had made in only a few months. The outer Bailey was large and completely encircled by a solid, high, wooden palisade fence, and dozens of buildings and walkways were attached to this. There were stables, barracks, blacksmiths and several stalls selling fresh foodstuffs. Messengers seemed to be continually galloping in and out. It was a large, bustling area full of Norman troops, villagers and animals hobbled and grazing on the centre's massive grassed area.

The arrival of a large, armed group and wagons caused a stir, especially as the Barbican horns had announced their arrival to the Donjon ahead. Even more so, as Malvais was a famous figure, his recent exploits and escape had only enhanced his reputation and the legends that surrounded him. His name spread like wildfire as he entered the Bailey, the impressive Breton Horse Warriors with signature crossed swords on their backs following behind him; within minutes, the Norman troops were cheering his entry. Simultaneously, local crowds gathered to watch his arrival on his splendid, steel-grey, dappled horse with its black flowing mane and tail. He acknowledged the cheers, raising a clenched fist to shouted greetings and then he dismissed most of his men, sending the wagons full of wheat to the granary before riding on to the new Donjon and its enclosure with his covered wagon and its guards. Arlo followed on; dismay was written clearly on his face at this vast display of Norman power and control, it was the first time he had been to Richmond since the arrival of Alain Rufus, and he remembered only a small village on this spot before.

Luc dismounted from Espirit and addressed the Serjeant at Arms outside the Donjon. 'There are two prisoners. However, they are the son and daughter of a notable Saxon Thegn', indicating Arlo, who with his Huscarls was watching like a hawk. 'They will be treated well while confined.' The man nodded. The guards went to the wagon, released the bonds, and helped the prisoners out of the wagon. Garrett was out and trying to support Merewyn; by the time they had reached the River Swale and moved into the busy town, Merewyn was exhausted, and retching; the guard was helping her down when she collapsed on the ground in a dead faint. Luc's heart leapt with dismay, and he stepped forward to help her, but Garrett was there first and had swept her up into his arms. She was deathly pale, and Luc eyed her with concern.

'Is she alright?' he asked Garrett.

Garrett gazed down at his sister, who was now coming round. 'It was the journey and the heat; neither was good for her in her condition,' he said. Luc frowned.

'What is wrong with her?' he said.

'She is carrying your child, Malvais,' he said with a grim smile and then followed the Serjeant into the coolness of the

248

Donjon, leaving Luc standing in shock, rooted to the spot.

Luc was reeling, his thoughts in chaos. 'With child?' It had to be his child; he had interrogated Helga; he knew what Merewyn had told him was true. Braxton had lied about taking Merewyn purely to try to break his spirit, and he might have succeeded if Garrett had not brought about his rescue. Merewyn, whom he still loved, was carrying his child, and he had brought her here to go on trial. The pain Luc felt at the thought of losing her, of losing them, was unbearable. He whirled around and saw Arlo behind him, looking equally concerned. 'Did you know?' he snapped at him.

Arlo just shook his head in dismay. 'You have to try and save them, Malvais,' he pleaded.

A wave of panic enveloped Luc, his stomach knotted, and he took a deep breath. He had to go and greet Alain, and he needed his wits about him to plead for the case of Garrett and Merewyn. He had realised some weeks ago that he still loved her, with every fibre of his being, and Luc knew he was ready to forgive her, but he also knew she would have to go on trial with her brother. He would have to play this very cleverly to save her life, if possible, Garret's life as well, and the life of his unborn son or daughter.

Chapter Twenty

Luc strode through the great hall to present himself to Count Alain. At least twenty of Alain's knights were present, and many called greetings or came to grasp his arm in welcome at seeing him alive and almost recovered. Luc walked purposefully towards the dais at the far end of the hall, smiling at his friends and compatriots. He knew how important it was to put on a show in his present situation. He dropped to one knee in front of Alain; his head bowed, his fist clenched on his breast in salute. Alain immediately stood and raised Luc to his feet, embracing him like a brother.

'Malvais, it is so good to see you back here and in one piece. We feared for your life for several days.'

Luc smiled, I am a Breton, Patron, and as one, you should know we are difficult to kill.'

Alain laughed but gave Luc a searching look, he was no fool, and he could see the change in Luc, the pain lines etched onto his face. 'Well, we have much to speak of later. Come and report to me in my solar this afternoon. Meanwhile, there is one brother-in-arms who has been awaiting your arrival.'

Luc turned, and there, emerging from the crowd of knights, was Bodin. Luc felt a massive wave of relief; Bodin was his closest friend, Alain's half-brother, and a highly influential courtier. If anyone could help him with his plea for Merewyn and her brother, it was this man. Bodin stepped forward with a huge grin and grasped Luc's forearms.

'Malvais! I leave you alone for a few months, and you almost get yourself killed,' he laughed, but his eyes showed genuine concern as he gazed searchingly at Luc's face, seeing the pain and suffering still etched there. 'Come, let's go and get some decent wine,' he said and, bowing to Alain, they headed over to a table near the stairs. Once settled with a cup of wine in their hands, Bodin looked critically at his friend.

'So, how are you truly? I can tell by the way that you are moving that you are still strapped up. Broken ribs?' he asked.

Luc nodded and tried to joke, 'They tried to smash them all, but I managed to restrict it to two or three.'

Bodin gave a grim smile, folded his arms and, sitting back, said, 'So you can now tell me the real story of what happened. I have read the sketchy report from Gerard and the brief one you sent, but there seem to be several gaps.'

Luc took a deep breath. Bodin was several years older than he was and now a skilled diplomat, but he had been his mentor and friend for over seven years, many of which they served together as mercenaries in European disputes. Luc knew he could hide nothing from him, and he desperately needed his help and advice on how to deal with presenting the case for the two prisoners.

He related the tale of the increasing rebel raids, his capture and ordeal at the hands of Braxton and his lucky escape with the help of Garrett. Bodin's expression hardened when he heard what they did to Luc. 'You are fortunate to be alive, Malvais; not many men could survive such a beating, followed by over forty lashes.'

251

Luc sighed, 'I know, Bodin, and a large part of that is due to Garrett Eymer, who stopped Braxton from killing me on several occasions and then risked his life to go and bring Gerard and my men to rescue me.'

Bodin narrowed his eyes, 'But this is the same rebel who has fought against us for two years, attacked patrols and raided other villages.'

Luc raised an eyebrow, 'You seem very well informed.'

Bodin shrugged, 'The tales of your capture and escape have spread like wildfire and become more exciting in the telling each time, if that is possible, now having heard the truth.'

Luc smiled, 'The truth is, he only stayed with Braxton for the last nine months to try and mitigate the damage and impact of Braxton's actions. He tells me he has fought several but never killed a Norman.

'Are you sure of that Malvais?' Are you influenced by the fact that he is the brother of the woman you were to marry?'

'I both believe and trust him, I owe him my life, Bodin, and I will do whatever I can to try and save him,' said Luc.

Bodin looked thoughtful, 'And the leader of the rebels… it is unfortunate he escaped, this Braxton Le Gunn, he would have made a good example, when put on trial and executed, which would have helped you in your difficult situation.'

'Yes, he escaped, but I promise that I will find him and kill him,' swore Luc clenching his fists.

'He is a Saxon Luc. Dozens of different villages may be hiding him. He comes from a powerful, respected family, and the people will want to help him; he will now have fame and prestige from the attacks on us and from your daring capture,' said Bodin.

Luc looked downcast at that thought, 'Alain has posted a

large reward that may prove fruitful, and his father Thorfinn Le Gunn has disowned and is I believe still searching for him.'

Bodin looked sceptical, 'These people, they still hate us, Luc.' They sat in silence for a few moments. 'So what of the Saxon girl, Merewyn Eymer?' Bodin asked.

'I loved her Bodin. As you know, we were to be married this week before Braxton drove us apart by attacking and threatening her and her family.' Bodin stared intently at Luc, who had dropped his eyes to stare into his wine.

'And now? After she has betrayed you and handed you over to this rebel leader, a man she was once hand-fasted to?' he asked.

Luc raised his head, his eyes full of pain, as he looked back into Bodin's face. 'I love her more than ever. I understand, to some extent, why she chose the path she did, and now, she is carrying my child,' he said.

'Mon Dieu!' said Bodin, shocked at the news and the situation in which his friend now found himself.

'This is a problem, indeed. Alain's hand will be forced to make an example of them. William is on his way north as we speak; he will be here in just over a month; he plans a war in the borders against the Scots who helped the Northern Earls in the rebellion. Alain's decision may be influenced by how any leniency to rebels might look at this current time.'

'That is why I depend on your help and advice, my friend,' beseeched Luc.

Bodin turned and gazed across the hall to where a group of his knights was still entertaining Alain Rufus. 'You have two things in your favour,' he said.

'Firstly, you are Luc De Malvais; you are one of his favourites, his champion. Use the truth and your loyalty

253

to him over the past ten years unashamedly when you meet with him. Secondly, William desperately needs money; he has paid a fortune in Danegeld over the past year to keep the Danes from our shores. Now he needs money for this war against the Scots that he is planning. It will do Alain good if he can provide some of that money.'

'Arlo is a very wealthy Saxon Thegn, owning large amounts of land in Denmark, he will pay large ransoms for their release,' said Luc hopefully.

'That will certainly help, but I must warn you, there will be some punishment. The Eymers have both rebelled against or betrayed us, and they will not get off lightly. I will talk to my brother and try to mitigate those punishments, given the circumstances, but I cannot promise anything,' he said.

Luc nodded, but he knew that even the mitigated punishments could be as harsh as mutilation, flogging or slavery. William often let knights live who had rebelled against him, but in the past, he had blinded them, or they had lost the hand that held the sword they raised against his forces.

Luc left his friend, clasping his hands and thanking him for his advice. He walked into the new Donjon enclosure to clear his head before his audience with Alain in an hour. He desperately wanted to go to Merewyn, but he knew that would be foolish, as he could offer them no hope yet. Every time he thought of Merewyn and his child facing execution or slavery, the pain in his breast was unbearable.

Finally, the sun rose high enough to be close to the appointed time, and he made his way to stand outside Count Alain's solar. He could hear voices inside, and he waited for some time until there came a lull, and he knocked on the door and entered. The room, richly furnished as befitted the nephew of King William, had colourful tapestries on the walls and the best-carved and engraved furniture that Normandy had to offer. Tables at the far wall held high mounds of scrolls and official documents, and a young clerk worked at a table beside them. Bodin was sitting, in a window embrasure, looking down onto the River Swale below. Bodin nodded at Luc, but he seemed unusually grave as Alain waved Luc over to the table.

'Come in, Malvais, and take a seat. Ralph, Bodin, would you leave us please?' said Alain. He smiled pleasantly at Luc, 'So tell me of your progress at Ravensworth, and on my other manors, I hear that Gerard has been carrying out your plans while you were recovering.'

This was safe ground, and Luc outlined the progress made on the castle and the completed mill. He detailed the large tithes from all of the manors paid in September, after a bountiful harvest. Alain was delighted at the amounts in both wheat and in gold from the local Thegns; this, of course, would form part of the sixty per cent he would send to William.

'The King was very pleased with the way we dealt with the rebellion in Northumberland. I am sure Bodin has told you of his new campaigns; William has ordered a castle built at Durham; Waltheof, the Saxon Earl of Northumberland, is undertaking the project, now he has been restored to favour. The King will be here in a month or two and will collect men to enhance his numbers from York, Durham, and our Breton contingent. I intend to send you to lead the Breton Horse Warriors against the Scots; you know the borderlands very well, do you not Malvais?'

Usually, Luc would be pleased and would greet this with exuberance; after all, he was first and foremost, a Breton warrior, and he had scores to settle with the Scots, but Merewyn was at the forefront of his mind.

'Of course, my Lord, I will be honoured to lead our men for the King,' he said, bowing his head. When he raised his head, Alain was watching him critically, 'That is, of course, if you are fit enough by then.'

Luc knew he had to lay any doubt to rest immediately, so he exaggerated slightly.

'I am almost back to full fitness, and I have been at sword practice every day this week with Gerard and the men,' Luc assured him.

Alain raised an eyebrow and smiled, 'I would expect no less, Malvais, but this has been a bad business, and now you have brought me two rebels that must go on trial for heinous crimes. I have imprisoned twenty of the camp rebels; they are to be executed tomorrow morning in the Bailey. It will be a public execution to send out some messages to the people of this region. I am aware that William is now following a policy of conciliation and integration. Still, this small uprising, and more importantly, the capture and savage beating of one of his Lords, cannot be tolerated. Harsh punishments must follow.'

'I am aware of that, Patron, but I wanted the chance to explain, in person, the mitigating circumstances of Mistress Eymer and her brother Garrett.' Alain poured them some wine, and then, giving Luc a piercing glance, he sat back with an enigmatic smile.

'So tell me,' he said.

Luc took a deep breath; Alain was only five years older than he was, his commanding air of authority was unmistakable, but he had fought alongside this man, and so he told the truth, which included his own doubts and feeling of betrayal. As

Alain knew him, he spoke from the heart, as his Patron would see through any ruse or deception. In the end, he sat back and looked at Alain with an earnest expression. Alain was pensive.

'I am aware that bringing them here to me was not an easy decision, and you have shown your loyalty to the King and to me by doing this when you are emotionally involved. You could easily have let the two of them escape in the last few weeks. However, I believe they stayed to receive my judgement in a trial rather than leave for Denmark, which is in their favour. Luc nodded. He found himself holding his breath while he waited for the following sentence.

'I am honoured by your trust, Luc, and the ordeal you went through, I now know, that it was far worse than Gerard had originally told me; in fact, I am amazed that you are here; most men would be convalescing for months, many would never recover or would have died from such a beating. However, I believe you have left out one important fact, which Bodin felt he had to share with me. I admire you for not using it to try and sway my judgement,' he said.

Luc let out the breath he had been holding, 'Yes, my Lord, Merewyn is carrying my child.'

'You are sure it is yours?' he asked.

'I am, Patron; she has lain with no other man,' said Luc emphatically.

Alain pushed his chair back and stood up. 'Leave it with me, Luc, but be in no doubt that they will be on trial in the main hall at noon tomorrow. There, they will have the chance to make their representation, and we will judge their case in light of their admissions and plea. Nevertheless, they are guilty of treason and rebellion.'

Luc, his mouth in a grim line, nodded. 'I thank you, my Lord.' When he reached the door, however, he turned. 'My Lord, it may be useful for you to know that Thegn Arlo Eymer, their father, is very wealthy in his own right with extensive lands in Denmark. He is willing to offer a considerable ransom in gold for any leniency for his children.' Alain stared thoughtfully at Luc for several long moments.

'That would have been helpful, Malvais, if their crimes had not been so serious,' he said, dismissing Luc with a wave of his hand.

Luc headed for the guardroom with his heart in his mouth, mentally thanking Bodin for his advice. He had done everything he could; now, he now needed to prepare them to present their plea to the tribunal.

He greeted the Serjeant at Arms, went down the steps and entered the long, dark passageway in the bottom of the Donjon. The Serjeant had kept his promise of providing comfort and keeping them together and unshackled. Both of them rose to their feet as he entered, and the door was firmly closed behind him. Merewyn looked better for the rest and raised her large green eyes to his in hope. He took her hands in his; this was the first time he had touched her since before her ordeal with Braxton in the orchard. He dared not hold her, or he would carry her out of there. He glanced around the room; he was glad to see that they had provided a table and chairs and some wine. There were thick pelt and blankets on the wooden beds. The light came from a small high window with a metal grill at the ground level above.

'Now listen to me, carefully. I have done my best with Count Alain, and Lord Bodin has helped, but you will appear at the rebel sentencing tomorrow morning; you will find that harrowing,' he said, looking at Merewyn. 'After that, they will announce that you go on trial at noon. It would be best if you spoke clearly and, above all, be repentant;' he looked significantly at Garrett as he said this. They both nodded. Garrett looked understandably grim and was clearly worried for his sister as well.

'I must go. Garrett, look after her for me,' said Luc, as he raised her hands to his lips and kissed them.

Garrett nodded and then followed Luc to the door, 'Is there any hope, Malvais?' he whispered, hoping that Merewyn could not hear what he was saying.

'There is always hope, Garrett. However, you need to be aware; they will be executing the rebels from the camp tomorrow morning, out in the Bailey before your trial at noon. You will hear the crowds baying for blood. I am hoping, however, that such killings may assuage the demand for revenge before your trial.' He clasped forearms with the young man, and turning on his heel; he left them.

Luc spent several hours at dinner that night with Bodin, Alain and over twenty of the Breton knights in Alain's entourage; he knew that it was essential to put on a front for his friends. Alain would expect him to be the Breton Lord and champion that they loved, and so he laughed, drank, and related tales of skirmishes in the northern rebellion with the rest of them. He made light of his capture, although he could see that his men had talked, and many were aware of the fact that he had survived a brutal beating and flogging. He played it down, saying that no Saxon could detain him for long and, of course, Breton warriors are made of steel; they never give in. This brought cheers, loud thumps on the tables, and more toasts, as most of the knights were Bretons; Count

259

Alain nodded encouragingly. Bodin watched the performance that Malvais was giving with a wry smile, but he was worried for his friend.

Inside, Luc was hurting in a way he had not thought possible, he drank copious amounts of wine, but the food was tasteless. His heart was in his mouth at the thought of what might happen to Merewyn and Garrett tomorrow; he felt that he had no control over their destiny. He had made representations on their behalf, and he would do so again at their trial, but the outcome was so uncertain.

He had a restless night and rose early to swim in the river. Returning to the Donjon, he saw the preparations going ahead in the Bailey for the executions after sentencing. He decided to go looking for Arlo but was dismayed to hear that he had ridden back to Ravensworth the previous night after an urgent message. Luc pondered on what that could be, but he prayed that Arlo would turn up in time for the trial to confirm the ransom offer, which could be crucial.

Merewyn had also slept only fitfully, sharing the bed with Garrett, who seemed to be awake all night tossing, turning, and then pacing the cell. Her spirits had soared after the visit from Luc. He had tightly grasped her hands, and she could see the love shining out of his eyes as he had gazed down at her. It was the first time he had looked at her like that since her world had shattered in the orchard. Surely, this must mean that he wanted to forgive her. It was bittersweet; if the trial went badly, that could be the last time he would ever touch her. She was aware that he now knew she was with child. She was dismayed at first; her head told her that she had not wanted this knowledge to sway his feelings for her, but her heart said to her that Luc still truly loved her, and he would have attempted to save her no matter what.

Garrett had made her aware of the options that Luc had related. Rebellion and treason carried the death penalty, and she knew about the sentencing and executions. They were to appear briefly early tomorrow morning– the same time as the rest of the rebels. She was aware that if she and Garrett were found guilty, even if the sentence was to be manumitted slightly, they could still face the loss of their liberty or even mutilation of some kind. She was aware that she would fetch a good price as a slave in southern Europe with her light skin and hair, but it would mean her child would be born into slavery too. They made a point of eating the frugal breakfast, and then they sat, arms around each other, as they listened to the cheers and shouts of the angry crowds waiting outside for the executions to begin.

Chapter Twenty-One

T
he smell of new wood assailed Luc as he entered the substantial new Great Hall with trepidation. He clenched his jaw as he viewed the ongoing preparations. A long, covered table was at the far end of the Hall on a dais, and to the right, there were chairs for any witnesses or interested parties. The clerk, Ralph, was there at a table to record the proceedings. It was an impressive new building of immense size, with wooden pillared aisles down the sides. There were benches along these sides of the Hall, as this was to be public sentencing, which were rapidly filling up with a mix of Norman knights and townspeople. Luc was worried that the crowd, made up of predominantly Norman retainers, would be baying for the two Saxon rebels' blood. He thought that this could influence the tribunal, especially when most insurgents would be executed after the sentencing this morning. He was equally worried that he might condemn Merewyn and Garrett with his own testimony if he didn't have a chance to explain when called upon to give witness and to tell the truth under oath.

As indicated, he took up a position next to Ralph the clerk, on one of the chairs provided to watch the proceedings. Alain Rufus and Lord Bodin arrived with two older knights that he knew, and they stood surveying the packed Hall; Bodin nodded in a silent but restrained greeting to Luc. Alain had a powerful voice that immediately quelled the excited crowd.

'Bring in the prisoners, Serjeant.'

A buzz rose in anticipation as a group of shackled men shuffled in. Some were downcast and dejected; others stood heads held high and glared at the Normans in defiance. All were dirty and sweat-covered from their close incarceration in an underground cellar. The lucky ones had already been ransomed or sold as slaves. Most of this final group of Braxton's men were directly involved in the capture and beating of Malvais. Luc recognised several of them, including two of the enormous Huscarls who had flogged him. He felt no sympathy for these men. Behind them, unshackled, Garrett and Merewyn stood with their guard at one side near the front. Both of them looked apprehensive as their eyes darted nervously around the Hall.

The clerk, Ralph, read the list of Saxon names from a large vellum sheet to announce sentencing; the evidence against them had been considered and heard the previous day. With due deference, Ralph handed the document to Alain Rufus, who declared, in stentorian tones, that they had been found guilty of rebellion and would go to the Bailey where they would be executed. A large mumble of excitement went through the crowd, but they quietened as Alain continued to announce that the trial of Garret and Merewyn Eymer would be separate and would commence at noon. With that concluded, the Serjeant returned the two shaken and apprehensive rebel captives to their cell.

Luc knew he should go out and attend these executions, but, strangely, he had no stomach for it, although he was aware that

263

some of these men were the ones that kicked him unconscious in the clearing and had then taken it in turns to flog or beat him. However, to him, they were just pawns in a game. His thirst for vengeance seemed to centre wholly on Braxton, who was still roaming free and who would cast a shadow over their lives until caught. He watched as the rebels were led out towards the gallows, followed by the excited crowd from the Hall.

By noon, he was back in the Hall, dressed in full military array as a Marechal, for the formal trial of Merewyn and Garrett Eymer, and he noticed that the Hall was packed again. There was a stir as he entered. The story of his kidnapping and torture, now combined with his love for the beautiful daughter of a Saxon Thegn, had spread like wildfire. Luc headed towards his former chair and nodded to Ralph as Alain Rufus, and two other notables took their seats on the dais.

Luc was relieved to see Bodin was one of the tribunal again, but he was concerned that, unexpectedly, the two knights were gone and in their place, there was a third man, one he did not know very well. He recognised him; he was a prominent senior Norman Prelate attached to William's court. He shook his head in bewilderment and tried to catch Bodin's eye. What was this senior churchman doing up here in the north, he wondered, and why was he now part of the tribunal who would decide Merewyn and Garrett's fate? Luc knew him to be an arrogant, intolerant man. He wore a richly embroidered cassock, his head was shaved in a tonsure, and he looked down at the crowd in the Hall with disdain and dislike.

Luc could feel the panic rising in his chest. Was it possible that William had sent him as his representative to punish the rebels and ensure the executions took place? If so, then Garrett and Merewyn were in grave danger of losing their lives. He moved one of the witness chairs close to Ralph and quietly asked him what he knew of this Prelate. Ralph's answer was not reassuring. 'He arrived unexpectedly this morning. He is the envoy of King William, on his way from York to Durham, to visit the shrine of St Cuthbert and to establish the site for the building of a great, new, northern cathedral. He will remain in Durham until the arrival of the King, my Lord.'

Luc was right; he was from William's court and could indeed have a great deal of influence over the decisions. He did not know the back-stories behind Garrett and Merewyn, and he would only see two Saxons who had rebelled against the King. Luc sat back, frowning and folded his arms, watching the three men settle at the table. He thought Bodin was looking uncharacteristically grim as he poured some wine.

Alain gave the Serjeant-at-Arms an order to bring the first prisoner, and Luc watched as Garrett came in, his hands bound, to stand alone in the centre of the Hall. He looked uncertainly round the Hall and then met Luc's eyes. Fear and apprehension were apparent, but he stood proudly, holding his head high as Luc nodded confidently back at him.

Suddenly, there was a stir at the back of the Hall, the crowd parted like a wave as two impressive Saxon Thegns and their many Huscarls made their way to stand at the front of the crowd. Arlo Eymer was this time in full battle regalia, and he had brought Thorfinn, similarly attired. They were dressed to intimidate but also to reflect their position and their wealth. They wore huge, gold torcs around their necks and on their arms. The Hall buzzed with noise as it spread like wildfire that this was the famous Thorfinn Le Gunn. Luc noticed that

Thorfinn had brought the boy, Rolf, in his entourage, standing shyly among the huge men. Gerard had freed the boy into Thorfinn's custody until his story was heard.

Alain Rufus looked slightly apprehensive at their arrival with a sizeable Saxon contingent, and he glanced at the reassuring sight of his Serjeants and their men around the chamber. The Prelate had also pushed his chair back in alarm, only Bodin smiled, reassuring the Prelate about their identity. Alain called for silence in the Hall and nodded to Ralph to begin.

'Garrett Eymer of Ravensworth, you are here today on trial for rebellion against King William. How do you plead?'

Garret spoke clearly, when he replied, 'I am guilty, my Lord, of taking part in the rebellion in Northumberland, where I was summoned, in fealty, by the Northern Earls.'

Luc allowed himself a small smile. That was a very clever answer, and he knew that Alain and Bodin would appreciate what he was saying, that he was following the orders of those he believed to be his true overlords.

Alain acquiesced, 'I am aware that some rebels have been pardoned and ransomed since that rebellion.' He turned and glanced at the Prelate for confirmation, and the churchman reluctantly nodded. 'However, I believe that since then, you took part in the attacks and raids in this area that led to the direct capture, imprisonment, beating and attempted murder of my Breton Lord and champion Luc De Malvais.'

A low grumble of discontent and hissing began in the room as many mistakenly thought this man had imprisoned and tortured Luc De Malvais. There were cries of, 'Hang him!' Many of Alain's knights looked over at Luc for confirmation. He firmly shook his head in denial. Garret went on to refute this, and he tried to explain how he had stayed with Braxton Le Gunn to prevent the killing of Norman troops and that he had gone for help to rescue Malvais.

The Prelate was not convinced. 'Do you have any witnesses to this?' he sneered.

'Yes, Sir. Luc De Malvais himself.' He said.

The Prelate looked disappointed, and more so when Alain asked Luc to describe what had happened and explain how Garrett had saved his life. In a clear carrying voice, Luc stood up and related what he knew about his rescue. Following this, the three men conferred for some time, with several glances at the intimidating Saxon Thegns at the back of the Hall. Then Alain spoke. 'Thegn Arlo Eymer, I believe you wish to pay a ransom in gold to the King to spare this man's life. Arlo stepped forward, a large leather pouch in his hands. 'I do, my Lord.'

Alain Rufus contemplated the young Saxon rebel standing in front of him for several long minutes, Luc could feel the tension in the Hall, and he found himself holding his breath, he had got to know Garrett Eymer quite well in the last few weeks, and he liked the young man. He also owed him his life, so although he knew he would not be set free; Luc hoped he had done enough to get the young Saxon a lighter sentence.

Then Alain spoke, 'Garrett Eymer, you rebelled against your rightful King and his Lords, and for that reason, the Serjeant will take you into the Bailey after this trial…' There was a pause as Ralph questioned something Alain had said. At that point, those in the Hall held their breath; they all expected a sentence of execution or maiming…

'You will receive ten lashes. In addition, it is decreed that you are given in fealty and servitude to Lord Bodin for five years. Your father will pay a ransom of twenty gold coins to the King for your life.'

A murmur of astonishment went round the Hall as Alain turned to placate the dissatisfied Prelate, the crowd were astounded not only at the lighter sentence but also at the ransom, which was a tremendous amount of gold, most would never see a gold coin in their lives. Arlo nodded, and Luc let out a sigh of relief; Garrett turned and gave him a grateful smile as he walked behind the guard to the side of the Hall. Luc now had hope in his heart; he had done what he could to save Garrett's life, the sentence paying lip service to the King and, of course, acquiring a considerable amount in gold. Garrett would survive ten lashes, and Bodin would treat him well. As the son of a Thegn, he could become a squire during his sentence and later, even a knight; his knowledge of horses would serve him in good stead with Bodin. Now Luc just hoped that they would similarly consider Merewyn's case.

Chapter Twenty-Two

There was a hum of excitement as the crowd waited for the next prisoner; many of the crowd in the packed Hall had come to see what would happen to the beautiful Saxon Thegns daughter, who had been due to wed their hero Luc De Malvais. Most of them had now heard of her betrayal of him; many asked what else could you expect from a Saxon and hoped they would execute her; only a handful in the Hall knew the truth.

Merewyn came in proudly; she held her head high, but her heart beat wildly in her chest, and her pulse raced. Her father had brought her best dress and overtunic, and she wore a large gold broach pinned on her shoulder to show her status. Her hair, brushed until it shone, hung down her back, and she wore a thin gold circlet on her head to hold her hair veil in place. Luc gave a sharp intake of breath as he saw her. She had never looked more beautiful, and he saw the effect she had on the large crowd, who were mainly men. He glanced at the top table, and he could see that her beauty stunned Alain. Bodin, of course, had seen her several times, but the officious Norman Prelate immediately narrowed his eyes in dislike.

Merewyn was not short of courage or spirit; her father was a renowned warrior, and her mother was the daughter of an

Irish Chieftain, a minor King. She was determined to show them that she had no choice in betraying Luc that she had acted under duress and because of the threats against her family from Braxton Le Gunn. The charges were read out by Ralph the clerk, 'Merewyn Eymer; you stand accused of treason, kidnapping, seditious revolt, the killing of Norman troops and the attempted murder of your Norman overlord.'

The crowd gasped. Any one of those charges could carry the death sentence.

Luc went stone cold as the charges were being readout, and he turned and stared at Bodin, who refused to meet his eyes. Alain sat back, still staring at Merewyn, and the Prelate who contemplated this Saxon rebel over his steepled fingers was smiling. Luc wondered how much influence he had exerted over Alain, for this list was unexpectedly far worse than Garrett's crimes. He glanced at Merewyn, who had gone deathly pale, but she was standing tall and keeping herself together, her eyes respectfully lowered. Luc heard Alain Rufus's voice, 'What is your answer to these crimes, Merewyn Eymer?'

Merewyn began in a low voice as she related to the tribunal precisely what had happened to her that day in the orchard. She described her fear, not for herself but for her five-year-old brother with a noose around his neck and for her older brother already in Braxton's clutches. She described her love for Luc and her promise to marry him, but she could not tell Malvais what had happened because Braxton had half a dozen men staying in the village, who could report her actions, and who could and would snatch her brother Durkin at any time. She explained that she had never felt so vulnerable in the whole of her life; this had made her equally terrified and utterly desperate to save those she loved.

Luc's heart went out to her as she implored Alain to believe her. Luc could see that he was affected by her story.

However, the Prelate was not convinced. 'A fine performance, as good as any strolling player I have seen,' he said in a loud voice, spreading his hands wide to the two Norman Lords beside him and then to the crowd. Luc noticed that some of them laughed and nodded.

'Are there any witnesses left to confirm this incredulous tale?' he continued. Luc was incensed by the Prelate's implication, and he was only slightly mollified when he perceived that Alain Rufus was not pleased with the Prelate, either.

However, Thorfinn pushed Rolf forward. 'Here, my Lord!' he bellowed. 'A witness, this is a young harvest boy, kidnapped, beaten and bullied by my rebel son, Braxton Le Gunn.'

The young Saxon boy was terrified, but Arlo and Thorfinn had coached him; all he had to do was to try and not incriminate himself when they asked him a question. Luc stood up and nodded encouragingly to Rolf to come forward, and he did so, standing in front of the raised dais, wringing his hands nervously. Merewyn smiled at him, and she explained Rolf's role in the orchard while skilfully questioning Rolf so that he confirmed that all she said was true. He admitted that he had twice accessed Arlo's house at night on Le Gunn's orders, and he could have easily carried the boy away if instructed by him to do so. He also confirmed that Braxton had returned on two occasions to gain access to the house to swive Merewyn but was unsuccessful each time.

The Prelate's lips drew back in an expression of distaste. 'How can we know that this is not just part of the set-up?' he

271

asked. 'Some cock and bull story to save their skins?'

This was too much for Luc, and he leapt to his feet again, his eyes flashing anger, bowing swiftly to the panel. 'With your permission, Patron,' he said, and he went on, with some fire and emotion, to describe the brave, scrawny, Saxon boy who had positioned himself in the barn doorway to try to prevent entry to Braxton Le Gunn and his huge Huscarls. He explained that this delay had given Garrett more time to bring back help and prevented Braxton from flogging him to death. He pointed out that Rolf was kicked senseless and had his nose broken for his pains. The crowd enjoyed this tale of David and Goliath, and a cheer went up for the bewildered Rolf, who, when dismissed, scuttled back behind Thorfinn's colossal bulk. Merewyn looked gratefully at Luc, and he gazed back at her, his heart in his eyes.

Alain Rufus looked thoughtfully at both of them and then turned to confer with the other two at the table for some time. Luc watched Bodin explain several things to the discontented Prelate. Then Alain called for silence, and Luc could hardly restrain himself as he waited for their judgement. A myriad of possibilities went through his mind; if she were to be executed, he would fight his way out of there with her, they would take a ship to her family in Ireland, and she would have to become a mercenary's wife. However, as his eyes scanned the twenty-plus armed knights and guards in the Hall, he knew that in reality, it was not possible; they would never get out alive.

Then Alain spoke: 'Merewyn Eymer, you are accused of treasonable acts; however, due to the extenuating circum-stances, the sentence will be manumitted from execution as I believe that Arlo Eymer is, again, willing to pay a large ransom for you. Given the serious nature of your crimes, I will set that amount at forty gold coins which he will pay to the King for his daughter's life.' There was a huge gasp from the assembled crowd as this was more than a fortune, and most of them would never see a fraction of it in their lifetime.

Arlo stepped forward and nodded, agreeing to the ransom with a worried look at the amount, but he knew it had to be done, and he would have sold all of his lands in Denmark several times over to save the lives of his children. However, unexpectedly, Thorfinn strode forward and walked purposefully towards the dais. The apprehension on the Prelates face was clear to see, and two of the Serjeants walked along to the table in front of the huge Saxon. Thorfinn looked at them and laughed up at Alain Rufus, 'As if they could stop me if I wished to do him harm,' he said, indicating the nervous Prelate. Alain nodded, seeing the joke and smiled at the warrior Thegn, who stepped forward, glaring at the Serjeants to move, which they did, and he placed a large bag of gold on the table. 'It was my son who is responsible for these crimes, so it is I who will pay Merewyn Eymer's ransom', he said before giving a slight bow of the head to Alain, and he turned to stride back to his men at the back of the Hall where Arlo gratefully clasped his arm.

Alain waited for the commotion in the Hall to die down, and then he continued, 'I thank Thorfinn Le Gunn for the generous ransom; however, Merewyn Eymer, your deliberate acts endangered the life of one of our bravest knights. You knowingly betrayed him, even though I believe you are possibly carrying his child.'

This news brought another intake of breath from the crowd. Muttering broke out, and many looked in Luc's direction; some could still not accept a Norman bedding a Saxon girl.

Luc felt himself go hot with embarrassment for Merewyn
as he realised that many of his fellow knights were grinning
and nodding at him. Luc was far more concerned about the
information being made public, as he thought this would
enrage the religious Prelate even further. A child born out
of wedlock, the church had so much influence and power;
this information would affect the Prelates views; it was even
possible he may now influence the tribunal.

He saw Merewyn's distress at what Alain announced, Luc
wanted to go to her, but he could do nothing until Alain had
finished. Yet again, the Prelate interceded, talking heatedly
with much hand-waving at Alain and Bodin. Luc watched in
concern as Bodin's face became grimmer, and he was shaking
his head in anger.

Silence hung in the air for several minutes as Alain sat back,
his head bowed, his hands clasped in front of him until the
restless crowd began shuffling their feet. Then he continued...

'Therefore, this tribunal has decided we will sell you into
slavery for ten years...'

There was a prolonged hush as the sentence sank in and
disgruntled muttering from the Norman Knights who thought
this was unfair on the woman of one of their own, especially
a woman who was carrying his child, a Breton child.

The Prelate was now sitting back and smiling. He had his
way, and Luc could hear him saying to Bodin that several
middle-eastern traders would pay very high prices for such a
blonde female slave such as this. He insisted, to Count Alain,
that a message be sent to one of them in York at once; the
King needed such an amount of money.

Luc was distraught, and he shot to his feet, his fists clenched.
He could not lose Merewyn and his child, but what could he

do. He looked frantically at his friend, but Bodin shook his head emphatically at him, telling him not to intervene, so he tried to stay calm. The thought of Merewyn owned by another man, his child brought up as a slave, was too much for him, and he stared, heartbrokenly across at Merewyn, who was standing in shock, gazing at the ground.

Merewyn could barely believe her ears; the word slave had descended almost like an axe on her head, and absolute panic fell on her. It took a few moments for her to realise what had happened. She looked across at Luc with tear-filled eyes as the guards came to lead her back to the cell.

'Stay strong, no matter what happens,' he mouthed at her. 'I will free you. I will rescue you.' As Merewyn and her guard turned to go, Luc realised that Alain Rufus was continuing to speak.

'However, given the circumstances and the fact that she took these actions under duress, she will not be sold beyond England, but instead to any person, apart from her family, who will pay to this tribunal, one hundred silver pounds within the next two days.'

Alain rapped on the table twice with the handle of his dagger, in conclusion, then he turned and stared at the Prelate with distaste; the man sat back with a sour expression on his face. This again was a considerable sum of money, and, once again, a hush fell on the crowd.

Luc was stunned. He felt a ray of hope, but then he mentally assessed his wealth and what he had available in England. He knew he did not have enough, and he certainly would not be able to raise more money in only two days. His stomach was in knots that he might still lose her. Frantically, he scanned the room; then he realised that Arlo and Thorfinn had disappeared, which was odd, as this was a critical moment. True, Thorfinn had pledged the hefty sum for her ransom, but he was surprised that they had not stayed to the end for sentencing. Luc dismissed the idea of borrowing from Arlo as that would not be allowed. However, he could borrow from Thorfinn, who was still exceptionally wealthy, despite his change in circumstances. Then, from the corner of his eye, he saw Bodin repeatedly gesturing at him and holding up a substantial leather purse. All suddenly became clear now to Luc; he blessed his friend for his generosity and stepped forward.

'My Lord, I would like to buy Merewyn Eymer. She will be giving birth to a child who will be a Breton Knight or maiden, and it is not right for her to be sold elsewhere,' he said, glaring at the Prelate. As Luc watched in fevered anticipation, a small smile played at the corners of Alain's mouth. 'Is there any other interested party who may want to bid for her?'

Luc turned and glowered around the Hall at the assembled crowd, daring anyone to speak.

'She is sold to Luc De Malvais,' said Alain Rufus.

Bodin nodded in satisfaction. However, the unhappy Prelate was determined to have the last word, 'I warn you, Malvais, this rebel will be a traitorous viper in your nest,' and he turned, tight-lipped, to Alain and added, 'I will make sure the King hears of this.'

Everything went quiet around the dais, and the Prelate suddenly realised he had gone too far; Alain Rufus was one of the wealthiest men in Europe and known to be a powerful and ruthless man with quite a temper; he was also a nephew of King William. The Prelate suddenly realised what he had said and tried to mumble an apology, which Alain ignored while pushing his chair violently backwards, his dagger still in his hand. 'I think not,' he spat, narrowing his eyes at the churchman as he turned to leave.

However, Luc was now striding towards Merewyn, his eyes blazing with happiness as the Serjeant-at-Arms was untying her bonds. Luc swept her up into his arms; she could not breathe for joy as she gazed up into his handsome face and shining grey eyes. However, before they could celebrate, there was a stir and much shouting from the back of the Hall near the massive double oak doors. The large crowd, gathered there, parted as Arlo emerged and strode into the centre of the Hall, Alain who was about to mount the stairs to the solar, turned back to stand at the table. Luc watched with concern and bated breath –what was Arlo doing?

Arlo stepped bravely forward. 'Count Alain Rufus, as you know, I am Thegn Arlo Eymer, and I am sorry for disrupting your proceedings, but we have brought you a prisoner.'

The crowd parted further, and Thorfinn Le Gunn came back in. Head and shoulders above all other men, he strode into the centre of the floor, an impressive presence, to stand beside Arlo. Behind him, two of his men brought a bound prisoner whom they threw onto the hall floor in front of them. Thorfinn nodded at Alain and Bodin and then looked at Luc. The crowd were silent, awed by what they were watching. Then Thorfinn's voice boomed around the Hall.

"My lords, I bring you my son, Braxton Le Gunn. I have disowned him after his actions concerning Merewyn Eymer and his capture and torture of Luc De Malvais. He is no longer a son of mine. My ancestors are warriors; we do not have to sink to underhand means to gain our victories.' At that, he turned and went back to stand with Arlo at the rear of the

Hall, leaving Braxton sprawled on the floor, his hands roped tightly behind him at wrists and elbow.

Chapter Twenty-Three

L uc stared in disbelief at the bound prisoner on the floor, who was now struggling to his feet. Luc would not have immediately recognised him; gone was the thick blonde beard and the long, plaited locks. He was now clean-shaven with a powerful square jaw and short, cropped hair in almost a Norman style; this was a recent disguise to enable him to escape. Had he gone to his father for money, for help to escape, pondered Luc, or had Thorfinn set out to capture him? He remembered Arlo telling him that Thorfinn was still searching for his rebel son.

Even though Braxton's hands were bound behind his back, Luc could see the fear and horror on Merewyn's face as she stared at her tormentor.

Luc leapt to his feet, but Bodin, out of his seat in a flash, got there first, his hands-on Luc's shoulders, holding him back. 'You will not help her by attacking him; this is Alain's Court,' he hissed at his friend.

Luc nodded with reluctance and stood while cold fury coursed through his body at the sight of this Saxon rebel who had tortured him for days and tried to destroy his future with Merewyn. Alain Rufus also stared, through narrowed eyes, down at this huge, bare-chested Saxon, the rebel who had caused so much damage in his lands, captured and attacked Malvais and murdered his men. He had to admit to himself, Braxton Le Gunn, like his father, was an imposing specimen.

'Braxton Le Gunn, you are charged with treason against your King and of assailing my lands and men. In addition, you deliberately captured and attempted to murder my Marechal, Luc De Malvais. The only sentence I can give will be death by beheading. A far quicker death than you deserve, but, unlike you, we Normans are not savages; we rarely torture our captives to death,' he said.

The large crowd in the Hall stared in excited fascination at the events playing out in front of them; even with his hands bound behind him, Braxton was an impressive sight. Stripped to the waist, with only rough linen chausses and braies covering his powerful legs, it revealed his massive, muscled torso and arms. He now straightened up to his full six-foot four-inch height, taking a step forward and squaring up to Alain Rufus on the dais, his narrow, pale blue eyes full of hatred as he stared at these Norman Lords. He swept his gaze sideways, over to Luc, and he smiled at him before his lip curled into a sneer of loathing.

He turned back to Alain Rufus. 'Norman Lord', he spat in a tone of mockery, 'I am the son of a noble Danish Thegn, and I have direct descent from the Kings of Denmark. As such, because of my birth, I demand my right to trial by combat. Luc De Malvais besmirched my name, took my inheritance and swived my hand-fasted virgin bride, despoiling her. It was his actions, which forced me into acts, which I would not normally have committed. I demand satisfaction with him and the return of my hand-fasted bride; she is mine as is the child she is carrying.' Braxton then stepped back, feet planted firmly as he glared unafraid at the three men at the table. There was a sharp intake of breath from the assembled crowd, and then a loud clamour of excitement broke out.

Luc was staggered by the audacity of the man. He saw Arlo start forward and raised a hand to stop him; he could not allow Arlo to do anything, which would put Merewyn's trial in jeopardy. Luc could still feel Bodin's hand on his arm, holding him back, and he shook it off. 'Do not do anything stupid, Luc,' he hissed. 'If you fight him and he wins, he may walk out of here with her and your unborn child while you lie dead or maimed.'

However, Luc was burning for revenge with a sword in his hand, and Bodin, watching him, knew he was not listening to reason, only to the cold anger inside him. Alain Rufus sat on the dais, looking pensive for some minutes as he contemplated Braxton and his demand. The noise slowly died in the Hall again. Then he waved Bodin and Ralph, over to him. The three men on the dais discussed the demand for some time while Luc paced behind them. 'He has the right, unfortunately,' Bodin informed Alain. Ralph, always a stickler for protocol, nodded. 'His case is that he only launched these attacks on the village and patrols after Luc's unreasonable actions in deflowering his betrothed, which seems to be true. If you turn him down, he has the right to appeal, because of his birth, to the King himself, which will take some time.'

Alain Rufus nodded in agreement. He understood it; he did not like it, but they were Normans who believed in a fair and proper justice system. This was the message they were instilling into the Saxons they now ruled, and William was adamant that the law be upheld. He realised that even more complicated would be the situation with Merewyn, who now belonged to Luc as a bought slave. 'If Braxton wins, can he claim her back,' he asked.

Bodin shook his head, 'I do not think so; Merewyn hated Braxton and was glad when he was declared dead or missing, she had moved on, and she was formally betrothed to Malvais, sanctioned by you, when Braxton tried to rape her.

'However again, he can appeal against that, as in Saxon law, a hand-fasted bride is perceived to be a man's wife and property as are the children. It is almost as binding as marriage,' added Ralph shrugging his shoulders apologetically.

Bodin glanced back at Luc behind him; he knew that Luc had probably heard all of this. He turned back to Alain, 'What is more, it will be an unfair contest if Luc fights, he has not recovered, his broken ribs are still tightly strapped which would restrict his movement, many of the scars on his body, inflicted by Braxton are still open and are only just healing.'

The Prelate broke in. 'It is a situation of his own doing; Malvais had brought this on himself by taking this woman out of wedlock, when in fact, she belonged to another. Now the Saxon is claiming the child is his, so who is telling the truth here.' He asked with open hands.

Alain ignoring the self-satisfied Prelate nodded his understanding at Bodin. Still, the crowd were growing restless, and Braxton was now openly grinning at them and leering at Merewyn, an expression of triumph on his face. Luc's fists were clenched, his knuckles white, he believed Merewyn; he knew it was his child. He wanted to walk over there and smash his fists into Le Gunn's face, but he knew he had to try to stay calm for Merewyn and Garrett's sakes. Alain stood up and raised his hand, and the clamour died down. 'Braxton Le Gunn, you have asked for a trial by combat, and I am prepared to offer one of my champions to do so. Each of you will be given a sword, and you will fight here and now in this Hall to resolve this matter. If you lose and you are still alive, you will be taken out and executed for your treason against the King.'

Braxton's eyes narrowed, and he let out a growl, 'There is only one man I want to fight, that is Luc De Malvais, he owes me reparation unless he is too much of a coward to face me.' He said, directing a contemptuous glare at Luc.

Luc started forward and stepped down off the dais. He heard, vaguely, in the distance, a woman repeatedly screaming 'No! No!'

Alain Rufus raised a hand and stopped Luc in his tracks. 'Malvais, are you sure you are prepared to take on this challenge? If I agree to a 'Trial by Combat', you do know it will be a fight to the death.'

This time, it was Luc's turn to smile tight-lipped at Braxton, and he nodded, 'Yes, my Lord, I would be honoured, with your permission to defend our honour, and it will be my pleasure to kill this Saxon renegade and murderer,' he declared in a voice that rang around the Hall. This initiated huge cheers from the assembled men, many of whom had fought with Malvais, many who just knew him by his fearsome reputation and expected him to win. However, none of them realised just how hurt and injured Luc De Malvais still was from his recent time in Braxton's hands, However Braxton knew, and this was what he was banking on as he slowly nodded and smiled at Luc.

'Clear the space!' ordered Alain Rufus, and the guards pushed the crowds back to the sides of the Hall in the aisles behind the pillars, moving any furniture out of the way.

Luc walked to the side of the Hall with Bodin and began

peeling off his leather doublet and chain mail hauberk; he left the thin, linen shirt on underneath as he had no wish to display, to the crowds, the many scars that Braxton inflicted on his body. He tied his braies tightly. Luc decided to fight barefoot to give him more purchase and speed. Then, he pulled up his shirt and removed the tight bindings around his ribs.

'Do you think that is wise, taking them off, Malvais?' Sighed Bodin, noticing the stains on the bindings where several wounds were still open and weeping. Privately he thought Malvais was mad to consider fighting, but he had known Luc since they were boys, and he knew in his heart that Luc had to see this through to the end one way or another.

'Yes, I need to be able to move and weave, Bodin, You have seen his upper body strength, and I have recently lost weight and muscle while I was recuperating, so I must be swift, supple and light on my feet. Just promise me one thing, Bodin,' said Luc, staring long and hard into his friend's eyes, 'if by any chance I lose, rescue her and my unborn child, and do not let him take her.'

Bodin grasped Luc's arm, 'I promise I will do my best, my friend,' he said.

Luc stood and watched as they undid Braxton's bonds, and they gave him a sword. A cohort of guards was posted in front of the dais to protect Alain, the Prelate and Bodin. Luc had one of his own blades, and he swung it a few times, in a figure of eight, to loosen his shoulders and feel the effect on his still painful ribs. The two men moved into the centre of the newly built Great Hall. Light streamed in from unshuttered windows high in the walls, and shafts of sunlight beamed down and lit the centre while the sides were still dark in deep shade. Luc purposefully kicked some of the fresh rushes out of his way, as he knew how deadly it could be to slip on them. As the two warriors faced each other, the crowd fell silent.

'Begin!' announced Alain Rufus.

The two men circled each other warily. Luc's face was a mask of concentration as he tried to anticipate Braxton's move. He knew from Garrett that Braxton was a good fighter, but he also knew that he tended to rely on pure smashing power rather than speed or skill. As he moved, Luc was very aware of his own vulnerability; he would have to try to finish him quickly; he knew he was not physically up to a long onslaught of powerful blows from the huge Saxon.

Braxton was aware of Luc's reputation as a swordsman, but he also knew that Luc's mobility would be compromised by the damage he had inflicted on him. After warily circling each other, Braxton suddenly attacked without warning, delivering a flurry of overhead blows. Beating down heavily on Luc's raised sword, the clang of steel on steel echoed across the Hall, and then slowly, Braxton brought his sword with force, down against Luc's blade, holding it there he pressed hard against Luc's body. The two men strained against each other. Luc could feel Braxton's rank breath in his face and the unbelievable power of the man as he pushed Luc backwards. His face was a mask of hatred as he stared at Luc with ice-cold eyes. 'Did you tell them Malvais,' he shouted into Luc's face, 'that you screamed and begged me for mercy when I had you strung up in that barn?'

Luc managed to push back and disengage, and he danced away from Braxton to cheers from the Norman Knights and soldiers. 'You must have been dreaming, Le Gunn; it was never going to happen. Bretons never beg or ask for quarter,' he shouted to more cheers from the large Breton contingent. The Saxon came swiftly after him, swinging the sword at his head, but Luc bravely ducking, dropped to his haunches, he turned and slashed his own blade under the Saxon's sword hand, opening up a deep cut on Braxton's thigh while, again, backing swiftly out of range. The Saxon roared with rage and then came on with purpose, seemingly oblivious to the injury.

Repeatedly, Braxton attacked with force. The man had a formidable amount of energy and power in his downward slashes, and Luc knew, having felt his strength, that he had to bring him down soon, as he managed to dance back away from him again.

Bodin, watching intently, could see the frustration on Braxton's face as he forced Luc back yet again, with crushing strokes, but this time against one of the pillars, each man straining against the other, their swords crossed and grating between them. Then, without warning, Braxton moved and used his left fist to punch Luc hard in the right side of his torso, where he knew he had broken the Breton's ribs previously. Luc let out a cry of pain and dropped to his knees in agony as Braxton smiled, stepped back, and raising his sword; he prepared to plunge a killing blow into Luc's neck.

Bodin leapt to his feet, and Merewyn was screaming at Braxton to stop, but Luc, though obviously in a lot of pain, suddenly rolled to his left side and leapt back up, his sword still in his right hand… as he backed quickly across the Hall, his left hand holding his ribs. The crowd breathed a collective sigh of relief, and then they roared in approval. Braxton, unperturbed, just laughed and came after him again, heedless of the blood running down his leg, knowing he could finish this now; he knew Luc was severely injured. It was just a matter of time.

Luc was in agony as he gritted his teeth; the sweat was standing out on his brow. He knew he had to do something quickly; another blow like that could kill or bring him down again. He straightened up and gazed coldly at Braxton, who was striding towards him with purpose. Luc needed something to make him even angrier, to make him reckless.

Luc suddenly relaxed and leaned both hands on his sword, laughing at the huge Saxon, 'You are losing your touch, Braxton, having all those girlish locks cut off has halved your strength.' Braxton, who had been taken aback by Luc's stance, let out a roar and then ran at him. Luc nimbly sidestepped and brought his sword down hard across the back of Braxton's legs as he passed so that he fell forward onto his knees. These were deep cuts but not severe enough to hope that the loss of more blood would weaken him. The pain and lack of movement in his right side prevented Luc from following through with speed, and he backed well away again.

Braxton leapt to his feet and faced Luc, breathing raggedly, his face contorted with hate for this man. 'I am going to gut you, Malvais and then I am going to take Merewyn back. I know she is carrying your child, as soon as it is born, I promise I will expose it on the hillside to die!' he shouted, and he suddenly raced at Luc. There was no time to dance further out of range. No way that he could meet that onslaught and survive with his re-broken ribs, so Luc chose the only path he could and launched himself straight at Braxton. He narrowed his eyes as he ran and estimated that they were about twenty feet apart on the rush covered floor.

It seemed as if these two powerful men would meet with a crunch in the centre to the onlooking crowd, and there was a collective gasp. Many of the Breton Knights there, who knew the extent of his injuries, believed that Malvais would not survive that clash, badly wounded as he so obviously was. Luc met Braxton's eyes as he raced across the Hall towards him, and he could see the triumph there. He expected to kill Luc quickly. Luc prayed that what he was about to do would work, or he would die a gruesome death, on the floor, in front of Merewyn and his friends.

The crowd held their breath and waited for the collision and clash of swords, but at the last minute, Luc dropped, launching himself, feet first along the floor, sliding on the new green rushes and straight at Braxton's lower legs. At the same time, using both hands, he brought his sword down and back to stab upwards, with all his might, through Braxton's unprotected groin and into his body.

Braxton, his feet taken away from him by the unexpected move, fell forward, arms outstretched, meeting the upraised sword. He dropped, in a writhing heap, pinning Luc below him and drenching him in his life-blood as it pumped out of him before he groaned loudly and finally stilled. For a few, frozen moments, there was a deadly silence in the Hall, as many thought both men had perished, in the final blows. Then, Luc, taking a deep breath, managed to push and roll the considerable weight of Braxton's body off his body and emerged, covered in Braxton's blood but still gripping the sword hilt that had delivered the killing blow. Luc knelt up, pulling his sword free to wild cheers and applause from the crowds, and Bodin rushed forward to help Luc to his feet. He embraced his friend. 'The legend that is Luc De Malvais lives on,' he said, shaking his head in amazement.

Alain Rufus came over and grasped Luc by his bloodstained

arm. 'Only you could pull off a clever move and thrust like that Malvais,' he laughed. 'Was it one of Sir Gerard's many ploys?'

'Of course, my Lord,' lied Luc, the relief evident in his voice but happy to give Gerard the acclaim.

'Well, he would be very proud,' said Alain, and he held Luc's arm up for all to see, declaring him the winner.

Merewyn stood and stared at him, her eyes devouring him. She had not believed that he could win while he was still so injured. She turned to Garrett, who gazed at Luc with open astonishment and admiration. He took her hands. 'He is an amazing and brave man, Merewyn; I would be honoured ever to call him a friend or even to serve with him if he will have me when I have finished my time with Lord Bodin.'

There was only one person Luc wanted to see, and he walked over to where Merewyn stood with her brother and the Serjeant. As he walked towards her, he could see her radiant smile through the tears streaming down her cheeks. He bowed to her and took her hand.

'Braxton Le Gunn will not be bothering you again, my lady,' he said and smiled. 'I would embrace you, but as you can see, I need to wash and change,' he said, indicating his blood-soaked shirt and braies. 'I will be back here at your side shortly,' he said, and nodding at Garrett, headed to salute Arlo and Thorfinn and, of course, to offer reparation to Thorfinn for killing his only son. Thorfinn refused but appreciated the gesture, and Luc headed, first for the pump outside and then to Alain's physician to strap his exceedingly painful re-broken ribs.

Chapter Twenty-Four

When he returned to the Great Hall in clean clothes, he gathered Merewyn in his arms, the crowds had cleared, and Alain had retired to the solar with the officious Prelate, but Bodin waved them over to join him on the dais. They reluctantly stepped apart and joined Bodin, who stepped forward and kissed Merewyn on the cheek. 'You did well, Merewyn Eymer, such a brave performance. And you will need to be brave to be married to this man, who will drag us all from one scrape into the next; I have had nearly seventeen years of him doing that to me.' He smiled and handed Luc two documents that were on the table. Luc looked down at them in some confusion at first, and then he realised that one was a certificate of ownership for Merewyn Eymer, and the second was a certificate of manumission to free her from the next day.

'I had these drawn up by Ralph as soon as I knew what Alain intended to do, but the Prelate arriving nearly scuppered us all, he demanded that both you and your brother be executed to make an example of you. Fortunately, Alain did not hold his opinions or advice in great store, and he disliked the churchman on sight. I know you will be staying here as Alain's guests tonight, which means you can be married tomorrow with Merewyn's family here. You never know, our stiff, unbending Prelate might even officiate. However, I somehow doubt it; I think he plans to leave for Durham much earlier than we expected. He was as white as a sheet after the trial by combat. He kept saying, 'So much blood, so much blood' over and over.' Luc clasped his friend to him, laughing. 'I cannot thank you enough, Bodin, for what you have done for us, and I will repay you every silver penny when I return to Brittany, I promise.'

Bodin smiled wryly and shook his head. 'Think of it as a wedding gift; just try and keep her under control and both of you out of trouble, Malvais!' He laughed and then left them to it.

'My Saxon slave for one day only,' Luc whispered in her ear. Then, suddenly he held her at arm's length and glowered at her. 'I love you very much, Merewyn Eymer, but lie to me, or disobey me again, or even hide things from me, and I promise, I will beat you,' he said, as he moved in to kiss her passionately. As she came up for air, she smiled wickedly at him.

'My Lord, as I am still your slave for tonight, doesn't that mean I have to do everything and anything you want, without question?' Luc frowned at the word slave, his blue eyes turning stormy, but then her meaning dawned on him, and he laughed, pulling her to him. He kissed her deeply, his body quickly responding to the warm softness of her. She opened her eyes and gazed up at him; she so wanted him to make love to her, her Breton knight. She thought she had lost him forever, but now she could see the passion in his eyes, and she thought with anticipation of their night together after being so long apart. Luc sighed; he knew they would have to sit through a boisterous celebration dinner this evening with

Alain and his friends, but after that, they would be alone, and she would be all his.

However, there was one more essential but unpleasant duty he had to carry out. He sent Merewyn up to Count Alain's solar, and he joined the two Saxon Thegns waiting at the door. The three men were grim-faced as they followed the Serjeants outside with their prisoner. Within minutes, they had stripped off Garret's tunic and tied his hands to the top of the two posts in the Bailey. The young man was clearly apprehensive, but as he glanced at the scaffolds with their still swinging corpses in front of him, he felt relief. Garrett realised how close it had been; he could have been on that scaffold. One of the Serjeants gave him a piece of thick leather to bite down on, and Garrett closed his eyes as the first lash descended. Luc watching with apprehension, could not help wincing as he heard the crack of the ox whip; his own ordeal was still too fresh in his mind.

Before long, the count to ten was over; the young rebel had taken the lashes with grit, but he had cried out, and his knees sagged as they released his hands. Arlo was there immediately to help his son, as was the castle physician; they held him up until he could walk. Garrett stopped, his face tense with pain; he turned to Luc. 'Thank you for doing what you did to save our lives, Malvais, I thought I had got away lightly, but now I have no idea how you survived your harrowing ordeal with such courage and fortitude. I only suffered a fraction of it, but the pain was and is unbelievable.'

Luc put his hand on the young rebels arm and gave a tight smile; strength comes in many forms, Garrett, as you will find out, and I was lucky that I had you looking out for me'. He said, waving him on to have his wounds bound. Luc grasped arms in a farewell to Thorfinn and thanked the Thegn for his part in the day's events. Then lighter of heart, he headed up to re-join Merewyn.

That night they enjoyed a passionate reunion underneath the large sumptuous fur coverlet on the bed; afterwards, they stood together in the window embrasure looking out over the River Swale under a crisp, cloudless night sky. Luc pulled her close; her head nestled under his chin, her arms were around his waist, as he thought about their future: he would be going away again soon to fight in the borders against the Scots, but he hoped he would be back in time for the birth of their child in May. Tonight, Alain Rufus had asked him to stay on for a few more years at Ravensworth before it was handed over to his younger brother Bardolph. The latter was presently serving King William's interests in Germany at the court of the young Emperor. For the moment, Luc was happy to stay in Ravensworth, and he looked forward to living here peacefully for a while in the north of England with Merewyn and her family.

He knew that he would have to go away repeatedly; after all, he was Luc De Malvais, the legendary leader of the famous Breton Horse Warriors. As a Breton Lord and knight, he was loyal to both his Patron Alain Rufus and their King, and he knew that he would be at their beck and call for some years to do their bidding until in the future he might be released from their service. However, deep in his heart, he knew that he would return to Brittany with Merewyn and his child to his own lands on the wild western coast of Europe before too long. Once there, he would continue to establish the bloodlines and breed the huge sought after War Destriers, such as Espirit Noir. This would be their future together on his lands, and these warhorses would become a legend in their own right.

The End

Glossary

- Bailey - A ward or courtyard in a castle, some outer baileys could be huge, encompassing grazing land.
- Braies - A type of trouser often used as an undergarment as well, often to mid-calf and made of light or heavier linen.
- Chausses – Attached by laces to the waist of the braies these were tighter fitting coverings for the legs.
- Destrier – A knight's large warhorse, often trained to fight, bite and strike out.
- Donjon – The fortified tower of an early castle later called the Keep.
- Doublet – A close-fitting jacket or jerkin often made from leather, with or without sleeves. Laced at the front and worn either under, or over, a chain mail hauberk.
- Hauberk – A tunic of chain mail, often reaching to mid-thigh.
- Liege lord – A feudal lord such as a Count or Baron entitled to allegiance and service from his knights.
- Marechal – A military officer or noble of the highest rank, to control or administer an area.
- Mead – An alcoholic drink made from fermented honey.

- Motte – An earth mound, forming a defensible platform on which a Donjon would be built, initially this would be made of wood until the earth settled and compacted.
- Palisade – A defensive wall made from wooden stakes to create a secure enclosure, often found around the inner and outer bailey of an early castle.
- Patron – An individual who gives financial, political, or social patronage to others. Often through, wealth or influence in return for loyalty and homage.
- Pottage – A staple of the medieval diet, a thick soup made by boiling grains and vegetables and, if available, meat or fish.
- Prelate – A high-ranking member of the clergy, often a cardinal, abbot or bishop.
- Serjeant – The soldier Serjeant was a man who often came from a higher class, most experienced medieval mercenaries fell into this class, they were deemed to be 'half of the value of a knight' in military terms.
- Vavasseur- A right hand man who is chosen for his dignity, valour and prowess.

Author Note

The Norman Conquest is a fascinating period of history, and I give thanks to the work of such eminent historians as David C. Douglas. His publications and many others certainly helped with the months of research into Norman life and politics both here and in Brittany and Normandy.

While bringing us Norman culture, buildings, language and bloodlines that shaped England for centuries to come, the Conquest was also a story of occupation, rebellion, domination and slaughter. The 'Harrying of the North', the ruthless suppression of rebellions by the forces of King William and his half-brother Odo is one of the darker periods of our history.

England in 1069-71 was a time of fierce rebellions in the north; Alain Rufus was tasked to put these down while establishing himself and building a large Motte and Bailey castle at Richmond. Alain Rufus is a fascinating character, becoming one of the wealthiest men in England at quite a young age by attaching himself to the tail of King William's comet. Alain is mentioned in the Domesday Book in 1,017 different entries as a landowner, behind only King William with his half-brother Robert in wealth. Alain's father, Eudo

De Penthievre, an interesting Breton character in his own right, provided hundreds of men, ships and cavalry to enable William to undertake England's invasion. Evidence shows that Alain and his knights led the Breton Horse Warriors at the Battle of Hastings, where they had a significant impact.

Ravensworth is a beautiful village that nestles in the Holmedale Valley, about four and a half miles north-west of Richmond's lovely market town. It has a large picturesque village green and the impressive ruins of a later castle on the site where the original Motte and Bailey castle would have been built. The original settlement was called Ravenswath, wath being a Norse word, meaning ford, so it translated as the ford of the Raven. In the 11th century, at the time of this novel, it was called Raveneswet, but I decided to use the modern name.

While the main characters in this novel are fictional, many of them, such as Alain Rufus, Bodin and Thorfinn Le Gunn of Austwicke, existed in North Yorkshire and were linked to Ravensworth.

Alain's half-brothers Bodin and Bardolf were prominent at William's court, and they did go on to become the Lords of Bedale and Ravensworth respectively in what is now North Yorkshire, although later Bodin did become a monk. Alain did encourage marriage between the Saxon and Norman families. Many chronicles state that he had a relationship, if not marriage, with Gunnhild of Wessex, King Harold's Saxon daughter; there are even suggestions that they had a daughter called Matilda.

Thorfinn of Austwicke, who was indeed a very wealthy Saxon Thegn, did own approximately 58 of the hundreds of manors given to Alain Rufus, in what was known as the

'Honour of Richmond.' Thorfinn was Lord of the Manor of Ravensworth in 1066 and was disenfranchised of his land, becoming one of Alain's tenants; he went on to live to a ripe old age.

I was delighted when I heard that Sir Ian Botham had become 'Baron Botham of Ravensworth', so establishing the newest 'Lord of Ravensworth'.

S.J. Martin

Read More

Rebellion
Book Two

The second book in the Breton Horse Warrior series continues the tale of Luc De Malvais and Merewyn, this time in war-torn Brittany, five years later. However, they face threats and betrayal from all sides. Luc's marriage, and even his life, is on the verge of being destroyed as he and his brother Morvan fight for King William against an array of enemies, rebel forces, but also friends that want to destroy them.

Read the first chapter on the next page...

Rebellion

English Channel – late autumn 1075

Merewyn, her knuckles white, tightly gripped the gunwale of the sturdy Cog that was taking them south across the English Channel to Brittany. The fine salt spray from the front of the boat occasionally splashed over her, and she threw her head back and gasped with exhilaration while licking the salt water from her fingers. To any onlooker, she seemed unconcerned that they had spent several hours at the mercy of a sudden storm.

She was mesmerised by the endless white-topped waves that stretched to the horizon, the smell and noise of the sea, the movement of the creaking boat. This was the first time she had ever seen the ocean or been on a ship. Despite misgivings and anxiety about her quest, she was thrilled to be on deck, even in rough weather, to experience as much as possible. She glanced along to the sturdy but rugged accommodation at the stern; she should have been there with her son Lusian and his nurse, but she needed to be able to breathe; her tension and excitement were too much to contain in those cramped quarters. The sea journey was just as rough as they thought at this time of year; as the small boat climbed and fell with the giant waves, Lusian's nurse Helga was suffering from a bout of seasickness, another reason for Merewyn to risk being out on the deck. Travelling across the sea in November weather was dangerous. Still, it was a risk she had to take, and the irritable captain was paid a considerable amount of silver to undertake this journey with his important passengers.

Sir Gerard, her husband's Steward and veteran Horse Warrior, stood beside her, his feet firmly planted on the heaving deck, one hand on the rail, but silent disapproval emanating from every pore in his body. She knew she was deliberately disobeying her husband's instructions by crossing from England to Brittany, and Gerard did not expect it to end well. He had painstakingly told her several times that no matter how much Luc De Malvais loved both her and his son, he would be furious that Merewyn had left the comparative safety of their home in Ravensworth to try and find him. By insisting on travelling in late autumn, she had put them all in danger. Crossing the channel was a huge risk at this rough time of year, without further peril in war-torn Brittany.

However, Merewyn felt that she had no choice but to make the journey. It had been eleven long months since Luc was recalled to his homeland on his liege lord's orders. Alain Rufus sent him to serve King William on the unsettled borders of Brittany, Maine and Anjou. She had been devastated to see him go, but he had promised to be back by early summer. It was now late autumn, and no one had heard anything from him for over five months. Her stomach knotted when she thought of Luc, her handsome Breton Horse Warrior, her husband, friend, and lover. They had been through difficult and often life-threatening times together, but she had never

302

been apart from him for this length of time before. It had left a hole in her life, and she knew that she had to go to Brittany to find him, to get some answers, to be by his side, no matter what he was facing. That is, if he was still alive, nobody seemed to know where he was... but there was no doubt that he was missing.

They had been married for over four years, and they had a beautiful son Lusian, a miniature Luc with an almost black mop of hair but with his mother's startling green eyes. He was growing up so fast and was already developing his parents' firm and almost wilful characteristics. She was worried that Luc would hardly recognise him; it had been so long now since he had seen him. Merewyn was not afraid; she knew she was capable of facing whatever dangers she would find in Brittany. She had been raised in a warrior's household; her father was a Saxon Thegn, who had fought at Hastings, so she was not short of courage. She had also matured early, managing her father's household and home farmlands when her mother died in childbirth.

Above all else, Luc was a Breton knight and Horse Warrior; the champion of Alain Rufus, heir to the wealthy House of Rennes, but they both also served William, Duke of Normandy, King of England. Luc De Malvais was the Marechal of vast lands around Ravensworth in the north of England; he was also the leader of the formidable Breton Horse Warriors, the most fearsome troop of cavalry in Western Europe. She knew that Luc loved her deeply, they had a deep connection between them, but she recognised that he had other obligations as well; he owned extensive estates around the port of Morlaix and also down at Malvais in Vannes.

Suddenly, there was a shout in Breton from the Cog's bows, and Gerard took her arm. 'Land has been sighted; at last, thank the Lord; I thought we would be driven down to Spain by that storm. We will see the shores of Brittany and the bluffs of Morlaix soon,' he said, gazing at the thin strip of coastline in the distance and willing the little boat into safe harbour.

Merewyn's stomach tightened, and she held her breath, raising her hands to her cheeks as she gazed at the dark line on the horizon. This, then, was Brittany, the wild region on the western Atlantic coast of France and the ancestral home of Luc and the De Malvais family. She hugged herself in anticipation. In a few hours, if he was alive and not mortally wounded, she might be with Luc and would feel his strong arms around her. However, Merewyn was not naive; she knew that Luc might not be in Morlaix at his home when they docked. According to Gerard, he could still be fighting elsewhere in Brittany, Maine or Normandy, defending the borders, so inside, she steeled herself for disappointment but prayed he was still alive and unharmed.

From listening to Gerard, she knew that King William had been fighting a campaign on Normandy's borders in Maine and Anjou's provinces. They were fighting against Count Fulk of Anjou and his allies. William had previously claimed the Province of Maine in 1063 despite opposition from Count Fulk and Conan, Duke of Brittany. Before he invaded England, William was determined to defeat his enemies and secure his borders in Normandy. So he had seized Maine's bordering province and the fortress and stronghold of Dol before finally agreeing to a peace pact with Count Fulk. However, Duke Conan of Brittany had refused to be pacified by William, whom he saw as an upstart, and he promised to attack

Normandy while William was invading England. Conan had signed his own death warrant by saying this, and low and behold, he was mysteriously poisoned in late 1066 whilst using a pair of new riding gloves.

This assassination conveniently removed him from Brittany, leaving no heir or Duke of age to take his place, and it left William free to concentrate on invading England. The finger of blame was firmly pointed at William, as he was not only ruthless in getting what he wanted, but he had a long history of poisoning and removing his enemies. Following this, years of war ensued in Brittany and the surrounding provinces, between those who supported William and those who did not.

Merewyn could understand the conflict; she knew that these independent feudal lords in Brittany and other provinces were a law unto themselves. They formed and changed alliances and sides constantly, as it suited their need. However, she could not understand why Luc had not returned home when the recent war had been resolved. Why had he not sent her a letter or message for over five months? This was so unlike him; she was terrified that something had happened to him. He could be badly injured or even dead for all she knew. She could not, and would not, imagine life without him.

Merewyn turned; she smiled at the relief on Gerard's face and returned to the cabin at the stern of the sturdy Cog. She found Lusian full of excitement and energy, galloping his beautifully carved wooden horse along the rough decking while his poor white-faced nurse tried to restrain him. Looking at the horse, she smiled, for it brought back bittersweet memories of life in Ravensworth, the scene of so many happy times for her and her family. She would never have believed that she could fall in love with the enemy of her Saxon people, a hated Norman knight. However, from the moment they had met, there had been an incredible magnetism and attraction between them, which they found difficult to deny or ignore. She was taken aback by how this Norman overlord was slowly accepted and even respected by her people for his firm but fair approach.

She soon discovered that he was a Breton warrior allied to King William; so she knew that one day they would have to leave her Saxon family and return to Luc's lands and estates in Brittany. Luc had returned to see his mother and young brother on a few occasions over the last four years, but this time it was different. Alain Rufus, Luc's liege Lord, had arrived with his entourage at Ravensworth and had spent several hours closeted with him. A week later, Luc had packed up and gone. He had ridden out last December on his beautiful Breton stallion, 'Espirit Noir', with his troop of Breton cavalry behind him, leaving a massive hole in her life and an ache in her heart.

At first, some periodic messages and letters had arrived through Alan Rufus at Richmond castle to let her know Luc was well and hoped to be back by the summer. Sir Gerard acted as Luc's Steward during his absence, and they spent a bitterly cold yuletide together at Ravensworth with Merewyn's father Arlo and her young brother. Still, Luc was sorely missed by them all. Early spring brought a positive message from him that lightened their steps and gave them the hope that he might be back for the summer.

Merewyn knew that Gerard missed Luc almost as much as she did. He had been Luc's mentor and friend since he was a boy in Brittany; he had taught him much of the swordsmanship for which Luc was now famous. Yet, by the end of the summer, there was still no word and no sign of Luc and Merewyn lived with an ache for the man she loved so much. Sleeping alone every night in their large wooden bed, she would often wake with tears on her face and put a hand out to the cold, empty side of the bed where his warm body would usually lie. When she closed her eyes, she could almost feel his touch, remembering how he would curl around her and pull her close as they settled to sleep.

It was at the harvest feast last month that things had come to a head; as the sturdy boat approached the dark Breton shoreline, she thought back to that night...

She had sat at the top table in the Great Hall that was full of her people. There was laughter, good food and flowing drink, and it had brought back memories of other nights in the Great Hall with Luc by her side. In particular, she thought back to the very first night he had arrived, when he had followed her outside to teach her a lesson for her insolence to her Norman overlords. His very touch as he pulled her roughly to him had sent waves of passion through her body, and even now, after five years, his lightest touch still sent fire racing to her loins.

As Merewyn sat in misery, her father, Arlo, had leaned in towards Sir Gerard, and she heard him say, 'Do you have any idea why we have heard nothing? It has been nearly four or five months since his last message; could he be dead,' he asked.

Gerard's mouth became a thin line as he snapped at some of the serving boys behind him for more wine, but he did not answer Arlo at first; he just shook his head, shrugged and gazed down into the red wine as he swirled it around in his goblet. She had clutched the edge of the table as she heard his next words. "Malvais is missing on the borders of Brittany

Arlo, there is no doubt of that. Even at his home in Morlaix, they have heard no word of him for several months. I try to keep my hope alive but I fear the worst, this is so unlike Luc."

Unexpectedly, they heard the sudden sounds of arrival outside the Great Hall and the large Irish dyer hounds set up a torrent of barking and howls. The doors were flung open, Merewyn was immediately on her feet, her hand to her mouth, and her face filled with joy, expecting Luc to walk into the Hall any moment. However, she was to be disappointed as Bodin, the half-brother of Alain Rufus, appeared with his retainers and another man, a stranger, at the back of the Hall. The anguish on Merewyn's face was clear to see, but, as the host, she quickly recovered and smiling, she had moved gracefully down the Hall to greet their friend Bodin Le Ver, who was now Lord of Bedale.

He had settled at the table with them and related the court's gossip; all the news was about the recent rebellions in the north. He had introduced the confident auburn-haired young man as Bardolph, his younger brother. Looking directly at Gerard, he explained that Bardolph was to take over the reins as Marechal of Ravensworth, and he thanked Gerard for his service to date while Luc was away. Merewyn's hand went to her heart as she wondered if Bodin knew that Luc was injured, or even dead, for Ravensworth to go to another Marechal.

Bodin, having seen her concern, quickly explained. This had been the plan for when Luc returned to Brittany; they were bringing it forward because of the rebellions in England and the threat to Normandy and Maine's borders. He knew that they had heard nothing from Luc and admitted it was unusual and troubling. He had taken her hand and reassured her that while Luc may have disappeared if someone had killed him, the news would have spread like wildfire; after all, he was Luc De Malvais, his name known across Western Europe.

Merewyn sat there, a fixed smile on her face as the conversations flowed around her, her mind in turmoil while Gerard arranged to show Bardolph around the estates. However, Merewyn only half listened, for her mind had been in Brittany. Luc was not returning, but she could not understand why he had not let her know; why had he not sent for them?

It was now October; she knew that it would become too dangerous to cross the seas very soon. She had determined to act; she refused to spend another yuletide and the long winter months without him. The arrival of Bardolph had made it easier for her to leave Ravensworth and go to Luc. She was his wife, Lusian was his son, and they needed to look for him, to be by his side. She had decided that they were leaving for Brittany immediately, and nothing and no one would stop her, not Gerard and not Lord Bodin. She was Merewyn De Malvais, no matter the barriers in her way; she knew she would find him wherever he had gone.

The Breton Horse Warriors Series

Rebellion
The Breton Horse Warriors - Book Two
It will be published by Moonstorm Books on
Amazon in May 2021

To find out more and to join S.J. Martin's mailing list and
newsletters, contact us at:
Website: www.moonstormbooks.com
Email: enquiries@moonstormbooks.com
Facebook: S.J.Martin Author
Instagram: S.J.Martin_author
Twitter: @SJMarti40719548

About the Author

S. **J. Martin...** is the pen name of a historian, writer and animal lover in the north of England. Having had an abiding love of history from a very early age, this influenced her academic and career choices. She worked in the field of archaeology for several years before becoming a history teacher in the schools of the north-east, then in London and finally Sheffield.

She particularly enjoys the engaging and fascinating historical research into the background of her favourite historical periods and characters, combining this with extensive field visits. Having decided to leave the world of education after a successful teaching and leadership career, she decided to combine her love of history and writing as an author of historical fiction. With her partner and a close friend, she established Moonstorm Books, publishing The Breton Horse Warrior Series…

When she is not writing, she walks their two dogs with her partner Greg on the beautiful beaches of the north-east coast or in the countryside. She also has an abiding love of live music and festivals, playing and singing in a band with her friends whenever possible.

Printed in Great Britain
by Amazon